A figure ghosted out of the darkness, directly in front of Doc's crouching figure

The movement was so sudden and so silent that it startled Doc. He nearly squeezed the Le Mat's trigger, but his better judgment asserted itself in the nick of time. Instead he stood and thrust with the rapier, aiming slightly upward, feeling the needle tip slide between the protecting ribs on the left side of the intruder's body.

It was a perfect, clean kill. The flagellant dropped to the floor, shrouded in rags.

Doc withdrew the blade, stepping confidently out into the open space between the stalls, aware only of the sudden restlessness of the animals, disturbed by the hot reek of freshly spilled blood—to find himself confronting a second assailant who stood ten feet in front of him, holding a long-hafted hatchet.

At that frozen moment, Doc remembered one of the Trader's sayings that Ryan had often quoted. *Pull the trigger too soon and you'll probably be fine. Pull it too late and you'll probably be dead.*

But the three and a half pounds of steel, lead and gold remained unfired. "Move and I'll fill you full of holes," Doc warned shakily.

"No, unbeliever," said a cold voice behind him. "*You* move and I'll fill *you* full of holes."

**Also available in the
Deathlands saga:**

JAMES AXLER

DEATH LANDS®

Road Wars

A GOLD EAGLE BOOK FROM
WORLDWIDE®

TORONTO • NEW YORK • LONDON
AMSTERDAM • PARIS • SYDNEY • HAMBURG
STOCKHOLM • ATHENS • TOKYO • MILAN
MADRID • WARSAW • BUDAPEST • AUCKLAND

This is for Sandy and David. Good friends with whom we have some of the very best times going. With much love and affection.

First edition October 1994

ISBN 0-373-62523-5

ROAD WARS

Printed in U.S.A.

In the end, we'll all finish up in the cold, cold ground. But, until then, bloody Hell, babes, don't we have fun!

—From *Wine, Theatre and Friends*, by Archie Pellaggo, Goldhurst Press, 1992

Chapter One

The piece of paper was crumpled and stained, but it was still perfectly legible.

Ryan laid it out on the kitchen table and read it through, for the twentieth time. It was now two days since the seedy packman, passing through the small ville of Patriarch, had handed it to Ryan Cawdor.

Success. Will stay around Seattle for three months. Come quick.

Abe.

The note had been on the road for just over six weeks before it eventually found Ryan, which gave him about a month and a half to make the long and dangerous overland trek to the far northwest of Deathlands to try to meet up again with his old friend Abe and his old leader, the Trader.

THE FIRST FRAIL LIGHT of dawn had been edging over the jagged crests of the mountains to the east of Jak Lauren's homestead when Ryan slipped from his bed.

Krysty Wroth had still been sleeping, her flaming red hair fanned out across the floral pillow, seeming to glow with a vivid fire of its own. Her bright green eyes were closed and one hand lay, fist clenched, across the top of the covers.

They had made love three times during their last night together—their last night together for a limitless time. Ryan's hope was that he and the Armorer, J. B. Dix, would be able to make the fifteen hundred miles to the northern Cific coast in a week or so, trouble permitting, take a few days to contact Trader and Abe, and then all return securely to old New Mexico. Call it three weeks, at the outside. That was the theory.

As soon as he'd set his eye on the note, Ryan had known that he would have to go. Since he couldn't use the gateway to make a jump to Seattle, it was going to mean some hard traveling, cross-country. It wasn't the kind of journey where he'd want to take Doc Tanner, Mildred Wyeth or his son, Dean, with him. Jak needed some time to get his head together again after the brutal slaying of his wife and baby.

That meant someone had to stay behind and keep an eye on things. Krysty was unarguably the best for that. And he needed someone to go with him on the road.

Trader used to say that a man traveling alone traveled fastest, but that two good men traveling together would travel safest.

John Barrymore Dix and Ryan Cawdor had ridden and fought together for more years—mostly with the Trader—than either cared to remember. Five feet eight inches tall and one hundred and thirty-seven pounds soaking wet, J.B. had forgotten more about weapons than most people in Deathlands would ever know. Sallow, bespectacled and terse, he seldom used one word where none would suffice.

In bed, the previous night, with the noises of the house quietening for the dark hours, Ryan had begun to try to explain the plan to Krysty Wroth.

THEY WERE NAKED, close together, yet back to back, a thousand miles apart. There was the faint golden glow of an oil lamp flickering under the bedroom door, and outside the window they could see the sickle moon, floating behind ragged clouds, low in the black velvet sky.

"Want to sleep, lover?" he whispered.

Krysty didn't answer him at first, but he could tell from the fast, shallow sound of her breathing that she was still very much awake.

"Want to talk about it?"

"No."

"Sure?"

She turned to face him, her breath warm on his skin. "We've talked it through, Ryan, talked this kind of thing through a hundred times since we met."

"I have to go."

"You stupe bastard. Think I don't know that?"

"Then . . ."

Krysty stretched an arm across his chest, then nuzzled her face into the hollow of his neck. Her right hand touched him, feather-light, on the lips, then traced a firm line down his throat, brushing past the legion of seamed scars and weals, over the flat muscular wall of his stomach.

Lower.

"Sure you want to?"

Krysty stopped him with her mouth, the tip of her tongue darting between his parted lips. Her hand grasped him firmly, bringing him to an instant diamond-hard readiness.

"Cut out the talking and get on with the doing, lover."

Their first time that night was over quickly, each taking what was urgently needed from the other.

The second time was slower, both concentrating more on giving than taking. Krysty slipped lower down the bed, but Ryan also wriggled around, leaving them head to toe. He used his fingers, sighing with his own excitement as she took him in her mouth. Then he repaid the compliment, licking and kissing her delicate moistness as she rolled on top, thighs parted to receive him.

After the loving they had fallen asleep, wrapped in each other's arms. Ryan awakened first, feeling the pressure on his bladder from the beer they'd all drunk. He returned from the outhouse, seeing moonlight glinting on Krysty's emerald eyes. He knew that she was awake.

"I thought you were triple pissed at me," he said quietly, aware of eleven-year-old Dean sleeping in the next room.

"No. Not angry. Sad, hurt, lonely and worried. Those are the sort of words, lover. I won't sleep a quiet hour until you get home safely."

"I know that."

"But it's not going to stop me from sending you on your way with the memory of your body fresh in my mind. Let's go for the third strike, Ryan."

THE ROOM WHERE HE SAT carried the faint scent of the predark brass oil lamp that he'd lighted as soon as he closed the oak bedroom door behind him. But it was overlaid now with the wholesome smell of fried food.

The plate in front of Ryan held three eggs, over easy, with some strips of Jak's home-cured bacon, mushrooms and hash browns with fresh-baked bread and salted butter. Nobody else seemed to be stirring, though he was sure he'd heard the sound of subdued conversation coming from the room shared by J.B. and Mildred.

His guess was that they were having a conversation something similar to the one he had with Krysty.

If they were to make an early start, Ryan knew that he'd soon have to rouse his old friend. But that meant waking the rest of the household.

For a few moments, sipping at a scalding mug of black coffee sub, he enjoyed the solitude, a time out of the perpetual war of surviving in Deathlands to sit and think and gather his private thoughts.

Fifteen hundred miles. They had the LAV-25 locked away in the large barn, and there was enough gas to take them a good part of their journey in the eight-wheeled light-armored vehicle. He and J.B. had checked out the few tattered maps available, trying to pick a good route that would keep them clear of any of the pesthole frontier villes that they knew from previous experience to be potentially hostile.

The reputation of having been one of the Trader's lieutenants didn't always mean a smiling reception. And when you looked like Ryan Cawdor—two hundred pounds of honed muscle and over six feet of one-eyed mean—then folks tended to remember you.

Ryan heard a floorboard creaking in the hall behind him, and his right hand dropped automatically to the butt of the big SIG-Sauer P-226.

"Only me, my dear chum," Doc said.

"Join me in a cup of coffee?"

"I don't believe there'll be room in it for both of us." He started to cackle, remembered the earliness of the hour and clapped a gnarled hand over his mouth. "Nothing like the old jokes, Master Cawdor. And that was nothing like one of the old jokes."

Ryan smiled, feeling a sudden rush of genuine affection for the old man.

Old man?

It was a recurring puzzle, trying to work out how old Doc really was. With his mane of white hair and lined face, wearing an ancient frock coat with a strange green sheen across the shoulders, and cracked knee boots, he looked to be closing in on seventy. And the ebony sword stick with the Toledo-steel rapier blade, the hilt a carved silver lion's head, gave him a nineteenth-century dandyish swagger.

Dr. Theophilus Tanner had been born in South Strafford, Vermont, on February 14, 1868. So that would make him well over two hundred years old.

He had married Emily Chandler in June of 1891, and they had two children—Rachel in 1893 and little Jolyon two years later. With his doctorate of science from Harvard, and doctorate of philosophy from Oxford University, England, Doc's academic career was already flourishing.

Until a bitter, leaden day in November of 1896.

In another time, the scientists of the United States government were laboring with a highly secret series of experiments. Code-named Operation Chronos, part of the Overproject Whisper, itself a small cog in the mighty machine of Totality Concept, they were trying to travel men and women from past to future.

And Doc was their star subject.

Some of their failures were horrific enough to make a man vomit blood, so ghastly and inhuman were what came through the temporal gateways.

You could count their successes on the fingers of both hands, and even some of them were of dubious merit.

Doc had been in Omaha, Nebraska, when his mind blurred and he collapsed, to awaken in a sterile laboratory in the year 1998, surrounded by a convocation of faceless scientists in masks and gowns.

At that moment you could have reasonably suggested that he was twenty-eight years old.

Nobody who'd ever encountered Doc Tanner would have said that he suffered fools gladly. Or, indeed, that he ever suffered them at all.

As soon as he found out what had happened to him, Doc devoted all of his considerable intellect to trying to make the chron jump back to his own time. But his keepers were too alert for that to happen.

But he consistently made himself a serious nuisance for the authorities.

Eventually, only a matter of days before the nuke holocaust of January 2001, the adminstration committee of Operation Chronos ordered Doc drugged and pushed forward in time. As far as they were concerned, the thorn in their side was gone forever. If he eventually made a temporal landing safely, a hundred years or so ahead, then he wasn't likely to ever come back to haunt them.

As it happened, they saved his life. Within twenty-three days, they were all dead.

But it was that jump that changed Doc forever.

Nobody had ever quite understood how the process of trawling worked. Now he looked a sparky sixty-odd years old, with a mind permanently tipped by the horrific experiences that he'd suffered, experiences that made him totally unique in the history of the human race.

"Penny for your thoughts, my dear fellow?"

Ryan realized that he was holding an empty mug, and that he'd been miles away. "Just thinking about memories, Doc. Nothing important, though."

"Things past, not worth forgetting, my friend. Things to come, not worth anticipating. You and John Barrymore Dix are ready for your journey?"

"Pretty well."

Doc poured himself some of the bitter coffee sub, grimacing as he raised it to his lips. "I disbelieve that I shall ever find this turgid sludge acceptable to my palate. Oh, for a muse of fire to sing of finest Java and the Blue Mountain blend."

"Wake others?"

Jak had come into the room so silently that even Ryan's razored combat reflexes hadn't detected him. The albino teenager was barefooted and wore only cotton pants and a short-sleeved shirt, open all the way down. His stark white hair blazed like a mag flare in the dim light of the oil lamp, and his red eyes glowed in sockets of wind-washed bone like the embers of a dying fire.

Ryan nodded. "Might as well."

"Sure don't want me come with you?"

"No, Jak. Not your fight, this time."

"Wasn't your fight, Christina and Jenny bein' chilled. Didn't stop you. Wouldn't stop me."

"I know that. But there's work to do here on the spread, Jak." Ryan lifted a hand. "I know that you keep telling me you don't intend to stay here. Not now. When we move on, in a few weeks, after I find Trader, then you can decide. Stay or come. Whichever you want, Jak. But for now, there's things to do here."

"Yeah. Guess so."

He went out as quietly as he'd entered, and they heard him going to rouse the rest of the household. Doc blew his nose on his swallow's-eye kerchief.

"Grief burns to the very core of his soul, Ryan. By the Three Kennedys! I know the feeling well enough. To lose a wife and a child..."

He paused as Krysty strode along the hall and joined them. She was wearing a white silk blouse, hanging loose over dark blue riding breeches. The heels of her blue leather Western boots clicked on the wooden floor.

"Good morning, gentlemen," she said. "Don't suppose you fried up enough breakfast for anyone else, did you, lover? Of course you didn't."

Doc rose and bowed. "I would deem it an honor to be allowed to go and cook some—"

Krysty laughed. "No, thanks, Doc. Best wait until everyone else is up and around. Then we can get organized."

J.B. appeared, wiping his wire-rimmed spectacles on a length of clean linen cloth. "Weather tastes good," he said. "Fresh northerly. Go at first light."

"That smells almost like coffee." Mildred stood behind J.B., one hand resting on his arm. She was stocky in build, with her hair knotted into tiny beaded plaits.

Like Doc, Mildred came from another time.

She'd been thirty-six years old, unmarried, one of the leading world authorities on cryogenics and cryosurgery. Her other claim to fame was that she had won

the silver medal in the free pistol-shooting in the last
ever Olympics in Miami in 1996.

Then, in December of the year 2000, the black
woman had gone into the hospital for some minor
abdominal surgery.

Things had gone wrong.

Badly wrong.

With the monumental irony that the blind lords of
chaos so love, Dr. Mildred Wyeth had been frozen in
an attempt to preserve her life.

Then the missiles had blackened the skies and civilization disappeared up its own nuclear-powered fun-
dament.

Along with a number of other patients, Mildred had
been locked into the dreamless sleep for nearly a century, until awakened by Ryan and the others, and
brought back to life in Deathlands.

Now everyone was up and bustling about.

Except for the youngest of the group, Dean Cawdor.

It had only been in the past year or so that Ryan had
known that he had a son. His brief sexual encounter
with Dean's mother, Sharona, had occupied only a
few minutes of Ryan's life. Then, like a bolt of lightning at a summer picnic, he found the boy, then ten
years old.

"Anyone seen Dean?" he asked, wiping his mouth
on his sleeve and getting up from the table.

"Heard movement when I came past," Mildred replied, looking around. "Here he is. Morning, young
man."

"Hi." Dean's black, curly hair was glistening, flat against his head where he'd stuck his head under the pump.

Ryan looked at his friends. They were all together.

Chapter Two

The dawn air tasted of sagebrush.

It was a heaven of sunrise, the first spears of light darting into the golden tops of the cottonwoods alongside the small creek. A trio of delicate-necked deer turned as one at the sound of the front door opening and boots ringing on the planks of the porch. For a frozen moment they stood there, sniffing the damp-scented air. Then they darted away toward the rising ground to the east of the ranch house.

Jak watched them go. "Freedom," he said.

"Looks like being a good one." Krysty took a deep breath, sucking in the freshness.

The squat shape of the LAV-25 stood ready and waiting in the shadows to the west of the spread. It had been loaded with all the supplies and gas that could be spared, along with tools, water and ammo.

Everyone stood in the morning sunlight, nobody quite knowing what to do or say.

Doc broke the awkwardness.

"Despite the sun, I fear that the chill air will play the old Harry with my lumbago," he said. "So, friends, stand not upon the order of your going. But go, in the name of God, go!" He offered a firm handshake to J.B. and then to Ryan. "Take the best care of yourselves."

"What's plumbago, Doc?" Dean asked eagerly. "Sounds like something you eat."

The old man ruffled the boy's hair. "Not quite, young man. Rather something that eats you, but let that pass. Yes, let that pass."

Ryan stooped to hug his son. "Look after things," he said. "Back soon."

"Don't worry, Dad. I'll be fine."

"We'll all be fine," Mildred added, standing on tiptoe to kiss Ryan on both cheeks. She smiled at J.B. "We said our goodbyes earlier."

"So did we," Krysty said. "Look after him, J.B., and bring him safe back to me."

"Sure." The slightly built figure nodded to everyone, the light sparkling and dancing off the polished lenses of his glasses.

Jak was leaning against one of the uprights at the front of the long veranda. Ryan turned, caught his eye and waved a casual hand, getting a nod of the white head in return. J.B. clenched his fist in a salute to the albino.

"Bring Trader back," Jak called. "Heard a lot. Be double great meet him."

The goodbyes were done.

Each man made sure that his own personal weapons were safely aboard the armored combat vehicle.

J.B. put his Uzi machine pistol on the metal floor of the vehicle, beside the driving control position. Carefully he placed his pride and joy alongside it. The Smith & Wesson Model 4000 12-gauge looked at a quick glance like a fairly ordinary 8-round scattergun with a pistol grip and a folding butt. But its ammunition was a country mile out of the ordinary. The blaster fired murderous Remington fléchettes, each round containing twenty of the tiny, inch-long arrows.

Ryan had his panga with the hand-honed eighteen-inch blade sheathed at his belt. The pistol balancing it on the right hip was a SIG-Sauer P-226. Just under eight inches in length with a barrel that was just a bare thumb's width below five inches, the weapon weighed in at a sturdy twenty-five and a half ounces. It held fifteen rounds of 9 mm ammunition, and had a push-button mag release. It's built-in baffle silencer had seen better days.

The rifle went behind the codriver's position, where the navigator would probably have once sat. There was a scratch on the walnut stock and Ryan spit on it, rubbing at the mark with the heel of his hand. The Steyr SSG-70 was a bolt-action blaster, with a mag of ten rounds of 7.62 ammo. It carried a beautiful Star-lite night scope, as well as a laser image enhancer. Though Ryan lacked Mildred's uncanny skill with firearms, he figured that he could still put a bullet through a man's head with the Steyr, in good weather and visibility, at a range in excess of six hundred yards.

The LAV had once had a powerful 25 mm Bush-master cannon, but there was no ammo for it, though they had a couple of belts of 7.62 mm rounds for the coaxial machine gun.

J.B. reemerged and gave a last wave to the remaining friends, getting a blown kiss from Mildred. Then he slipped back down through the hatch. Ryan remained on top, hanging on as the six-cylinder turbocharged diesel engine kicked in, with a surging roar and a cloud of blue-gray smoke from the exhaust, generating nearly three hundred horsepower.

He'd put on the miniature earphones and throat mike that enabled him to communicate easily with J.B., inside or outside the cacophonous steel box.

"Ready, Ryan?"

"Ready as I'll be."

Krysty put her hands to her mouth and shouted at the top of her voice, the words barely reaching Ryan's ears. "Gaia go with you, lover."

Everyone else waved, Doc framed in the doorway, Jak on the porch. Mildred and Dean stood close together, turning away from a dust devil thrown up by a gust of wind. Krysty stood very still, her dazzling hair blowing out behind her, one hand high above her head.

The gears meshed noisily and the LAV began to move slowly across the sandy dirt, the eight wheels leaving a complex pattern behind them.

Ryan stood up on top of the slow-moving armawag, staring around him, capturing the scene in the camera of his memory. He held on to how Krysty looked, the last grin from his son, Doc flourishing the sword stick, the silver hilt catching the desert sun, Mildred punching the air, Jak, his face in shadow beneath the tumbling mane of snowy hair.

His friends.

Chapter Three

"Where is Trader?"

"What?"

The sepulchral voice, coming out of the blackness of midnight, jerked Abe awake. He had been dreaming of a fabulous gaudy slut from Canon City who'd been the proud and notorious owner of sixty-inch breasts. The owner of the filthy gaudy, when a customer asked what her speciality was, used to reply that with a little help she could sit up.

Abe had been lying spread-eagled in a meadow of lush grass, while the whore sat astride him and lowered her breasts over his face, nearly suffocating him.

It had been a good dream, and Abe was reluctant to return to real life.

"What?" he repeated irritably. "Who said that?"

"Where is the man called Trader?"

The fire had long died, leaving only the ghostly residue of powdery white ashes. Abe knew that there were trees around them, mixed conifers, thicker than hairs on the back of a hog. But they were invisible. There had been a moon earlier, while he and Trader sat around eating the chunks of charred rabbit meat, telling familiar tales to each other. Then a bank of cloud had come up from the west, dropping the temperature and leaving the bitter flavor of salt, flat on the tongue, from the Cific Ocean. Trader had warned that there might be rain before dawn.

Abe felt a burning deep in his belly, which he figured came from a crock of home brew that an old woman had sold them two days earlier. She'd claimed that it was real pulque, distilled south of the Grandee. It had the right, slightly milky color, but it tasted of kerosene.

He belched, trying to ease the pain, but all that happened was a spurt of sour bile filled his throat. He spit it out, still not fully awake.

"Trader, that you?"

The voice had sounded like Trader's, but why in the name of skydark would the old man be asking where he was? It didn't make much sense.

"Trader? You havin' some kind of black-dog dream over there? You feeling all right, Trader?"

"Where is he?"

"Who?"

"Trader of course, you triple-stupe mutie son of a bitch!"

"You're Trader, Trader."

There was a long stillness.

Abe waited, aware of the endless nocturnal sounds in the forest—the light breeze sighing through the tops of the pines, a dog howling far off, in the direction of the small ville, the faint breath of a hunting bird ghosting past, its large eyes circling in its ceaseless quest for prey.

"I know that. I know I'm Trader, Abe, for Christ's sake! Why did you say that?"

Even in the few weeks that he'd spent with Trader after his long quest to find him, Abe had learned that the old man's temper hadn't improved with the passage of time.

"Must've been dreaming, I guess."

His waking vision was improving, and Abe could actually make out the shape of his companion. He saw the powerful figure, sitting up, the quilted sleeping bag falling off the broad shoulders, the mop of thinning gray hair and the pale blur of the lined face, the right hand fumbling for the stock of the ever-ready Armalite at his side.

"I never dream, Abe. Did I ever tell you that?" He didn't wait for the reply. "Man who dreams is a soft man, and a soft man is the one you see lying under six feet of cold, cold ground. I ever tell you that before, Abe?"

The skinny ex-gunner from War Wag One shook his head. "Don't believe you did."

"What's the finest meal you ever ate, Abe?"

That was something else about the new Trader.

He was far more occupied with the past than Abe remembered him being when he had been the scourge of the ungodly and the unrighteous, the length and breadth of Deathlands.

"Don't recall. Must've been ten thousand shit meals. Not many come back as being any good."

"Once had red snapper, cooked on a little stove on a boat out of Mobile, down on the Gulf. Caught it, fried it and ate it, all in a half hour. Sunshine on the deck and the sea as flat as Kansas. It was the afternoon of the morning we took out that camp of stickies near a shingle beach. You recall?''

"Can't say I do, Trader."

"Sure you do. Old mutie, chief of the tribe, got a knife through his belly. Spilled out a piece of his gut. You gotta remember this, Abe."

"Not properly, though it rings a kind of distant bell, Trader. Go on."

"Where was... Yeah. Shithole bastard falls down in his panic to get away from the guns of the war wags. Sort of snags this loop of his gut on a jagged hunk of a broken tree. Might've been a sycamore. Or a piñon. Anyway, up he gets, screaming shrill like a pig at the fucking gelding."

Now the story was making sense to Abe, but he was sure it hadn't been stickies by the Gulf. His memory was that it had been a camp of scalies up in the Rockies, and the victim had been a woman, not a man.

But he wasn't about to contradict Trader when he was in full flow.

"Doesn't notice that a part of his intestines was caught up tight as a tick. Off he runs..." Trader laughed, a slow, grating sound in the darkness.

The woman had been naked, breasts jiggling as she tried to get away from the withering fire from the brush around the camp. Her mouth had hung open like she was trying to swallow the world around her. Now Abe remembered it real well.

"He starts trying to run for the sea. Expression on his face like the earth's turned upside down. Trips a couple of times, but he doesn't look down. By now the piece of stomach's around thirty feet long. No, forty feet if it's an inch. Still see the color of it. Course, in the end it pulled him short like he was on a cutting rope. Sat him down on his ass, with the stupest look I think I ever saw on a man's face. Couldn't believe what had happened."

Abe remembered that Ryan Cawdor had put a bullet smack between the wretched woman's eyes from the M-16 he was carrying in those days.

"I took my Armalite and chilled him with a single round through the middle of his piggy mutie face. Don't never say that the Trader doesn't show mercy, Abe."

"I wouldn't, Trader. I wouldn't."

The figure lay down again. "You reckon that Ryan and J.B.'ll come running, Abe?"

"We sent out enough of those messages. Only takes one to get through."

"How long ago was it?"

"Three weeks, give or take a couple days. Thing is with Ryan, nobody knows where he might be. Anywhere in Deathlands. Jumps here, there and everywhere."

Trader yawned. "I wish you wouldn't wake me up in the middle of the rad-blasted night, Abe. Just because you want to wag your jaws, chewing over the old meat."

"Sorry."

"Don't apologize, Abe. You know that it's a sign of double weakness."

"Yeah. We going hunting again tomorrow, Trader?"

"Thought we might pay a visit to that ville where the old woman sold us the pulque. Or whatever mutie piss it was."

"We don't have any jack, Trader."

"Day that Trader needs jack is the day they lay the lid down on the long wooden box."

"What we got to barter?"

The man alongside him moved, and Abe heard the unmistakable sound of a rifle being cocked. "That answer your question, Abe?"

"Yeah, Trader."

"So, did you say you figured that Ryan would be up here soon?"

"Can't promise it, Trader. But I'm sure that he'll come, as long as he gets the message. Can't say fairer than that."

"Good. Ryan was the best, you know. I always figured that he'd be the one to pick up the cards when I laid them down."

"Shit doesn't always hit the bowl like you expect, Trader, does it?"

"It doesn't, Abe. Still, I gotta get some sleep. Tomorrow's another day."

Chapter Four

"Been a long time since we did this."

"Too long?"

Ryan considered the question. "I guess that what Krysty says about life is right."

"What?"

"You shouldn't ever close yourself off from trying new experiences. Or reliving old ones."

J.B. was leaning back against one of the eight wheels of the LAV, his hands folded across his stomach, his eyes closed behind the glasses. "Guess that's true. Mildred says change is healthy. Then the next minute, she says that she likes things staying the same. Never know with women."

"You can say that again, friend."

"I said that you never know with women."

Ryan laughed. "Like Doc said, there's nothing like an old joke, and that's nothing like an old joke."

The morning had passed easily, both men finding it easy to pick up the threads of their close relationship.

In their early days with Trader, as fiery young bloods, they had often been sent off on dangerous missions as a twosome. Later, as they rose through the war wag hierarchy, there had been less time alone together.

And more recently, since they had broken from Trader and traveled across Deathlands through the mat-trans gateways, there had always been others with them.

J.B. yawned. "This riding along sure gives you an appetite. Any more of that shortbread?"

"We eat at this rate, and they'll find us starved by the side of the highway before we're even across the state line into Colorado. Yeah, there's a few crumbs."

"Love the vanilla flavoring that Mildred put in them. She's a real good cook, you know, Ryan."

"Course I know it. Eaten enough of her food, haven't I? Think we should be moving on?"

"Trader's waited years for us. Figure he can wait a few minutes longer."

"Easy to say that when the old terror's not standing in front of you."

The Armorer laughed. "Remember that pompous baron of the ville near the Washington Hole?"

In the last of all wars, Washington, D.C., had been the first of the major casualties, vanishing into dust, spray and lethal radiation in the initial seconds of the final conflict, though it was to be followed into infinity in the next three or four hours by most of the other heavily populated centers of civilization throughout the predark world.

Now there was a crater, a huge basin of total desolation filled with a vast lake of noxious, muddy water. It was still a notorious nuke hot spot, where once the Capitol and the White House had stood. In that great wilderness of dirt, devoid of any life, nothing remained.

Nothing in the Washington Hole.

"I remember him. Dark-skinned with a rad cancer eating away his nose."

"That's the one, Ryan. Got drunk and started lipping off. Said that Trader was a fish-eyed cowardly bastard. Thought the old man was back with the war wags. Said he wasn't frightened of him and he'd say the same to his face."

Ryan nodded. "Yeah. Next thing he knows he's got a mouthful of the butt of the Armalite and he's spitting teeth and blood all over the place."

J.B. stood, brushing a few flakes of the vanilla shortbread from his leather jacket and adjusting the angle of his well-worn fedora.

"Move on?"

"We've made real good progress since dawn. Your turn to drive again."

"Keep it an economical average and we can stretch the gas twice as far as putting the pedal to the metal."

Ryan nodded. "Been lucky with the weather so far. Get us good tans sitting up on top."

It had been truly beautiful. The sun had risen gently into a sky of finest blue. Once they were off the dirt road from Jak's spread, they'd been on blacktops all the way. Apart from the occasional ribboning effect of the undulating quakes, there'd been no problem.

During the first five hours of their journey, they hadn't seen a single living person, seen hardly any living creatures.

A pure white carrion crow had adopted them for several miles, wheeling and darting only a few feet above the head of J.B., who'd been out on top of the turret at that point. There'd been the ubiquitous coyotes, always looking as though they had some important and rather dubious business to transact, slinking along at an easy lope, devouring the miles, dodging the fragile balls of tumbleweed. They'd only once given the vehicle a sideways glance, then carried on and ignored it.

Once a massive mutie rattler had coiled itself across the highway, only a hundred yards in front of the armored wag, whipping its fifteen feet of speckled brightness out of the way at the last moment, its angry rattle clearly audible above the roar of the engine.

Apart from the usual desert lizards and scorpions, scuttling across the sand-blown roads, that was the full extent of what they'd seen.

But there was a dramatic change, an hour after their midday break.

RYAN WAS AT THE CONTROLS, looking through the ob slit, cruising at a comfortable fifteen miles an hour and watching for any sudden end to the pavement.

J.B. sat on top, his hat clamped firmly between his thighs, not wanting to risk losing it to the light northerly breeze that had sprung up.

There was a sudden metallic rapping on the arma-plate above Ryan's head, and he immediately slowed to a walking pace, waiting for J.B. to tell him what the warning had been for. He blinked as the Armorer's face appeared, upside down, in front of the driver's ob slit.

"Folks ahead, fifteen or twenty on foot, spread out both sides the highway. They're in a dip. You won't see them from this low down for another couple hundred yards or so."

J.B. was right. Ryan eased off the gas until the LAV was barely moving. "I see them."

He heard the hatch of the turret clanging open and J.B.'s boots clattering on the ladder. "Just taking basic precautions, Ryan. I'll keep the lid up unless they look hostile. Can you make them out, yet?"

There was a small magnifying periscope to Ryan's right and he used it, focusing the cross hairs on the group of men and women standing still, right across the blacktop, around five hundred yards ahead.

"Look a raggedy bunch," he said, using the mike now that he knew that J.B. had plugged himself in again.

"How do you want to play it? Drop the hatch and sail on through?"

"Negative. They might have some news of what it's like farther down the line."

"Yeah. I'll buy that, Ryan."

The big eight-wheeler crawled cautiously forward, with J.B. waiting patiently, his index finger on the trigger of the M-240 machine gun.

"I make it fourteen," Ryan said, hearing his own voice crackling on feedback through the ancient earphones. "And I think all male."

J.B. had his own scope. "Agreed."

"See blasters?"

"No. Doesn't mean there aren't any. Finest pie crust can easy hide—"

"Stinking fish. I know, J.B., don't I? One of Trader's best sayings."

They were stationary, eighty long paces from the silent group of watchers.

"One's carrying a big cross," J.B. stated. "The one near the back on the left. Down on his knees."

"And some of them got whips." Ryan whistled through his teeth. "Fireblast! They're penitentes, I reckon. Some kind of religious crazies."

"Flagellants! Dark night, remember how much Trader used to loathe them? I never seen him do it, but there was talk he'd personally flogged a half dozen of them to death."

"Said he was speeding them to their own Paradise and how come they kept screaming and not thanking him. Yeah, I heard that story, too."

"Believe it, Ryan?"

"Put it like this, J.B.—I don't exactly say it happened. But I reckon it *might* have happened."

"One in front's shouting something."

"Should I cut the engine?"

"No. I'll put my head out the top and relay what he says down to you."

''Fine. Switch the automatic relay for the machine gun through to me.''

Ryan edged forward another fifty yards, bringing them within easier hailing distance. He knocked the engine out of gear, and held it on the hand brake.

Now it was possible to see the men much more clearly. All of them wore torn cotton pants or skirts, with their feet bare. Each had a multithonged whip at their belts, some with tips of plaited wire or tiny knots, clotted with black blood. Most of them were stripped to the waist, their chests and backs baked deep brown by exposure to the southwestern sun.

Ryan noticed something else, which didn't surprise him at all.

The bodies of the flagellants were seamed with countless scars and weals, most old, layered upon older wounds. A few were obviously new, open cuts, like dozens of hungry red mouths, each one leaking fresh crimson.

Their leader was very tall and lean, his thinning hair and long matted beard a gingery color. The skin of his face was peeling from too much sun.

He carried a long staff with what looked to Ryan like a twisted and tortured figure of Christ at its head.

The man was gesturing toward J.B. with the rod, his mouth working. But Ryan couldn't hear a word, relying on the hissing earphones.

''Says that they want water and food.''

''Want?'' Ryan queried

There was a short pause of ten or fifteen seconds. ''He's changed the word to 'demand' now.''

"Tell him from me to go take a flying leap into a brimming cesspool!"

"Want me to say that, partner?"

"Better not. Ask him who they are and where they're going." He had a fresh thought. "And what the roads are like up toward the north. That sort of thing."

There was another pause while the conversation was relayed, then some talk among the penitentes. The one at the back, supporting an enormous rough-hewn cross, had slipped forward onto his face in the hot sand in a dead faint. But the remaining thirteen members of the sect totally ignored him.

"Says that talk costs in food and water."

Ryan nodded grimly to himself. He swiveled the machine gun a little to the right and saw that every head followed the movement. He brought it back to center on the chest of the leader of the group.

J.B. chuckled. "He saw that. They all did. He's shouting again."

The air-conditioning inside the LAV wasn't functioning well, and Ryan was aware of a thread of sweat trickling down between his shoulder blades.

"Well?"

"Wait a minute."

Time slithered by. Ryan looked at the side of the cab of the LAV, where someone, perhaps bored and hot, had scratched his name—"Pete Haining."

He wondered what the man had been like and how and when he'd died. But his train of thought was interrupted by J.B.'s voice in his ears.

"Name's Apostle Simon, he says. His posse's called the Slaves of Sin."

"Pretty."

J.B. laughed quietly. "Isn't it? Says they're heading south and east. Want to pick up a boat on the Gulf and go to India."

"Say again? Sounded like you said they were planning to go to India."

"Right. Not my business, Ryan. Said the road north is clear. Some villes pay them to keep moving. Doesn't like being threatened by you."

"Tough. Tell them to move their asses off the highway. We're going through."

"Think we should chill a few of them?"

Ryan considered the question seriously, knowing that the years with Trader lay behind it. "No. They can't do any harm."

"Apostle says to tell you that they have the power to bless or curse us."

"Fuck them. They can curse me when I drive this baby smack over the top of them."

He heard the Armorer passing that on, and saw the angry reaction. The leader, followed by his supporters, made an oddly threatening sign to him, forking the fingers of his right hand, like twin horns, pointing them straight at Ryan, hidden behind the armaglass of the ob slit.

The gears engaged, and the machine began to rumble slowly forward.

For a dubious moment, Ryan thought that the religious maniacs weren't going to move and that he would simply crush them under the 25,000-pound weight of the LAV. He ducked instinctively as the leader thrashed out at him with his staff, rapping it smartly against the steel plating just to the side of the driver's ob slit.

The man's mouth was open, caked spittle at the corners of his cracked lips. For a moment Ryan was close enough to hear the screamed words of hatred and anger.

"The God of Pain and the Virgin of Blessed Suffering curse you and your children and their children, yea unto the tenth generation of the unbelieving bastards!"

Then the road ahead of the wag was clear and Ryan eased it up into a higher gear. Over the intercom, J.B. called through to him. "Did the right thing. Wouldn't have trusted them if we'd stopped to help."

"Right." In the rearview mirrors Ryan could see the tatterdemalion group receding fast behind them. "Last we'll ever hear of them. Can't do any harm."

And that was a serious mistake.

Chapter Five

A bullet-pocked sign, a mile back, had warned Ryan and J.B. that they were approaching Huston Wells, altitude three thousand eight hundred feet, population—that sign had been painted, repainted and overpainted so many times that it was now illegible.

J.B. knocked the engine out of gear, allowing the LAV-25 to roll forward under its own momentum, until he stopped it on the crown of the bend, a couple hundred yards from the edge of the frontier ville.

"Roadblock," he stated.

Ryan, higher up, had already seen it and was back inside the turret again.

"Over, under, through or around?" he asked, quoting what was probably the best known of all the Trader's favorite sayings.

J.B. laughed quietly. "By the look of it, we could probably do any one of three. Not so sure about managing to get under it, though."

The blacktop ran north-south, ruler straight, with no side trails visible in either direction. The roadblock was composed mainly of terminally rusted automobiles and pickups, welded together to almost fill the main street. The gap in the middle was just about wide enough for a war wag to slide through.

"Two men with hunting rifles," J.B. announced, peering through his magnifying scope. "Probably a few more around the place. Doesn't look like a sec zone."

"Another sign on the left, hand-painted. Can't make it out with the sun across it."

"Says that you pay a toll to Noah Huston for the way-leave of passing by."

"How much jack?"

J.B. read the sign again. "Doesn't say. Probably the old frontier toll. How much you got? Give it all to us. That's the toll here."

The diesel engine rumbled softly. Ryan looked at the country on either side of the road. It was fairly flat, but there could easily be a honeycomb of old irrigation ditches that would make it difficult driving, even for the powerful LAV.

"Through, I think," he said.

"HOLD IT THERE!" Ryan could barely hear the shout, but the gesture was unmistakable.

The man was of average height and wore a fur vest and denim pants. He carried what looked to Ryan like a bolt-action Winchester Ranger. His colleague, whose face was hidden under the brim of a battered Stetson, held a Model 848 Mossberg rifle with a remodeled stock. He was leaning against the hood of a rusted flatbed truck.

"We're coming through," Ryan yelled.

In his earpiece he could hear J.B.'s calm voice confirming that he had the guy in the fur vest covered with the wag's machine gun.

"Pay the toll and on you go, stranger."

One of the many things that helped to keep you alive in Deathlands was being a good student of behavior. How a person stood, spoke and acted gave you some clue as to what might be going down.

The speaker wasn't exactly brimming with confidence. He stood with his shoulders hunched, and his fingers drummed nervously on the stock of the Winchester. Twice in a handful of seconds he'd glanced behind him, toward the row of semiderelict houses and stores.

"He's looking for company to arrive," J.B. said.

Ryan held the SIG-Sauer in his right hand, just below the rim of the turret. There wasn't any point in wasting time here.

"Noah Huston says..." began the man by the roadblock.

But nobody ever got to hear just what it was that Noah Huston said.

Ryan brought up the automatic and fired at the shadowy figure in the Stetson. At a range of only twenty yards, it was a positive no-miss situation.

The bullet went within a quarter inch of where Ryan had aimed it, a finger's width below the jaw, exploding the air passage and the gullet, powering through and destroying the fragile cervical vertebrae, exiting out of the back of the neck as a distorted and mangled chunk of hot lead. Eventually it buried itself over the door of what had once been, in the nineteenth century, the finest sporting house in Huston Wells.

The Mossberg clattered to the dirt and the Stetson flew off, becoming splattered with arterial blood as it landed behind the flatbed.

Ryan stared at the mane of blond hair that cascaded from under the hat, across the young woman's startled face, vanishing as she fell dead at the back of the roadblock.

Almost simultaneously, the machine gun coughed into life. J.B. fired a triple-shot burst at the man in the fur vest, two of the bullets hitting him in the middle of the chest. The third one struck the barrel of the Winchester and spun howling toward the setting sun.

"Go!" Ryan shouted, his eyes raking the deserted street of the township.

J.B. was already moving, putting the wag into first gear and slamming his foot on the gas. The roadblock didn't leave much room on either side of the LAV. The gap was only around eight feet, to deter anyone trying to run it at speed. The armored vehicle was precisely seven feet, two and a half inches wide. There was less than five inches clearance on each side.

The dying man in his torn and bloodied fur vest had fallen across the gap, almost as though he had made the deliberate decision to try to use his corpse to try to check the escape of the outlanders.

All four wheels on the left side ran over the man's right arm, chest and head.

Ryan felt only the slightest jolt as the skull was splintered to shards of smeared bone, none of them any larger than a silver dollar.

"Company, right, thirty."

The voice of the Armorer whispered urgently into Ryan's ears, warning him that other residents of Huston Wells were coming out at them, thirty degrees from the front of the wag, on the right side. Three figures came running out of a movie theater, one holding a machine pistol like she knew how to use it.

"One ahead, hundred yards."

Ryan glanced down the street. There were alleys and narrow side roads along the western flank, each one with pools of bright sunlight spilling out across the street. There was a man, tall and white-haired, standing in one of those dazzling golden lakes, slowly bringing a bazooka to this shoulder.

"Fireblast!"

J.B. had spotted him. "Not much ammo left for the MG, Ryan. Want me to try and take him out?"

To have a safe shot at the man with either the SIG-Sauer or the rifle, Ryan needed a stable base to shoot from. The LAV, rocking and rolling over the humps and potholes in the street, wasn't going to be a help.

"Bust him, J.B., now!"

He snapped off a couple of rounds at the trio of attackers on his right, seeing the woman go down, clutching her leg, the Uzi skidding away down the seed-strewn sidewalk. A bullet screamed off the armaplating just behind the turret, and Ryan instinctively ducked a little lower.

"Get 'em, Noah!" The shout came from a window above one of the stores to the left, but Ryan couldn't identify which one and held his fire.

The silver-haired man seemed impervious to any threat of danger from the approaching armored wag, standing quite still, surrounded by the halo of brilliant light. He held what looked like an old M-72, the muzzle gaping toward Ryan, as big as the mouth of a mine shaft.

Against a soft target, the weapon had an effective range of more than three hundred yards. Less than half that if the target was on the move.

But the LAV was barely fifty yards away, coming straight at him, with no chance of veering to one side or the other.

"J.B., do it!" Ryan yelled.

The machine gun opened fire, but the wag had just hit an ancient speed-bump and tipped up and down, throwing Ryan against the side of the turret, dealing his right elbow a sharp blow that nearly made him drop the automatic.

He saw the stream of bullets tear into the shingled wall of the frame house just beyond the figure with the blaster, a figure that Ryan guessed was probably the same Noah Huston who ran the small ville.

From high up in the turret he heard the repeated clicking as the machine gun ran out of ammo.

It wasn't a time for hesitation.

Ryan braced himself as best he could against the yawing and pitching of the wag, raised the automatic and opened fire at the man by the alley, not pausing, pouring a river of lead, his index finger working at the trigger, until the mag was empty.

There was chaos all around.

J.B. fought the controls, as the vehicle swerved and clipped a supporting post from a storefront, bringing half the building down in a shower of dust and rotted timbers.

The two men from the old movie theater were both shooting, bullets sparking off the armasteel. The wounded woman was screaming at the top of her voice. Someone fired a shotgun from an upstairs window, but the aim was poor, though Ryan heard the hiss above his head of the pellets slicing through the dusk.

And the M-72 had been fired.

At least five of the 9 mm rounds struck Noah Huston—one through the left elbow, another in the groin, a third and fourth in the chest, toward the left side. A fifth round had ripped away a chunk of bone the size of an ax blade from the right side of his skull, taking the ear with it.

A dying spasm fired the bazooka. The 66 mm rocket roared diagonally across the street, missing the front of the LAV by twenty feet, hitting the front of an ancient funeral home.

There was a devastating explosion, and a sheet of flame with boiling coils of red and gold leaped skyward. Smoke billowed out across the main street of the ville. J.B. pushed the wag up through the gears, accelerating away.

Ryan looked down at the dying man as they thundered by the alley, blinking at the brightness of the setting sun.

"I can see hostiles coming after us, Ryan!"

"They're too far away to bother us."

"They look close."

Ryan was staring back at Huston Wells. It looked as if the rocket had been a flamer, packed with hi-ex and napalm, as half the ville seemed to be burning. There were two diminutive figures, way behind.

"Don't worry, J.B.," he said. "Remember that objects in the rearview mirror may appear closer than they are."

Both men started to laugh.

Chapter Six

They covered another eighteen miles north of Huston Wells, through the gathering gloom, before Ryan decided it was safe to call a halt and camp for the night.

"Fire?" J.B. had taken off his glasses to polish them, cleaning away the road dirt.

"Mebbe not. If that was Noah Huston I chilled, he might have kin eager to come after us. These frontier folk like to try the vengeance trail."

The Armorer nodded. "Could be. I'm sure I heard Jak mention that place once. Old man was supposed to put himself around a lot. Didn't much matter whether it was woman, girl, man or boy."

Ryan whistled softly between his teeth. "Sure. I remember now. Kid said that he peopled the ville with his own bastards. Slept with his own daughter and then, years after, bothered the child he'd fathered on her."

"Sick."

"Could be the safest for us to sleep inside the wag. Lock down the turret. Cold outside." He looked up at the clear sky, where the first bright stars were breaking through the layer of dusty velvet.

"Shall I gas her up?"

Ryan shook his head, sighing as he tried to stretch some of the kinks out of his spine. "Leave that until the morning. Way I feel now, a quick meal and then some shut-eye sounds like the ace on the line."

J.B. carefully put his glasses back on. "I'll second that."

THE LIGHT ARMORED VEHICLE wasn't all that well equipped in the sleeping department. The LAV-25s had originally been designed for a working crew of three, so at least there was a little more space for the two men.

There were vent slits and ob slits around the sides of the wag, and Ryan went around and carefully closed all but two—one at the front and one at the top of the turret, leaving a narrow gap in both of them.

"Don't fancy having one of the locals slipping a rattler in among us," he said.

"Or a scorpion."

"Or a black widow spider."

"Or a poison toad."

Ryan considered. "Or anything that might kill us." He grinned at his old friend.

J.B. looked around the darkling land. They had parked the LAV near the top of a ridge, among a clump of feathery tamarisks. The dying northerly was carrying the faint scent of a wood fire, elusive, untraceable. Both men knew well enough that a smell like that could easily have insinuated itself for twenty miles or more across the uninterrupted desert.

"You're enjoying this, Ryan," the Armorer said. It was a statement, not a question.

"Like the early times," Ryan agreed.

"You believe we'll find him, don't you?"

"Yeah. You?"

"I guess, for most of the time, I never believed the old man was still alive. The rad cancer, or whatever it was, that used to grip at his guts like a nest of red ants...seemed like it would chill him in the end. Then, the way he finally walked out on us without—"

Ryan yawned. "Time'll tell. Don't forget what Trader used to say about trying to guess what the future might bring."

"What?"

"Save your brain. He said it was as useless as trying to hold a conversation with a dead stickie."

RYAN FELT EXHAUSTED. In the old days he'd been used to traveling for endless miles in one of the huge war wags, surrounded by the highly trained crews of the twin vehicles. He'd been used to the cramped quarters and the stink of sweat.

Now it felt like all of the muscles in his body ached, and the marrow of every bone had become jelly from the ceaseless vibration of the big wag. His spine had been compressed by the jolting, and his eye still didn't feel as though it had settled properly back in its socket. Even his voice sounded odd to his ears, grating and harsh.

They had canned pork for their supper, from a hog farm and processing outfit up close by the Lakes, with some pickled cabbage. They'd washed it down with a couple of bottles of beer that Jak had dug out of his cellar for them.

There wasn't much conversation between the two men.

When you've known a friend for close to twenty years and you've spent most of the time within twenty feet of that friend, then conversation was sometimes superfluous.

"We got any more ammo for the MG?" Ryan asked.

"No. Got spares of the nine mill for your blaster. That wasn't bad shooting in the street there."

"Thanks." There was auxiliary lighting off the battery, but it gave only a feeble glow.

"Dawn start?"

"Before."

"Sure."

And that was about the extent of the conversation between Ryan and J.B. that evening inside the LAV-25 in northern New Mexico.

RYAN DREAMED OF A WORLD that he had never known, a world that vanished more than fifty years before he was born in the Shens, one that he only knew from the memories of the elderly and from fragile books and magazines—the world before the missiles blackened the skies and blighted the earth.

He was riding on one of the steam wags that had crossed the country on iron rails. The coaches were luxurious, with padded seats and silken draperies. It was difficult to know where he was, as it was deepest night and the bright electric lamps reflected from the dark glass of the windows.

There was nobody else in his compartment, though a table was laid for two people, with fine china and crystal glasses. But nothing there to eat or drink.

From behind the walls Ryan could hear the muted hum of conversation and the occasional laughter of other travelers. The train was moving fast, the wheels humming, the clicking sounding like whispered words—you can never go back, you can never go back, you can never go back...

Ryan pressed his forehead against the cold glass, trying to make out some feature of the land beyond the coach. But it was blankly invisible. For a bizarre moment he had the illusion that he could see a strange birdlike lizard, taller than a grown man, hopping alongside the train, its feather-crested head turned toward him.

He heard the sound of a gentle rapping on the door of his compartment.

"Yeah?"

A white-coated porter entered.

"Your guest sent a message, Mr. Cawdor, that he has been delayed forever."

"Thanks."

"You're welcome. Enjoy the rest of your ride on the good old Atchison, Topeka and Santa Fe Railroad."

He closed the door quietly and Ryan was left alone again, rumbling on through the night.

In the middle of the dream, he fell asleep, and dreamed, though he couldn't remember what it had been about when he jerked awake again in the luxurious train sleeper.

For a moment Ryan couldn't work out what it was that had awakened him. The lights had dimmed, and he could now see something of the countryside.

They were moving at a little better than walking pace through a dense forest of forbidding conifers, so tall that Ryan couldn't make out their tops.

Then he realized that Trader was outside the train, his head and shoulders level with the window of the compartment, moving steadily along and keeping up with it. He was smiling, his head turned toward Ryan, with a feathery crest of gray hair running down the center of his angular skull.

Ryan blinked—blinked both eyes.

The train was gathering momentum, its acceleration pressing him back into the embroidered cushions of the seat.

It was astounding the way that Trader was able to keep up with it, matching it for speed, the old Armalite resting across his shoulders. He was still smiling, his face closer to the glass than before.

Now Trader lifted his right hand and began to scratch on the window. Ryan noticed that the nails were hooked and as thick as horn, more like the claws of a big puma. They were leaving gouges on the glass.

The smile was still there, but it had become deeply sinister and vulpine, the lips peeling back, revealing crooked teeth, jagged and yellow, poking from raw and bleeding gums.

Faster.

Trader was floating effortlessly alongside the coach, nodding and beckoning to Ryan.

"You can never go back, Ryan... You can never go back, Ryan... Never go back, Ryan... Go back, Ryan... Ryan..."

It was the familiar voice of the Trader.

Terror held Ryan in thrall, paralyzed, frozen, unable to move a limb to escape from the prison of the compartment.

The rest of the universe was a blur.

Ryan couldn't turn his head away from the macabre specter that flowed with the train, now moving at unimaginable speed. So fast that the glass was beginning to melt, beads of it turning molten and starting to trickle toward the rear of the window.

Trader's hand was pressed against it, the flesh blackening from the intense heat, smoldering and smoking. Tiny blue flames erupted from each curved claw.

And the smile never wavered.

It had become so hot that Ryan was dripping with perspiration, feeling it trickle down into both his eyes, over his cheeks, across his stomach.

It was only a matter of seconds before the glass, the only thing protecting him from the ghastly apparition, would totally disintegrate.

One hand broke through and seized Ryan by the jaw, the broken nails digging into his flesh. Trader was laughing now, and calling out to him in a wild shriek of triumph.

"Dark night, Ryan, can you stop that rad-blasted noise and let me get some sleep?"

The train was still going, going...

Ryan opened his eye, finding that he had rolled on his side, so that the bolt of the Steyr was digging into his jaw. The compartment of the LAV was warm and he had been sweating.

"Sorry, J.B.," he said. "Sorry."

Chapter Seven

The two men walked quietly through the early-morning forest. It had been cold in the middle part of the night, and dew was dripping from the dark needles of the pines. The trail was soft with mulched leaves, making it easy to keep silent.

At a turn in the track they surprised a doe with a fawn, feeding from the tender shoots in the undergrowth. One of the men instinctively raised a weathered old Armalite rifle to his shoulder, then shook his head and lowered it again.

"Might as well beat a drum to let the sons of bitches know we're coming," he said.

The deer stared at the two human intruders with large, frightened eyes, then spun and darted off into the protection of the shadows, the little fawn following at his heels in a gawky, skipping leap.

"Your lucky day, young fellow," Abe said, his breath feathering out in front of him.

THE VILLE WAS a nameless collection of scattered huts, around the sides of a bowl-shaped valley. A wide river flowed flatly through the settlement, with plum trout rising to the swarms of flies in the muddy hollows.

The store was a converted church, though the weather had done most of the actual converting. Lightning had felled the top of the spire, and a quake had brought down the rear part of the tower. The small stained-glass window, dedicated to a long-dead worthy, had disintegrated into dusty, colored splinters. A sign, protected by the porch, still proclaimed: Today Belongs to Man but Forever Belongs to the Almighty.

There had been extensive logging in that part of the Cascades during the past few years before skydark, and the woods were still veined with the faint remnants of the trails. One of them brought Trader and Abe out onto a shallow promontory, overlooking the ragtag ville.

They stood together, concealed by the fringe of shadow, checking the place out.

"Man who rushes in is the man who gets hisself carried out," the older man muttered.

"True," Abe agreed, his right hand resting on the butt of the big Colt Python strapped to his hip. His left hand was plucking nervously at his drooping mustache.

On their previous visit, when they'd been given the pulque, there had been elements in the place that had made Abe feel distinctly uncomfortable.

In the old times, with the two war wags, Abe recalled visiting hamlets in the dark backwoods of the Smokies and the Shens, blue-misted, triple-poor places.

This place was reminiscent of those poverty shacks.

There'd been a boy, seeming close to fifteen, shuffling around the store with a broom. It had been several minutes before Abe had spotted what was wrong with the lad. His feet were on backward, facing behind him.

And there had been the group sitting around the potbellied stove, half a dozen men, all of them looking as if they were members of the same inbred family. They had thin hair, the color of rain-beat straw, and pale blue eyes with dropping lids.

When Abe and Trader had first walked into the place, there had been a sudden silence so intense that you could have heard a moth fart.

When they finally left, Trader had said that he had thought for a moment it was going to be a time to put the top up and the hammer down.

There'd been comments about outlanders, not quite loud enough to be heard, that produced noisy laughter and much spitting and hawking.

Abe had wanted to get out as quick and easy as possible, but it was like he feared. Trader wasn't the sort of man to turn his back on trouble.

After downing the first slug of the milky home-brewed liquor, Trader had walked to stand by the group.

"Sounds to me like there's some good jokes being told," he said, as quiet as a rattler moving through soft sand. "Like a good joke myself. How about telling them to me and my friend here?"

One of the men stood, uncoiling from an ancient armchair with rusting springs sticking out of it. Abe had put him at way over seven feet, with a myopic stoop. He carried a sword at his belt, with filthy golden tassels dangling from the hilt.

"Outlanders don't get to hear jokes." The voice seemed to come from the bottom of a dry well.

"That so?"

"Yeah."

Trader cradled the Armalite in his arms like a mother with her firstborn child. He stared into the man's face and nodded.

"Then you'd better keep the jokes quiet until after we've gone. That way we don't hear anything we shouldn't hear, and nobody gets to be hurt."

Abe waited while seconds stretched into millennia. The hairs at his nape were crawling with a life of their own. He was ready to draw and dive behind a sack of dried peas, putting a couple of rounds into the group of men.

But the moment passed.

The giant glanced at his friends, but he didn't see any great desire to get involved in something that would leave blood on the floor. Possibly their blood.

"TRADER?"

"Yeah, what is it?"

"We just going to walk in and take what we want?"

"Sure are ... Abe, isn't it?"

"Yeah."

Trader shook his head. "My memory's getting like an interstate sign. Crammed full of holes."

"What is it that we want?"

"Jug or two of that home brew. Salt. Saw some apples. Wouldn't mind if they got some fresh milk or butter and a new-baked loaf or two."

"Didn't see any of that when we were there before. Just a lot of dirt and some crazies who looked like they all had the same father and a load of different mothers."

Trader laughed and slapped Abe on the shoulder, nearly knocking him off his feet. "Might not be enough of you to feed a bear cub, Abe, but you're a ballsy little bastard. Now, let's go kick the rednecks' asses."

ABE BLINKED. It was like a bad dream, where you think you've been someplace before.

The store was precisely the same as it had been for their previous visit. Same old woman leaned on the filthy counter, and the same bunch of men sat around the stove.

And there was the same silence when he and Trader walked in, broken by the enormously tall man, sitting with his legs stretched out in front of him.

"Well, looky, looky here. If it's not Daddy Outlander and little baby Outlander, come to see who's been sleeping in their beds."

Trader ignored the man. He walked up to the counter and rapped on it with the butt of the rifle, jerking the old woman out of a daydream.

"Got any bread?"

"Makin' some 'morrow," she mumbled.

"So you can just fuck off in the forest and find yourself a good pile of bark and some dead beetles and make do with that, Daddy Outlander." The others greeted the man's heavy-handed attempt at a joke with sycophantic laughter.

Trader turned around. There was a tension to his wiry, muscular body that Abe remembered from times past. He readied himself for the violence that he guessed was waiting in the wings to run onto the stage.

"Enough," Trader said.

"Now, what does that mean, old-timer?"

Chairs scraped back and everyone got to their feet. The old woman behind the counter hastily took down a framed picture of a racehorse.

"It means that we came in here, real peaceable, not looking for any sort of trouble."

Which wasn't quite true. The idea had been to go in and take what they wanted by threat of arms. But things had moved so far and so fast that it didn't much matter.

"Might not want trouble, you gray-haired old bastard, but you sure found it now." A cackle of laughter erupted from the smallest of the litter, a youth with a scar at the corner of his mouth, skinnier even than Abe.

"Yeah. Insults our ville, don't he?" A fatter man cracked his knuckles while he grinned at Trader and Abe.

"This your ville, is it?" Trader asked, courteous and polite, as if he were asking a priest the time of day.

"Sure is."

"My mistake, friend. I mistook it for a shithole in the dirt filled with dead worms that used to fuck their grandmothers."

Trader's words, delivered with the same gentle calm, hung in the air, almost as if he'd somehow carved them into the slabs of dusty sunlight that filtered through the open door.

"That about does it," Abe whispered.

The immensely tall man drew his sword from its sheath and flourished it with such vigor that he sliced open a bag of nails, hanging from the rafters. He dodged them as they spilled around him, his blue eyes fixed on Trader.

"You... You're dead, old man. You're walking around and suckin' air, but you're deader than a rusty bucket. Was goin' to just kick you around some, but not now."

"Loudest-talking corpse I ever did see, Abe," Trader commented, firing the Armalite from the hip.

The boom of the blaster was deafening in the small building. The bullet hit the giant through the center of his belly and exited behind in a spray of blood and torn intestines, breaking a window at the side of the store.

"Land o'Goshen!" the old woman exclaimed, her eyes rolling up in their sockets as she fell to the floor behind the counter in a dead faint.

"You shot me, friend," the tall man said, left hand exploring the neat hole just above his belt buckle.

"I'll shoot anyone makes a bad move." Trader covered the other five with the Armalite. "Get us some food, Abe, if you can find anything in this midden worth the eating or drinking."

"You fuckin' killed me. No call... Hurts like a kinda spear in me." His face was working with shock and pain. "Pay for this, you will. Both of you. Won't just walk away...."

"Watch us. Better put that steel on the floor, young fellow. Right now!" The crack of command rang out.

The fat young man dropped the straight razor from his right hand, so clumsily that he almost managed to cut himself. "You'll be fine, Luke."

"Not unless you got a good doctor in this place, son," Trader said. "Hole that bullet made in his back means you'll be burying him before sunset."

The sword fell from the weakening fingers, point first, sticking in the splintered planks of the floor, where it quivered for a few seconds until it became still.

Abe hadn't found much worth taking, but he'd snatched two green bottles of what he hoped were pulque as well as some jerky and a handful of biscuits. "Best get out, Trader," he said.

The skinniest of the group facing them gave a short, barking laugh. "Trader! Who you joshin', stranger? Trader died ten years back."

"Then your friend here got himself chilled by a ghost," Trader replied, backing toward the door, making sure that Abe was covered by the Armalite.

"Company out here," Abe stated, peering through the dusty glass of the door into the street. "Old man, three women and one I ain't sure of."

"Carrying?"

"One's got a sawed-down. The old man." Abe felt a momentary pang of worry as he realized that the "old" man was probably younger than Trader. "The others don't have any weapons, but it won't take long."

"You bastards are dead for that," said one of the shocked group of men, watching their friend down and dying. "Hunt you like the dogs you are."

"Heard that a damned lot of times." Trader glanced over his shoulder at Abe. "Take out the guy carrying the scattergun, and we'll be able to shake the friendly mud of this wholesome ville off our boots."

Abe inched out of the door, aware of a hum of movement, like a wasp nest after someone's poked a stick inside it. The old-timer with the sawed-down looked at him, seeing the gleaming blaster in his hand. He turned on his heel and scuttled away, realizing that he was on a loser.

"Gone," Abe called.

"Fine." Trader swiveled the Armalite across the men. "First one to stick his nose out the door gets it blown away. Not a threat. A promise."

"You *are* the Trader, aren't you?" one of them said wonderingly.

"So they say." He fired a bullet into the ceiling, shaking down the mummified corpse of a large brown rat and several pounds of powdery rust.

Then he was outside, running fast, heading around the corner of the ruined church toward the trees, Abe close at his heels. Someone fired a single echoing shot from a black-powder musket, but the ball went nowhere near either of them.

A lean mongrel snarled and snapped at Trader, but he smashed its skull open with the butt of the rifle, not even breaking step.

"Was it worth it, Trader?" Abe panted, as they got among the friendly shelter of the pines. "Didn't get away with much worth having."

"Always worth it. You don't try, then you don't succeed, do you?"

Far behind them they could hear shouts and a single, piercing woman's scream. Abe guessed it was either the dying man's wife or sister or mother or daughter. In a ville like that it could have been any combination of the four.

And a man's voice, like a bear, bellowed, "You can run, but you can't hide from us, outlanders! We know the woods and the valleys, and we'll catch you."

"Fuck off!" Trader shouted, bending over, leaning against a tree, fighting for breath.

"Blood for blood . . ." The howl followed them as they struck the steep, winding trail that would lead back safely to their hidden camp.

The biting anger in the voice pursued Abe into his dreams that night.

Chapter Eight

It had been some years since Ryan and J.B. had ridden that part of northern New Mexico. A wild and barren land, a person could travel for three days in a straight line and never see a single living soul.

Their memories were of rolling hills, stubbled with sagebrush and mesquite, seamed by fresh rivers, with orange mesas and buttes dotting the higher ground and snow-tipped mountains away to the east.

The only life you ever saw, apart from the scattered and isolated villes, was the Navaho—a single horseman on the skyline, watching over a few dozen sheep; an elderly woman, head covered in a patterned scarf, trudging along a winding highway, looking neither to left nor right, going from one unimaginable place to another. And the empty hogans, left open and deserted so that the night spirits of the dead could move away from them.

The passing of time hadn't made many changes.

The region had been plagued by a number of fairly recent quakes, breaking open the blacktops and splitting the land into dark crevasses. One of them meant a change in plan, on the afternoon of the second day out.

Forty-four, as it wound through the Nacimento Mountains, had been wiped away, disappearing into a riven moonscape that even the off-road LAV would have found impossible.

J.B. had been at the driving controls of the eight-wheeler and he'd pulled over, switching off while he and Ryan consulted their precious old maps.

"There's a road east," J.B. said, pointing with his finger, "across to Coyote. Then north... No, east again to Abiquiu."

"Taking us the wrong way." Ryan shook his head. "Gas is at a premium. Look, there's a blacktop west through Chaco Canyon and then onto 371, toward Farmington or Cortez. Or Durango. Least it's in the right direction."

The Armorer took off his glasses and wiped them on his sleeve. "North and west. Probably only a dirt road. Still... Yeah. Let's go for that. Just one thing, Ryan, old friend."

"What?"

"We have a breakdown in a region like this and the chances of getting out alive are somewhere between one and zero. The ass end of nowhere."

"No choice, is there?" Ryan smiled, cracking the patina of dust that filled the fine lines in his face. "When is there a choice, J.B., tell me that?"

"I REMEMBER SOMEBODY once talking about this road, on War Wag One."

"Who?"

"Can't remember. Might have been Simon Lam. One was interested in the old Indian things. Said he'd visited Chaco Canyon when he'd been a young sprout in a ville on the edge of Monument Valley. Claimed that in predark days there were big arguments about this dirt road. Some said it should be upgraded to a smooth blacktop, to make it easier to visit the canyon. Others said it was good that only people who really wanted to go there would make the effort and keep the rough road."

There was the worst section of the trip since they'd left the ordinary highway, the LAV rising nose-up, like a breaching whale, then rolling to its left and sliding for fifteen or twenty feet, finally climbing again up over a series of bone-rattling humped ridges.

"Don't need to ask who won the argument," J.B. said. "And it's your turn to spell me, Ryan."

THEY REACHED THE RUINS of what had once been the Visitors' Center in the middle of the afternoon, stopping in what was the overgrown, sandy remains of the parking lot.

"Doesn't look the most hospitable place in the world," Ryan commented, pulling on the brakes.

"Lam say it was worth a look?"

"Sure did. I think he said it was about the biggest and the best of the centers of the Anasazi culture, over a thousand years ago."

"Mesa Verde," J.B. said, throwing open the hatch and sucking in great gulps of clean air.

"Right. This was bigger. Much bigger."

"Take a look in the building first?"

"Sure." Ryan switched off the engine, relishing the sudden, delicious quiet.

The drinking fountain stood just outside the broken entrance doors. Ryan pressed the chromed button on the top and a tiny red spider with green legs fell out of the spout. It was long dead, curled into a ball.

"Smell panther," J.B. said, hesitating in front of the shadowed center.

Ryan sniffed, catching the bitter scent of feline urine. "Yeah. Mebbe we don't want to go in after all."

The idea of going into a ruined and desolate building, with its linked rooms, like a maze of black caves, that was used as a lair by pumas seemed triple stupe.

"Back to the wag," J.B. urged.

THE TWO OLD FRIENDS stood together in front of one of the great marvels of the world, the red ruins of what was called Pueblo Bonito. Six hundred rooms, spread over four stories, were once home to well over a thousand of the old people. Deserted, said the carved information slab in front of Ryan and J.B., with inexplicable haste, leaving pots on tables and cloth on looms.

The shadows of Fajada Butte fell clear across Chaco Wash as the day crept toward its ending. The only faint sounds were those of nature—the wind through the dry grasses and the whispering of a lizard scuttling across a stretch of exposed stonework. High clouds skated from north to south, against the pink-purple sky.

"I don't get it," J.B. said, his voice unexpectedly loud in the stillness.

"What?"

"Says they had this culture here, way before any white men came to the place. Roads and stuff. What I don't get is where the water was. There wasn't a sign in this whole canyon that there was ever any water here at all. It's got to be a good forty miles or more to the San Juan."

Ryan looked around at the emptiness. "Quakes and stuff could easily have changed the land," he said. "Can't have houses holding a thousand people without good regular water. Wouldn't make any kind of sense."

J.B. scuffed at the dust with the toe of his combat boot. "Sure isn't any here now."

"Good job we got plenty in the wag." Ryan shuddered suddenly, hunching his shoulders. "Somebody must've just walked across my grave."

"Kind of creepy, isn't it? That guy, Lam, had good camp fire stories about the witches that the Navaho believe protect some of the ancient sites. Might be some of them around here, watching us, waiting for us."

Ryan grinned. "Thanks a lot, friend. Just what I need before settling down for the night. Still, take more than a few witches to move us on."

They stopped at three different places throughout Chaco Canyon to try to find a good campsite for the night.

But at each of them one or the other of the men found something to object to: too close to the overhanging butte, too far away from the cover of the cliffs, not enough scrub for cover, too much scrub for cover.

In the end, despite the failing light, Ryan and J.B. agreed that they would drive farther, taking the other dirt road north and then cutting west over an undulating dusty highway, until Chaco Canyon and all of its ghosts and witches were left safely behind them.

They found a long-abandoned farm trail cutting steeply off the old blacktop, following it for a mile until it reached a narrow stream set among a small grove of delicate tamarisks and stunted live oaks.

Neither of them said anything more about whether the place might be haunted.

Ryan started a camp fire, using only dry wood to minimize the risk of smoke being spotted. But there hadn't seemed any sign of life for a hundred miles around them.

The Armorer went down to the water, topping up their canteens and cans. He then checked over the engine of the wag, filling both gas and oil, so that they'd be ready to hit the road again, first thing in the morning.

Once the fire was crackling merrily, Ryan took the Steyr and walked away into the evening gloom, reappearing in less than a quarter of an hour with a brace of rabbits dangling from his belt.

"COULD'VE DONE with a pinch more salt," J.B. commented, leaning back expansively against one of the wag's huge wheels.

"I'm sorry that old Loz isn't here to do the cooking for you, partner."

The Armorer laughed. "Loz! Best cook that War Wag One ever had. Just about the only cook that War Wag One ever had. Only man who could burn a boiled egg."

"Had a way with buffalo meat, though. One of Loz's bison stews lasted you about a week, what with all the bits you kept on picking out between your teeth."

"Could be we might run into one of the big herds up Colorado way." J.B. was cleaning his fingernails with a saguaro spine. "Rumors a couple of years ago said the buffalo were coming back in a big way. Like they used to do in the middle 1800s before the hunters came along with the .50-caliber Sharps and butchered the lot."

"Be a sight to see." Ryan stretched. "Fireblast! I'd almost rather ride a lame mule than that white-nuked wag. Yeah, even that red-eyed Judas that Jak has at his spread."

"Wouldn't go that far. Though old Doc finally seemed to reach an understanding with the long-eared brute. Beats me. I'd have slit its throat, first hour out."

Ryan stood and walked a few yards away, unzipping and taking a leak, hearing the powerful stream of liquid hiss into the dry sand. He had once heard of a man on one of the wag trains west who'd done the same thing and had a rattler rear up out of the blackness and bite him on the end of his dick. And not a man there was prepared to try to suck out the poison.

So, he kept extra alert until he'd rejoined J.B. by the welcoming fire.

"I sometimes wonder, specially round the outskirts of big old villes, what it must've been like before skydark, whether there were any more folks around here."

The Armorer shook his head, the firelight reflecting off the lenses of his spectacles. "Read old guidebooks and stuff like that," he said. "Even in the last olden days, there wasn't much activity around here."

"Only group we saw were those flagellants. What were they called?"

"Slaves of Sin."

Ryan scraped a couple of spoonfuls of the rich gruel from the bottom of the cooking pot, still hanging over the flames on its iron tripod.

"Trader would probably have simply chilled the lot of them," he said.

"Probably."

After a companionable silence, Ryan yawned. "Think I might turn in now."

"Sure."

Ryan paused, climbing up onto the LAV. "Mebbe we should've chilled those religious sickos."

"Mebbe. Too late now. Good night, Ryan."

"Night."

Chapter Nine

The mule rolled its red-rimmed eyes and turned its head to peer at the old man sitting perched on the saddle.

"Look at me like that, you spawn of Satan, and I break my ebony cane across your brainless skull!"

Doc had been unsettled ever since Ryan and J.B. had driven off in the clumsy eight-wheeler, heading northwest to their date with the Trader.

If pressed, he'd probably have said that the inside of his brain was itching and his skin felt like it belonged to somebody else.

Now, with the sun sinking far away across the blank wilderness beyond the Lauren spread, he'd decided to try to get himself a little exercise.

He got Judas out of the barn, neatly avoiding a halfhearted attempt from the mule to break his knees with a sideways kick. Supper was still a couple of hours off, and Doc had chosen to ride toward the low foothills.

Over the past few days, the animal and the man had reached a sort of compromise. Judas wouldn't try too hard to bite or injure Doc, and the old man wouldn't smash it across the rawboned, angular skull with his sword stick.

Neither of them was particularly happy with this revised arrangement, but it was working fairly well, with just the occasional lapse from grace on one side or the other.

The whole house had been prickly and uneasy since the departure of the two men the previous morning.

Mildred had been waspish and snappy, and Dean had been slapped hard across the side of the head by Jak for carelessly leaving a corral gate open and allowing a couple of horses to escape.

Krysty had taken her troubles into herself.

Doc had come across her three or four times, sitting on the swing seat out on the porch with her emerald green eyes fixed on the distant horizon.

"Penny for them."

"Worth a lot less than that, Doc."

"Ryan'll make it back."

"Because he always does?"

Doc nodded. "I suppose that is partly the answer. He always does."

"But one day he won't."

"Ryan die?"

"We all do, Doc."

And there wasn't any answer to that.

"COME ON, JUDAS. Just a little farther up the trail and then we can reach that *vista encantadora,* across the universe. Top of the world. Mother of mercy, is this the end of Doc Tanner? Must try to check myself of this foolish habit of giving in to mental instability, Theophilus, my dear fellow." He patted the mule on the side of the neck. "It does, perchance, cross my mind that Master Cawdor and the other good, good friends might sometimes consider me a few cards short of a grand slam."

The track was narrowing, with yuccas towering on either side. Something rustled in the dry undergrowth down on the left, making Judas start uncertainly. But the sound wasn't repeated and they carried on.

"Steady there, steady," Doc said, keeping a firm grip with his skinny shanks on the animal.

It was comparatively rare for any of the group of friends to find themselves quite alone. Now, breathing in the slightly cooler air of evening, Doc was aware that his thoughts were carrying him back to the time that he had been a young married man with a beautiful wife and two adorable little children, a man with a career and excellent academic prospects. "Nostalgia is a fine place to visit," he said quietly, "but I doubt that one should aspire to go and live there."

The trail widened again, becoming more gentle. He'd hiked it before and knew that it became much more steep, just around the next corner.

But there was the cutoff to the left. Doc heeled Judas on, ducking under the low branches of an elegant sycamore, smiling at the amazing view out over the spread land.

The ranch and outbuildings were immediately below him, looking like a child's toy farm. Doc's sight was reasonably good, but he couldn't see anyone moving there. The mountains ranged along to right and left, rising and falling, their peaks and ravines already shrouded in the purple mists of evening.

"The blue remembered hills," Doc said, the sound of his voice making the mule prick up his ears.

A very large bird flew several thousand feet above him, its giant wings spread, hugging a shrinking thermal. It looked like some kind of South American condor, but Doc couldn't be anywhere near certain.

He swung his leg across and dismounted, rubbing the small of his back. He tied the reins to a broken lower branch of the sycamore, making sure that the knot was secure. He'd already experienced Judas's party trick of shaking loose a carelessly tied knot and vanishing in a cloud of dust, braying in triumph.

"Wait here. Won't be long." There was the suspicion of bared teeth and Doc glared at the animal. "I strongly urge you to set such thoughts aside," he warned, shaking the silver-headed cane at the animal.

There was some fresh and tender young grass sprouting below the shade of the tree, and the mule lowered its head and began to browse contentedly.

Doc sighed and walked the few steps to the edge of the overlook, waving away a few golden-winged flies and seating himself on the warm turf.

"What is happiness?" he asked. "It is a moment when the pain and desolation are briefly absent."

His face cracked into a broad smile, revealing his strong, faultless teeth. "Self-pity is a most excellent medicine. Would you not say, Dr. Tanner?" He turned his head to look the other way, toward the north, answering himself. "It is only truly efficacious for the patient who relishes wallowing in his own emotional detritus."

He lay back, resting his head on his hands. The late-afternoon sun was still pleasantly warm, and Doc realized that he should take care not to just slide away into sleep. The older he became, the more he seemed able to do that.

So he resisted the temptation to close his eyes. As he looked up toward the heavens, tiny specks floated across his vision. "Enzyme chains," he muttered. "Or are they the secret messages left for us by the inhabitants of faerie?"

One of the clouds was the shape of a large, old-fashioned hat, with a lacy feather sticking out of its top. His dead wife, Emily, had once worn a hat like that.

It had been purple silk, decorated with a white osprey's feather. The long pin that held it in place was silver, with a head of Whitby jet. She had worn it to a christening of a close friend's baby. But the names of the child and the friend had escaped Doc.

"Odd how the memories of so long ago are often as clear as finest crystal," he mused. "While what I ate to break my fast this morning is as misty as Nantucket in November." He thought about it. "Bacon and grits with scrambled eggs," he finally concluded. "And the child was christened Jonquil and the friends were called Tarquin and Hermione Rivett." He clapped his hands in triumph, making Judas stop his ruminative munching.

The air was heavy with the scent of wild mint, growing in a cluster near the tree behind him. Doc sighed, unable to shake off the passing feeling of melancholy that was lying over the entire group of companions.

"Be a good thing when Master Cawdor and Brother Dix return safely to us, Judas. They are truly our shield and our buckler against the ungodly." He yawned. "I shall have a quick look out at the valley of death before us, and then we might commence our downward journey."

He stood, knee joints cracking painfully, rubbed dust from his breeches and stared out over the New Mexico desert, first toward the south, then shading his eyes as he looked toward the coppery fire of the setting sun.

"Feel like Pilgrim, after his battle against the demonic Apollyon, gazing toward the far-off radiance of the... By the Three Kennedys! What was it? Was it the golden road to Samarkand? Or the unexpected stranger in the bustling marketplace of Somarra? I disremember."

Finally he looked toward the north.

It was impossible to guess how far the horizon was. It was bathed in a shimmering mist, with the distant mesas and buttes standing out from it like the beached wrecks of ancient, mastless vessels.

"All it lacks is a vast and headless trunk of stone," Doc said. "But I can do the looking and the despairing for... Now, what can that be?"

There was a faint column of dust, many miles away, rising a hundred feet in the air, the last rays of the sun catching it before the wind dispersed it.

"Is it one of those whirling dervishes of sand? No, it doesn't seem . . ."

Again his voice faded away as he saw the cause of the disturbance. Moving out of a shallow depression in the speckled desert was a group of people. They were much too far away for the old man to have any chance of making out any details.

"More than one and less than a thousand" was his best estimate.

Doc had lived enough of his disturbed time in Deathlands to know that strangers could often signify danger.

"Best be moving, Judas, and warn the others." He untied the reins and slapped the mule on the rump when it refused to budge from the fresh grass.

But the minuscule figures, dark-shadowed against the pallor of the land, drew him again and he stood on the narrow plateau, staring.

"The threat from the north," he muttered. "Always from the north."

Whomever the strangers were, they might have encountered J.B. and Ryan on the road. And they might easily be ordinary, pleasant travelers.

"Of course they are," Doc said, shaking himself. "Silly old fool. Seeing danger where there is none."

He climbed aboard the mule and started the descent toward the valley floor and the spread and his friends.

Chapter Ten

The third day of the journey began with a bright sun peeking over the hills to the east.

"Hope this weather lasts," J.B. said, wiping the skillet with a handful of fine white sand.

Ryan was busily stamping out the glowing, smoldering remnants of their morning cooking fire. "I figure that the farther north and west we drive in the wag, the colder and wetter it's going to become."

The Armorer blew into the pan, removing the last particles of dust. "Yeah. The other thing that it's going to become is hard traveling if we don't get ourselves some more gas in the next day or so."

"I always liked walking," Ryan said.

"I noticed that. Ever since we first met up, Ryan. I've known you as a man who liked walking. Just about as much as a pig likes flying."

DURANGO, AND THEN up on 666 across Utah and into Nevada. That was just about as far as they'd bothered to make any detailed plans. Both of them knew that trying to schedule a long journey of more than three or four days over any part of Deathlands was about as pointless as Russian roulette. Often with the same result.

There could be a severe chem storm, with teeming rain so acid that it would strip the paint off a wag in forty minutes or a man's flesh from his bones in a great deal less. Or quakes or one of the volatile volcanoes that had been brought back to life by the massive nukings of skydark, fires or flash floods, falling trees or major earth slips. Or you might even run into an unmarked radiation hot spot.

And that didn't include the strong probability of encountering big trouble from either four-legged or two-legged animals. Norms or muties. Or both.

Trader used to say that a man who planned anything beyond the end of his own nose was likely to have it hacked off.

"MORE TREES." Ryan was driving, watching the changing landscape through the narrow ob slit at the front of the LAV-25. J.B. sat in the top of the turret, head and shoulders out in the fresh morning air. His fedora had been jammed on tight to avoid its being snatched off by the breeze.

"Say again." The Armorer wasn't bothering to wear his earphones. Apart from a couple of tumbledown and isolated hunters' cabins set way back off the blacktop, they still had seen no sign of human life.

"Getting plenty of trees now."

"Yeah."

Ryan wished he hadn't bothered to say anything at all. It was such an obvious comment. But they hadn't exchanged a single word for over an hour, and he felt a slight social pressure to keep the contact open.

"Colder, too."

"Yeah."

There had been a faint drizzle falling for an hour or so, from about the time they approached what would have been the old state line into Colorado. It had made the highway slick and treacherous, particularly in places where the gradient had been affected by quakes or earth shifts.

At an isolated crossroads, miles from anywhere, Ryan had noticed the tracks of another wag. He'd slowed, drawing J.B.'s attention to them. The Armorer had climbed out on the top of the eight-wheeler, reporting that they looked like threadbare tires off a four-by.

Ever since the long winters, motorized transport had been at a premium. The metal-working skills were still there to repair the mechanics of the remaining vehicles, but making tires when the supply of rubber in Deathlands was almost nonexistent was a lot more difficult.

And gas that even remotely approached the purity of predark supplies couldn't be found anywhere. But crude processing plants down in west Texas and in Louisiana offered a product that just about reached acceptability.

One of Trader's great strengths had been based on the time he'd found vast supplies of gas from before skydark, a hundred miles or more north of Boston. Buried in a massive military installation, like a redoubt, there'd been enough to keep the pair of powerful war wags, which he'd discovered in the Apps a quarter century earlier, on the road for many years.

Ryan found his mind turning more and more toward the elusive figure of his old leader.

For many months he had been utterly convinced that Trader was dead, gone off like a wounded animal into the forest to seek a quiet, dark place to suffer through the last agonies of what most of the crews of the war wags had been certain was an abdominal rad cancer.

The whispers around the villes, frontier pestholes and gaudies that the Trader still lived had come to Ryan like bolts from the clear blue sky.

And his first reaction had been that this was all the stuff of legend.

Then the whispers had become more frequent, about a grizzled man, short on temper and long on nerve, carrying the ubiquitous battered Armalite— among the flaming fall leaves of New England; down on the coral keys of the extreme southeast; shuffling through the ghoul-haunted streets of the old Windy City; trapping beaver in the Shens; clearing out some *comanchero* bandits from a ville a spit away from the Grandee; fighting a duel with a trio of weird Mohawk sisters perched among the spidery remnants of a ninety-story skyscraper in the burned-out blocks of lower Manhattan.

Stories, stories, stories.

It was the repetition of these mythic tales that began to preoccupy the thoughts of Abe, until the skinny ex-gunner couldn't live with the doubts. He needed to go and turn them into certainties, one way or the other.

As the wag rolled toward Durango, J.B. was at the controls, leaving Ryan plenty of time for his own thoughts, riding shotgun across a deserted landscape.

But he still couldn't get his mind clear on what he *really* thought about Trader. The message now removed any doubts that the old man was still this side of the dark river. And that, if things went well, Ryan and the Armorer might be seeing him again within the next couple of weeks.

"Then what?" The words were whipped away by the afternoon breeze, into the pine-scented air.

Would Trader expect them to rejoin him? Or would he want to assume the leadership of their small group? Neither of them were ideal options for Ryan.

In fact, he figured that he didn't truly relish either of them at all.

THE BLACKTOP RAN across a stretch of open prairie, a broad plateau of sun-bleached turf surrounded by banks of tall, dark pines. J.B. was driving the big wag.

"Looks like someone's been farming the grass here," he called back to Ryan.

"Yeah. Noticed. But it seems from up here like some kind of army's been marching through. Grass is all trampled down and muddied."

There was a swath of worn turf at least four hundred yards wide, stretching from east to west, as far as

Ryan could see. As the LAV went closer, he noticed that there were piles of animal droppings everywhere.

"Cattle," he shouted. "See the hoof marks as well as the shit. Lot of cattle."

"Could be one of the local tribes of native Americans," J.B. replied. "Mebbe moving from one hunting ground to another, taking all their animals with them."

Ryan stood up higher to get a better look, steadying himself with both hands on the sides of the turret. If the Armorer was right, then it had to be a tribe of hundreds and hundreds of people to leave a track of that size.

To one side of the open space, nearly in among the fringe of the forest, he could see half a dozen coyotes, squabbling over a raggled carcass of what looked to be a calf. But it was too far away to be certain.

"Any villes round here?" he yelled.

"Don't have the maps with me. Can you come down and get them? Check it out."

Ryan found the tattered atlas and traced the thin wavering lines with his forefinger, trying to work out just where they'd gotten to. You didn't travel long in Deathlands before realizing the old road maps were only the most rudimentary guides to human habitation.

Some of the biggest cities of the predark United States, such as Washington, D.C., itself, had been vaporized in the first few hours of the final megawar. Most had been hit hard and repeatedly, sometimes destroying the buildings. In other cases the enemy had utilized neutron technology that chilled all life but left the artifacts untouched.

Many of the smaller settlements had vanished forever, particularly those that were sited close to any of the legion of missile bases that composed the bedrock for the Totality Concept of national defence.

"There's a place called Wetherill Springs. Dot on the highway. Ten miles or so from here."

"Engine's run...a...it hot."

"Say again. Use the mike." He dropped the atlas back down into the cabin of the wag and put on the earphones to listen to J.B.'s voice.

"Said that the engine's starting to run hot. I topped up the oil last night, and it took more than I figured it would. Could mean trouble."

Having originally taken the LAV-25 as part of the spoils of a firefight, Ryan knew how lucky they were to have it at their disposal for their odyssey to Seattle. It was a damnably long journey, and to try to complete it on foot would have come close to being impossible. If the wag broke down on them now, in such an isolated region, it would be difficult even to try to steal some alternative form of transport.

And it would likely mean the spilling of blood.

The highway passed across the plateau, then snaked away into the woods. It commenced to climb within the mile, going along the eastern flank of a narrow valley with a white river foaming at its bottom. There was a row of roofless, windowless vacation cabins on the far side of the water, reached by a rusting bridge.

Ryan considered suggesting an early halt there for the night, but the derelict buildings offered little cover.

"Good grade ahead," J.B. shouted.

Ryan had taken off the earphones again, sitting right out on top, one arm hanging onto the muzzle of the cannon. He'd hoped that they'd have reached the large ville of Durango by that evening, but the blacktop had been in poor condition earlier in the day and it had slowed them. If Wetherill Springs really existed, it might be the best they could hope for.

The road became steep, and Ryan could feel the shuddering of the big engine as it labored upward. Twice the gears slipped, and he heard J.B.'s fluent cursing.

He crawled cautiously forward and lay flat, calling through the driver's ob slit. "Think we should give it a break for a while? Sounds to me like it might burn out, way we're going."

"How far to the top?"

"Good three miles or more. Difficult to be certain with the way it twists and turns like a gaffed salmon."

"All right. Looks like a pull-off ahead."

RYAN COULD SEE the waves of heat shimmering above the engine as J.B. opened it up. And he could also detect the faint smell of overheated oil, so familiar from the years of riding with war wags One and Two.

"What's it look like?" he asked.

J.B. straightened and pushed back his fedora. "It looks to me like we might be walking the rest of the way to Seattle."

"Bad as that?"

He took off the spectacles and peered up at the sky through them. "Covered in dead flies," he said. "Bad as that, did you say?"

"Yeah."

"No. But something's burning out down there. I reckon we have enough oil on board to keep going another three or four days. Mebbe more."

"Mebbe less."

The Armorer nodded. "Right."

"Let her cool off."

"Sure. Better keep a real careful eye on the gauge tomorrow and the other tomorrows."

Ryan nodded. "Yeah. Longer we go without walking, happier I'll be. Just going for a leak."

"Right. Have one for me, will you?"

Ryan grinned. He walked across the blacktop and up a narrow dirt road that cut away into the trees. He'd just unzipped when he heard a noise behind him and turned around to see a full-grown African lion crouched less than twenty paces away.

Chapter Eleven

Ryan had seen pictures of carnivorous hunting animals like the lion, in several mags and predark vids. But he'd never thought that he'd encounter one while taking a piss in a Colorado forest.

It looked to be about eight or ten feet in length, from the huge maned head to the tip of the twitching tail. The eyes were a unique mixture of emerald and gold, flecked with a darker green. The mouth was just open, with a rope of saliva dribbling onto the carpet of dry pine needles below it. There was the faintest sound emanating from the predator's throat, like a powerful wag engine ticking over.

"Fireblast." The word was barely breathed.

The SIG-Sauer was snug on his hip, but he wasn't sure what kind of stopping power it would have on an animal of that size. But it looked like he was about to find out.

Very slowly, Ryan moved his right hand off his dick, toward the butt of the 9 mm automatic. The reaction from the lion was instantaneous. The purring turned into an unmistakable snarl and the jaws opened much wider, showing yellow curved teeth that looked as if they could easily go through a man's thigh in a single crunching bite.

"Better grab hold of your prick again, mister."

Ryan started, half turning to his right, where the woman's voice had come from. But he could see nobody beyond the dark barrier of the pines.

The lion was now in a half crouch, its hind legs cocked beneath it, ready to power the animal toward the watching man in a couple of giant bounds. The eyes had narrowed, and the snarling had stopped. Only the bushy tip of its tail kept moving from side to side, brushing at the pine needles.

Ryan's hand was down on the cold butt of the blaster.

The voice of the young woman came out of the forest again. "Balthazar'll have your throat out and your guts spilled in the dirt, before that pretty gun cleared leather."

"If you got some control over this animal, lady, then you best use it."

"Use it?"

"Or lose it. Fastest lion I ever heard of wasn't quick enough to beat fifteen rounds of full-metal jacket. You want it living, then call it off."

"Big talk for a one-eyed man, mister."

"Not a game, lady. I aim to chill your pet in about six seconds from now."

"Think you're good enough?"

"I know I'm good enough."

Ryan could actually hear the initial terror warming away from his voice. The shock had been so cataclysmic that he was actually surprised that he hadn't pissed his pants. Now he was regaining control. Whomever the woman was, her voice was also showing some changes, from an amused confidence to just the first shading of doubt.

"Time's gone, lady."

"Balthazar!" The crack of command made the lion hunker down again, eyes narrowing, mouth closing.

"Better." Ryan drew the SIG-Sauer just in case, giving himself a safer edge.

"If you feel so much better, mister, then you can zip up your breeches and put away that little white worm I see dangling out in the cold."

Ryan smiled, despite the tenseness of the situation, using his left hand to adjust his dress. "There," he said. "Now you can come out safely."

"Thanks."

Balthazar looked up, starting the deep-throated purring again, as the woman stepped out of the shadows of the trees, a little to the left of where Ryan had placed her.

She was tall and slender, with long hair, blacker than the wing of a raven, tied back in a ponytail. Her eyes were light blue, and she was wearing dark green pants and a matching jacket with black knee-length boots. She carried a riding crop in her hand.

"You can holster the blaster. He won't move unless I tell him to."

"How do I know you won't tell him to move?"

The woman laughed. "Chance you got to take, mister. No other choice."

J.B.'s voice came from the side of the clearing. "Always another choice, lady. Anything goes wrong, and you got a dead animal on your hands."

She turned around, unable to spot the Armorer. "How many are there of you?"

Ryan grinned at her, feeling confident that the situation was finally back under their control. "We come cheaper by the dozen, lady."

Yet another voice called out from a couple of hundred yards away, a younger woman, making the lion lift its head again, staring past Ryan into the forest.

"Ma? You all right?"

"Joking's over now, strangers," the woman said. "I'm Ellie Kissoon and I run an animal show. Balthazar's the star. Got his mate caged up over yonder."

"Ma?"

"Here, Julie! Couple of men with me as well."

"Need help, Ma?"

"No. But you could throw a couple more chunks of beef into the stew. Looks like we might have company." She turned to Ryan. "You and your invisible friend got names?"

"Sure, Ellie. I'm Ryan Cawdor and the ghost in the forest's J. B. Dix."

"I got three daughters, Ryan Cawdor. Oldest is Julie, at twenty-one. Then comes Nell, who's nineteen, and little Katie. She's eighteen. Just a word of warning."

"No need, Ellie. Both me and J.B. are spoken for. Your girls are safe."

She laughed, tapping the whip against the side of her boots. "You give me a pocketful of jack for every spoken-for man who's tried to get close to me or my girls, and I can retire for life." Her cold smile vanished clean away. "And there's men pushing up the daisies who thought a widow and three little girls would give them easy pickings."

"We hear you," J.B. said, stepping slowly out of the trees, keeping both the Smith & Wesson M-4000 and a careful eye on the lion.

"My, but you're a pocket hurricane, aren't you, J. B. Dix? That blaster fire fléchettes?"

"Yeah."

"Appreciate taking a look at it after we've all been properly introduced and wrapped ourselves around some meat. One thing about having Balthazar with you. Not many things on four legs can get away from him. Nor two legs, neither."

THERE WERE THREE WAGS, one with an extra trailer. Blazoned across the sides, in ornamented gold and crimson lettering, were the words: Satana's Animal Show.

"Me," Ellie said, pointing at the name. "If I called it Ellie's Show I reckon it'd sound more like a ladies' class in home cooking."

Ryan was a good judge of people. In a world filled with strangers, any of whom might want to take your life, it was a useful skill. A vital skill. Meeting up with Ellie Kissoon's three daughters, he realized that the woman hadn't been joking. Not at all. He'd rarely encountered three more self-sufficient young ladies in the breadth and length of Deathlands.

Julie had the shoulders and upper arms of someone who worked with weights. She had a long-barreled nameless revolver strapped to her waist. Nell wore crossed leather belts across her chest, decorated with a dozen throwing knives, each with a colored silken tassel. Katie still carried the remnants of adolescent puppy fat, but the twin tomahawks with honed steel blades on either hip belied her chubby smile.

They all shook hands with Ryan and J.B., making them welcome to their camp.

There was the delicious smell of a rich stew, bubbling in an iron caldron over a well-built fire. Balthazar was led through into his cage that he shared with his mate, Rosa.

"We got us a Bengal tiger," Ellie said. "Rajah. Handsome looking and he'll roar up a storm when you give him the signal. Trouble is, he's old and lost most of his back teeth. Getting blind as well."

"What other animals?" J.B. asked. "I see a black bear in that cage there."

"That's Brutus. Him, and his brother, Cassius."

Ryan didn't let his hand move far from the butt of his SIG-Sauer. "Where in Deathlands did you get the lions and the tiger from?" he asked. "I've seen most creatures, norm and mutie, but never anything like them."

Nell answered. "Then you never got to visit Loren Engel and his spread in the Cats. During skydark most of the zoos and places like that folded up. Animals got slaughtered for food. But not all. Loren's grand-daddy went into the mountains with some good breeding animals. Place is still there.''

''Running down, though,'' Katie said. ''Inbred stock and they get weak. Rajah's the last of the ti-gers.''

''How do you train them?'' J.B. asked.

Ellie laughed, followed by her daughters. ''Family joke, J.B., you understand. Way to train them is to start by being a mite cruel, then you can get more kindly. I tell the girls to work on the same system when they get them husbands.''

Julie opened her hand, then clenched it into a fist. ''Ma says it's the same method. Buckle a tight strap round their balls and chain them to a tree. Whip them eight times a day until they do what you say. Easy as that.''

Ryan shook his head. ''And you told us not to do any harm to your daughters, Ellie! Sounds to me like the warning works the other way.''

BEFORE JOINING the four women for supper, Ryan and J.B. walked back to the LAV-25, checking that it was secure against any passing intruders.

''What do you reckon?'' the Armorer asked.

''Reckon that any man tangles with that quartet and their pets is going to end up being badly mauled.''

''Yeah. Handsome, aren't they?'' The Armorer had a vague, ruminative smile.

"Sure. How about some food, J.B., before this conversation wanders into alleys we might both regret when we get home to Mildred and Krysty?"

THE FOOD WAS as good as it smelled. The only thing that put Ryan off a little was having the big carnivores watching him through what seemed peculiarly flimsy iron bars.

J.B. was more relaxed, lying on a faded quilted blanket, tucking into a third helping of the beef stew, his scattergun at his side, the Uzi ready by his left hand.

Ellie and her daughters were remarkable women. She had been married three times, each of her husbands having fathered one of the girls, which accounted for the fact that they all looked very different.

"Guess I've been unlucky with my men," she said, taking a swig from a bottle of moonshine. "Not one lasted longer than a month married to me."

"What happened?" Ryan wiped the tin plate clean with his last hunk of bread.

She ticked them off her fingers, relating each man to one of the daughters. "Julie's Pa was Renaldo. Bit of Mex in him. Stupe way to go. Shoveling shit from the lions' cage and he cut his ankle. Turned poisoned. Dead in a week. Father of Nell was Raleigh. Nice man from what little I recall. Claimed his folks came from Ireland. Not that I cared about that."

"Wish you'd have had pix of them, Ma," Nell said. "Liked to have known what they looked like."

"All real handsome is all I remember of them," her mother replied. "And we don't have any pix of a single one and that's an end to that."

"What happened to Raleigh?" J.B. asked.

Brutus—or Cassius—gave a roar that shook the forest, but none of the women took a shred of notice of him.

"Raleigh liked to fix himself up with jolt, now and then. I didn't know that when I met him." Ellie shook her head sadly. "I don't have a problem with folks that do drugs like jolt or spin. Trouble was, jolt made Raleigh imagine things. It made him imagine that he could swim across the Sippi, in a flood, near Memphis, when he couldn't swim a stroke. Never found his body."

"My pa was called Jake," Katie said. "And Ma cut his throat when she found him fucking a gaudy slut in the wag."

"What did you do to the slut?" J.B. asked curiously. "Chill her as well?"

"Course not," Ellie replied indignantly. "She was doing her job. Jake was the only one needed chilling." The woman drained the last few drops from the bottle, then laughed. "But I only paid the slut half of the jack she wanted. Told her that she only did half the job. Poor old Jake never got to shoot his load before I opened him up an extra grinnin' mouth."

"You coming with us tomorrow?" Julie had returned from throwing some meat to the tiger.

"We have to be on the road," Ryan replied.

"See our show." Ellie pushed her shoulders back, making her breasts jut forward. "Show worth seeing, boys."

J.B. stood. "We got to go." He paused. "Where are you doing the show, Ellie?"

"Wetherill Springs. Never been there. Someone on the trail said there was a bunch of buffalo hunters passing through right about now."

"That good for trade?"

"Mebbe, Ryan. Mebbe not. I done my Satana turn all over Deathlands. Done it for the blackest-hearted sec men you ever saw and never had a hair of trouble. Done it for some sort of closed-off church of religious monks up close to Sidalia, out west, and they rioted. Came after me and the girls with their cocks up and their pants down."

"What did you do?" J.B. asked.

"Loosed Rosa and Balthazar. Cleared the lot of them in six seconds flat. One tripped over his own breeches and provided the lions with fresh meat for a day and a half."

"You should come and see the show," Katie said. "Ma's the best there is."

"We were thinking of passing through Wetherill Springs." Ryan glanced at his partner. "What do you reckon? Might find some oil or gas there."

J.B. sniffed doubtfully. "Nothing to lose. We've made good time so far. Still have at least five weeks to get to Seattle and find Trader."

"Yeah, do it. Be nice to have some friendly faces in the crowd." Ellie kissed both men on the cheek.

"How can we refuse now?" Ryan said, smiling. "And we can lend a hand if there's trouble."

The woman tossed back her ponytail. "Trouble! Me and the girls just laugh at trouble. There won't be no trouble."

Chapter Twelve

"Blood for blood!"

The yell followed Abe as he scuttled along, trying to keep up with Trader's lengthy stride. Rain dropped off the low branches of the lowering pines as they moved quickly along the steep path, making for higher ground.

One of the inexorable rules of Deathlands about living and dying was that when the dying gets easy, then the living make for the high ground.

"Sure pissed on their ants' nest," Trader said over his shoulder.

"Sure did," Abe agreed, clutching the biscuits and the jerky.

"Those shit-eaters won't dare to come after us," Trader added, beginning to pant and slow down as the uphill grade became much harsher.

"Sure," Abe said, though he wasn't at all certain that Trader was right about that one. From what he'd seen in the store it seemed more than likely that there might be a general posse headed after them.

The heavy-lidded eyes of the rednecks as they saw their neighbor bleeding to death on the filthy plank floor had shone with a malevolence that had startled

Abe. It was a ferocious lust for vengeance on the pair of outlanders that wasn't likely to be quenched just like that.

A garter snake slithered across the path right in front of Trader, making the old man stumble and nearly fall. He leaped clumsily to one side, coming close to dropping the Armalite.

"Bitching reptile!"

He paused for breath, resting a hand on the moss-slick trunk of a larch. Abe also stopped, swallowing hard, tasting the bitterness of bile rising in his throat. Below and behind them he could still hear shouting and screaming.

And the deep-throated barking of a pack of hounds.

"Getting the dogs after us," he said.

"They'll give up on it." Trader hawked and spit in the wet mud at his feet.

THE TRAIL WOUND HIGHER, through chiffon layers of thin white fog. Every time there was a fork in it, Trader would unhesitatingly pick one and go haring up it. Abe was impressed at first at the way the old man's memory had given him such a photographic memory for the valleys and hills.

Until he suddenly spotted what Trader was doing—alternately picking right or left turns, regardless of whether they might be right or wrong for their head-long escape from the pursuers.

"Sure you know which way we're going, Trader?"

"Course. Got a gift like a homing eagle for finding my way through the wilderness."

"Pigeon."

"How's that?"

"Homing pigeon, Trader. Not an eagle."

"Who said anything about a fucking eagle, Abe? You losing the clapper out of your bell? Don't go soft on me, Abe. Just don't do that."

They ran on.

THE COTTAGE WAS BUILT into a wall of gray rock, on the right of the path, with a sheer drop of three hundred feet, down through the trees on the left. It had two small windows on the first floor and three on the floor above. A narrow door stood open.

Trader slowed, glancing behind, making sure that Abe was still with him.

"Smell cooking," he said.

"Yeah. But I don't think we have enough time to stop for breakfast, Trader."

The barking of the dogs echoed in the dark valley below them.

"Who's there?" A woman's voice, shrill and querulous, spoke from inside the little house.

The woman appeared out on the path, a dozen feet ahead of them, as if she'd been propelled there from a gigantic catapult. A broom made from ragged twigs was between her legs.

And she was naked.

The long blond hair that slithered over her pendulous breasts was plaited with all manner of herbs and wild flowers. Her face was smeared with streaks of soot, and her light green eyes were wide and staring, circled with yellow paint. She rode the broom as though it were a spirited stallion.

"Whoa back, Buck," she said, the narrow branches scratching on the stones of the path. "Gets spooked when he sees strangers. What's your business with old Meg?"

"Just passing through, lady," Trader said. "Though there's a good smell of baking coming out of your front door."

"No time," Abe whispered, getting increasingly antsy at the thought of the murderous vigilante posse storming up the trail after them.

"Always time for some food, Abe. Take it while you can, has always been my motto. Bread gets you through times of hunger better than hunger gets you through times of no bread."

Abe considered pointing out to Trader that this made no sense at all, but decided against it.

The woman dropped her broom, instantly losing interest in it and kicking it with her bare feet.

"Pretty hair, Meg," Trader commented, edging toward the door of her home.

"Rosemary for forgetting and rue for laughter. And here's the Deathlands daisy with its white coat and heart of gold. But it's sorely withered."

"Watch her, Abe." Trader slipped into the house, emerging ten heartbeats later with two fresh loaves in his arms, half a smoked ham dangling from his right hand.

"You thieving bastards."

"Dogs closing on us, Trader." Abe had his Colt Python drawn.

The nude woman dashed into the house and came out again almost immediately, brandishing a long carving knife with a serrated edge. "Cut your fucking balls off and braise 'em with gilly flowers!" she screamed.

"Bust her, Abe." Trader had the Armalite strung across his back, his hands filled with the food.

"Oh, shit."

Though he'd been a gunner on both war wags One and Two, Abe's speciality had been machine guns, wasting people who were some distance off. Not a crazed naked woman, who was so close he could taste her sweat.

There wasn't time for any argument. If he didn't pull the trigger, then the mad woman was going to open up Trader's guts and spill his tripes all over the track.

Abe pulled the trigger.

The blaster kicked in his hand, the jolt running to his shoulder.

The woman screamed, higher, louder and longer than Abe had ever imagined possible. The bullet had struck her beneath the right arm, sending the knife spinning away, striking a tiny fountain of golden sparks from the wall of her house. The .357 round exited near her spine, not touching any vital organ, punching out a hole the size of a man's fist.

She staggered backward, away from Abe, toward the Trader, blood gouting onto the path. Her mouth was jammed open in that piercing, endless cry.

"Again," Trader snapped.

It was nightmare city for Abe.

The noise of the hounds seemed so much closer, almost as though they were just around the last bend in the trail. Someone was yelling out "Blood for blood!" Abe could almost feel the whisper of the dark man's scythe.

The blond woman lifted her hands and tore wildly at her own face, gouging great scarlet furrows down her cheeks with ragged nails.

"Again, Abe!"

The Python boomed again, this time with greater success.

The heavy bullet hit the screaming Meg through the top of her right breast, smashing the shoulder bone on the way out. The impact was far more devastating, spinning her completely around through three hundred and sixty degrees, giving Abe a glimpse of the two massive exit wounds in her back.

She staggered to her right, stumbling over her own feet, disappearing over the brink of the drop with a startling speed. One moment she was there, whirling like a demented dervish, her shrill scream tearing the air apart.

As she vanished, she stopped screaming.

All that they could hear, above the northerly wind, was the wet flopping as her body bounced off the jagged rocks all the way to the bottom of the ravine, ending in a distant clatter of loose boulders and smaller pebbles.

"Took you long enough," Trader said, as Abe holstered the warm blaster.

"Let's go," the skinny gunner replied. "Sons of bitches getting closer by the minute."

Trader was off, his long legs eating up the ground, toward the top of the steep incline, Abe at his heels. As he ran past the open door of the little house, he was surprised to see a pair of small children peering silently out at him.

They had weirdly elongated skulls, tapering almost to points, and their eyes were stretched to slits. Neither of them showed any sign of emotion.

Abe tripped and nearly fell, recovering to follow the rapidly disappearing Trader.

Behind them, the dogs were howling like banshees.

THE NEXT COUPLE of hours were a blur of exhaustion for Abe.

As they reached the top of the trail, it opened onto a broad plateau. The ruins of a stone-built church dominated the space, surrounded by dark trees. A herd of twenty or thirty wild ponies were driven close to panic by the sudden appearance of the two panting humans. They rushed clattering past Trader and Abe, heading for the beginning of the path down.

"Give the bastards something to think about when they fetch up with them horses on a narrow twist." Trader laughed, dropping to his knees to recover his breathing.

They heard the noises of the meeting of horses and posse. The baying of the hounds changed its note, sliding up the scale to a frightened howling. Men shouted in alarm, horses whinnied, and someone fired a couple of shots.

After that, the sounds of the lynch mob's pursuit seemed less pressing.

Trader picked his way around the far edge of the plateau, until he discovered an almost invisible trail among the bracken that took them steeply down the northern flank of the bluff.

It was slippery and dangerous, with the roaring of water from somewhere below them, among the trees.

"Fuckers won't find it easy following us with their dogs." Trader was leaning against the tilted trunk of an aspen, waiting for Abe to catch up.

"Think there's a falls down there?" Abe asked. His breathing was painful, rasping and burning in his chest. His eyes kept watering and his mouth was dry. He had always been unlucky with wounds, and several of them were reminding him of their existence. Particularly his damaged knees and lower back and right shoulder. One of the bottles of pulque had broken when he fell against a tree, and his coat and pants stank of the fiery home brew.

"Sure to be. Once we cross that they'll lose the trail and give up on us. Must admit, Abe, that I'm surprised they keep on after us. You swore they wouldn't bother."

"No, I didn't."

"Sure did, Ryan. I mean, Abe."

"If you say so, Trader."

While they recovered, ears straining for the pursuers, they divided up the stolen food, saving some of it for later. Between them they managed to get through two-thirds of the remaining bottle of pulque.

"FOLLOW IT until we can find a way over." Trader eased the Armalite across his back. "Going faster than goose shit off a greased shovel."

The river was in full spate. A dozen yards wide, it was crashing over tumbled rocks, foaming and frothing, drowning out any other sounds.

It made Abe nervous, knowing that the hunters could be within ten feet and they'd never hear them.

Trader led the way, following it upstream, knowing from experience that pursuers would automatically assume that they'd gone the other, easier way.

"There." He pointed to a place where the jagged tips of two huge boulders were just breaking the surface of the racing, peat-colored river.

"I'd never make it," Abe said, feeling dizzy from a dangerous combination of fatigue and the effects of the potent alcohol.

"Course you can."

"Can't, Trader."

The older man turned to look at him, his eyes suddenly cold and dead, sending a chill of fear through Abe. He knew that expression from the old times.

"I say you can do it, Abe." His voice was like ice, velvet and steel.

"Then I guess I can."

His reward was a broad smile and a pat on the back so hard it nearly knocked Abe over.

And, as it turned out, Trader was right. Apart from a slip in midstream that soaked him to the skin, Abe made it across, blowing freezing water out of his mustache.

Trader followed him, hopping from stone to stone with the agility of a man a third his age.

"There," he said, grinning. "Keep moving and you'll soon dry out."

"Yeah." Abe felt sick, and the pulque had given him a ferocious headache behind the eyes.

Trader stared at the dark mountainside behind them, seeing no sign of life. "That's done then," he said confidently.

Chapter Thirteen

Wetherill Springs was typical of thousands of frontier pesthole villes. There was a narrow main street that choked you in dust during the summer and drowned you in thick, black glutinous mud throughout the rest of the year.

The boardwalk was mostly rotted through and was lined by tumbling, leaning houses. There were a couple of stores, remnants of a church or a school, a row of outdoor privies with their fetid odors and swarms of glistening flies, a saloon with bat's-wing doors and stinking brass cuspidors that overflowed onto the stained planks of the floor. Most time you found that the gaudy and the drinker were in the same building. Occasionally it might have a name like The Silver Dollar or The Lucky Chance. Other times there could be a hand-lettered sign, weathered by rain and wind and frost, that would simply read "Sluts."

Ryan and J.B. must have visited hundreds of similar places and knew the variety of common factors that you always found in them: faro dealers and barkeeps with false smiles permanently pasted in place; drink that would peel the enamel off of your teeth if you were too slow in swallowing it. Food was rudimentary, with grease as the common unifying factor—fried eggs, blackened at the edges, with fried bacon, fried bread, fried tomatoes, fried chicken, fried potatoes and fried mushrooms.

The gaudy whores all looked the same. Ryan had once read an old guidebook that said that the big motel chains were so cunningly designed that you could wake up in one and not have the slightest clue whether you were in Tallahassee or Nantucket or Chinle or Missoula.

Sluts were like that.

You could wake up in bed with one, the remnants of a hangover throbbing at your temples and the sickly taste of bile in your throat. You'd look around the cheap room with faded pictures tacked to the plasterboard walls, the jug and bowl, unmatched or chipped or cracked, the narrow bed and rickety chair with one leg shorter than the rest.

Tawdry clothes hung on a rail behind a half-drawn curtain, stained and torn underwear on the floor with down-at-heel shoes or midcalf boots, the leather cracked and grease-stained.

And the nameless woman snoring at your side. Her cheeks would be puffy from the booze, or haggard from the jolt that made life barely tolerable, broken veins in the backs of her thighs and across the face, mouth hung open to show the broken teeth standing proud among the gaps, like the old telegraph poles strung across the high plains country.

And the indescribably appalling cavern of Eros at the junction of her flabby legs, a valley that truly concealed the shadow of death.

Her customers would also be interchangeable, hardly varying from one pesthole to another. You might get more Hispanic types in the Southwest, more Asiatic-looking men up toward the far Northwest. Hunters and farmers. Cowboys and wranglers. Local good old boys with brains the size of teacups and an infinite capacity for drinking, whoring and fighting.

Yes. Wetherill Springs was much like any of the thousands of frontier pestholes.

Only it was currently hosting a couple of dozen buffalo hunters, following the herds of animals as they moved restlessly across the prairies and mountains.

THE CARAVAN ARRIVED from the south in the middle of the following morning. Ellie drove the first wag, holding the pair of lions, with her daughters bringing in the other rigs. Ryan came along at the rear in the LAV-25, J.B. perched in the turret, riding shotgun on the big armored wag.

The gaudyhouse rejoiced in the name of The Shangri-La. There was an old orchard out back, with a broken picket fence partly enclosing it. There were ancient, blighted apple and pear trees, all with immensely long, spindly branches, some of them with a single withered fruit at their end.

After a quick tour of the small ville, Ellie picked that abandoned paddock to put on their show.

"Miss Satana and her wild animals will be appearing here at noon, three and six," she announced to the crowd of drinkers in the bar of the Shangri-La.

"Drop your panties!" yelled one of the buffalo hunters, a huge mountain of a man in a fur coat, a jagged scar disfiguring one side of his face.

"Show us your tits!" screeched another of the hunters, involved in an expensive game of draw poker at a corner table.

Ellie tapped the quirt on her boots, keeping her smile going at full radiance. "Gentlemen out there seem real interested in what I got to show that I'm not showing right now." There was a roar from the crowd, overlaid with whistling and table-banging. The tall, bald barkeep looked around worriedly.

"Show us, lady!"

"Well, now, there's times that I do and there's times that I don't. But what I will promise to show you—" Someone bellowed something inaudible, and she dropped a curtsey in his direction. "Forgive me talking while you're interrupting, mister." The quip drew a burst of sympathetic laughter. "I promise to show you animals that none of you will ever have seen. A royal tiger, the meanest and most powerful carnivore in the entire ever-loving history of creation. A proven man killer with over thirty corpses to its name."

Ryan glanced sideways at J.B., who was standing at the bar with him and with the three daughters. "Good at it, isn't she?" he mouthed.

"Should see her when the shills are difficult," Julie said, downing a shot glass of whiskey in a single gulp.

"Shills?"

"The crowd, Ryan. Ma's at her best when her back's to the wall. This bunch is blind kittens for her."

Ellie was winding up her spiel. "Lions and bears and a tiger. Plus a dozen rattlers."

"Snakes?" asked J.B., who wasn't known for his love of crawling reptiles.

"Sure. Katie milks 'em every other day, but they got the fangs and Ma does get bit now and then."

"Out back!" Ellie shouted. "You know the times. Be noon real soon, friends. Come and be amazed."

WHEN RYAN and J.B. strolled over to their wag, they found four of the hunters standing around it. Another one was up on top, looking like he was trying, unsuccessfully, to lever open the turret hatch.

"What are you aiming to do if you manage to get inside?" Ryan asked, his voice friendly and gentle, his hand on the butt of the SIG-Sauer.

"Nothing, friend," the man by the turret replied. He had a straggling beard and wore a necklace of what looked like the skulls of minks. "Just sort of checking. Wouldn't object to that, would you now?"

"Yeah, we would," J.B. stated, noisily levering a fléchette round under the hammer of the shotgun. "Anyone touches our wag could get hurt."

"Two of you outlanders," another man said, looking uncertainly at his companions for support. "There's plenty of us buffalo boys in town. Could you and your one-eyed friend there that gets to be hurt."

Ryan had plenty of experience of this sort of prickly situation. Trader used to say that if you took one foot backward, then you'd likely end up with six feet of cold clay lying on your breast.

He didn't hesitate for a moment, utterly confident that the Armorer was ready for him to make the move and would back him all the way.

Ryan stepped in closer to the man, sizing him up. He was just on six feet tall, with his two hundred pounds centered around the belly and hips. He wore a torn vest, and a home-built single-shot flintlock pistol on the hip. His eyes were bloodshot, and Ryan could smell the 'shine on his breath.

"Hey, now..." the hunter said, seeing the cold anger in Ryan's face.

He was watching for the automatic that lay under Ryan's right hand and never saw the wickedly curving left jab that didn't travel more than about fourteen inches before it exploded into his midriff.

Having delivered the punch, Ryan immediately took three paces back, finally drawing the SIG-Sauer, covering the man on top of the wag as well as his shaken companions.

The other reason for moving out of the way was to avoid the spurt of stinking vomit that fountained from the injured hunter's mouth as he doubled over in the dirt.

He lay groaning at Ryan's feet, his legs drawn up, face the color of milk and grits, mouth wide open as he fought to suck in some air.

"Fuck'n chilled 'im," said the man with the uncertain beard. "No cause..."

Ryan looked up at him, gesturing with the barrel of the 9 mm blaster. "Down," he said. "You got a warning about being hurt. We only give one warning."

"You bastard." The words a painful whisper from the buffalo hunter on his hands and knees. "No call for that."

Ryan considered laying him out with a kick behind the right ear, but decided that the lesson had probably been learned by the group of men. Word of the lesson would spread quickly through Wetherill Springs.

"Now move away. Next person we see within spitting distance of our wag ends up hurt bad."

Two of the hunters helped up their injured friend, and they all shambled away, not even looking back at J.B. and Ryan over their shoulders.

"Nice punch," the Armorer commented. "Pretty. Trader would've been proud of you."

"Thanks." Ryan holstered the blaster. "We going to watch this show?"

"Sure. Sounds to me like it could be real interesting."

It was more than interesting.

Chapter Fourteen

The midday sun shone brightly on the sweating pate of the towering barkeep. He had led the applause after Cassius and Brutus, the black bears, had performed their rota of tricks. But Ryan had noticed that the man had brought his steel jackbox with him and kept it snug beneath his foot.

Virtually everyone in the little pesthole ville had come to the old orchard behind the Shangri-La to watch the noon performance of Mistress Satana and her deadly animals.

Ellie had begun with the rattlers. Nell had carried them on, wearing a short skirt that attracted the wolf whistles, the wind blowing the bright tassels on the row of knives sheathed across her breasts.

There were four of the reptiles, the shortest of them a good seven feet in length. Being kept locked away in a hot and dusty basket had done nothing for their tempers, and they writhed and hissed angrily. Ellie worked them with a hooked cane, no longer than a normal walking stick, constantly keeping her distance from them, dodging as they struck toward her booted legs.

It had silenced the jeers and bawdy shouts from the buffalo hunters, though one of them had queried loudly whether the snakes were really poisonous.

Ellie gestured to Katie, who brought on a mangy black-and-white cat. She laid it on the ground where it cowered down, not trying to run away from the brightly patterned rattlers. Ryan noticed that it seemed paralyzed, its legs clumsy.

"What did you do?" he whispered to the eighteen-year-old young woman as she rejoined her sisters, standing near J.B. and himself by the caged wags.

"Cut its hamstrings," she replied. "Otherwise you wouldn't see its ass for smoke."

Ellie nudged the snakes closer with the stick, watched in silence by her audience.

"But if the poison's been drained..." the Armorer asked quietly.

"Watch," Nell breathed.

Inevitably one of the snakes struck at the helpless cat, biting it near the shoulder. Though it hissed and squealed in pain and fear, the animal didn't try to escape.

Ellie stepped in fast and picked it up. A moment later it hung limp and dead in her arms.

"Are they poisonous?" she mocked. "Any of you bold gentlemen care to come and check them out?"

Ryan guessed that he and J.B. were probably the only ones who'd spotted the way Ellie had gripped the cat with her finger and thumb at its nape, giving a sudden squeeze to break the spine and chill it instantly.

The snakes had been returned to their basket before the bears came out.

The beasts played dutifully with a large wooden ball and staged a clumsy boxing match.

"How about your lions and tigers?" shouted the big scar-faced man in the fur coat.

"Here they come, mister," Ellie replied, beckoning to her daughters to release the animals.

Ryan was aware of his own conditioned reflex, his right hand gripping the butt of the blaster, seeing his own reaction mirrored by the audience. The gaudies screamed and clung to the arms of their pimps or lovers. A pretty little girl near the front closed her eyes and said, very clearly, "I like the good animals but not the bad animals."

Rajah belied his age and frailty, giving vent to a deafening roar as he was goaded down the ramp from his cage by Julie. His head turned from side to side, along the rows of watching men and women, as if he were in the process of selecting his lunch.

Balthazar and Rosa came close behind him, though the three big cats ignored one another.

"How does she train them?" Ryan asked.

Katie answered. "Mostly done when we bought them. Mainly tamed, but you still don't get careless and ever turn your back on them. Not even old Rajah."

Ryan had seen a number of performing bears, sorry, decrepit, flea-ridden creatures with collars of rusting iron that had worn septic wounds around their scrawny throats. Clawless and toothless, they would "dance," while being jabbed with a spiked prod or flicked with a barbed whip.

Trader had once violently lost his temper with a smiling young teenager in Kansas who had an animal that was barely alive. Trader had first put a merciful bullet through the head of the wretched bear and then stripped the youth and had the collar welded around his neck. He used the electric prod to make him jig and caper, weeping and begging for mercy, until he finally collapsed unconscious, feet pulped and bleeding.

Ellie's performance with the tiger and the two lions was nothing like that. It wasn't really very much like a traditional animal act at all.

The fact that these lethal creatures were free, unchained and not behind bars, gave a frisson of genuine danger to the proceedings. The knowledge that at any moment the tiger or either of the lions might break free of Ellie's control and run bloodily amok throughout the crowd provided an edge of danger that you could almost taste, salty and hot.

Nell was leaning against one of the wags, her shoulder touching Ryan. She was plucking at some of the loose strands of satin thread on her knives, vivid orange, turquoise, crimson and cobalt.

"You should travel with us, Ryan," she said, watching her mother. "You and J.B. here. We could all have us some real nice times together."

"All?" Ryan said.

Nell grinned, the pink tip of her tongue darting out between parted lips. "Sure," she breathed. "All of us."

He felt himself becoming aroused at the thought of the nest of tangled limbs, closing his eye for a moment to try to wipe away the vision.

Ellie was kneeling in the center of the open space, by a rugged pear tree, while Rajah levered his front paws, rather slowly and painfully, onto her shoulders from behind. Balthazar, snarling softly to himself, lay across her lap, while Rosa, her flanks heaving as she breathed, stood directly in front of the helpless woman and opened her enormous jaws.

"Everyone real quiet, please!" Julie called.

The chattering and nervous laughter died away. The only sound in the stillness was the large scar-faced man striking a match on the sole of his boot to light a fat black cigar.

Ellie leaned forward, one hand on either side of her face, to hold back the great flood of raven hair. Ryan wasn't certain, but he thought he detected the glint of metal in her left hand, as though she were gripping some kind of small knife.

Just in case.

Rosa's jaws opened wider, the green incurious eyes staring past its mistress, seeming to focus on the tall figure of the barkeep, who shifted nervously, the jackbox tinkling softly as he caught it with his foot.

Ryan found himself holding his breath, aware of the horror that would result if something went wrong.

Ellie leaned farther forward, submissively, until her head was completely within the framing jaws, the curved, cruel teeth brushing at her face. For a few heartbeats she held the pose, the group looking like the living embodiment of some heroic Victorian piece of commemorative statuary.

When she finally broke away, slapping the big lioness affectionately on the side of the neck, the crowd broke into a great roar of applause.

The fur-coated buffalo hunter waved his cigar in the air. "Easy. It's a trick. Mangy fuckers wouldn't even bite a shrimp in half."

"Then your dick'll be safe in her mouth, mister. Come and try it, why don't you?"

Ryan grinned, guessing that Ellie had honed her wit over the years of touring with the act and probably knew the likely things a drunk audience might throw at her, and the best replies to bring most of them onto her side.

The hunter scowled at finding himself the unexpected center of the crowd's laughter.

"Watch him," J.B. said. "Pot just waiting to boil right over."

Ryan nodded.

Ellie was on her feet again, bowing to the cheers, raising her hand to quiet them. "To finish this little show, I'm going to give you good folks of—" she hesitated a moment, trying to remember the name of the ville "—Wetherill Springs a chance to do something that you can tell your children and your children's children about. How you patted one of the most terrifying animals ever to stalk the earth."

Ryan straightened up, moving a couple of steps away from the barred wag, hearing the snuffling behind him of the pair of black bears.

"She really taking the lions in among them?" he asked Julie.

"No. Just Rajah. Old softy's harmless. Unless you get on the wrong side of him."

Katie and Nell had gone forward, each of them taking one of the lions with them, snapping thin chain leashes onto the leather collars.

They led them back to stand by Ryan and J.B., both of whom moved a few self-conscious steps away.

Ellie clipped a similar chain onto Rajah's collar, patting the huge head. The tiger opened its mouth and gave a halfhearted roar, loud enough to send the crowd swaying back, moving together in the gestalt unison of fear, like a school of fish that scented a killer whale.

A fat little man in a striped apron broke the spell by taking the crucial step in the front. He reached out with his hand, a gold ring gleaming in the midday sun, and touched Rajah cautiously on the top of the ruffed head.

"Well done," Ellie said. "Mistress Satana rewards you with a kiss." She offered her pursed lips to him.

But his supply of courage had been drained, and he shook his head shyly. "No thanks," he stammered. "Don't think . . . think wife would like that."

Ellie smiled understandingly. "You did good, anyway. Who else wants to stroke striped death?"

This time there were plenty of volunteers, including three or four of the little children, though all of them were only allowed to pat Rajah while their mothers or fathers tightly gripped their other hand.

The woman and the animal were working their way slowly around the perimeter of the orchard, nearing the hard core of the buffalo hunters, the scarred giant at its center. Exhaling a cloud of noisome smoke from his cigar, the man dropped his head and said something to his immediate group of cronies, something that made most of them snigger.

Ryan had the familiar prickling feeling at his nape, the feeling that something bad was about to go down.

Beside him, J.B. was starting to unsling his Uzi. Neither man spoke to the other. There wasn't any need for talking.

Now Ellie was only ten feet from the hunters. Six feet. Four.

"I wanna pat the fuckin' pussycat," said the leader of the group. "Can I do that?"

"Sure. Be careful with that cigar. Rajah doesn't much like smoke."

"Then I'll fucking stub it out, slut!"

Before anyone could move, the buffalo hunter leaned forward and stooped a little. He lifted Rajah's plumed tail with his left hand and jammed the glowing end of his cigar against the animal's tender flesh.

Chapter Fifteen

"I'd be the first to admit to being surprised by this, Abe."

The high-pitched cry came from somewhere behind them, threatening blood for blood, echoing off the peaks until it sounded like a hundred men were all shouting at once, encircling the two fugitives.

Abe started to wonder whether he was becoming seriously sick. The rot-gut liquor burned a hole through his intestines. Twice in the past hour or so they'd been forced to stop while he hastily dropped his pants by the side of the trail, feeling his stomach contract with the gripping pains.

Now he couldn't decide whether he was feeling too hot or too cold.

And all the Trader could say was that he was fucking surprised that the posse from the nameless shithole of a ville hadn't given up the chase after the brutal murder of one of their number. Well over half of the day had gone, and if anything, the sound of the tracking hounds was closer.

They had gone up another steep track, after the river crossing. Despite the patches of sunshine between the trees, Abe's clothes didn't seem to have dried properly and still felt damp and clammy.

The longer the day wore on and the nearer the vigilantes came to them, the worse Trader's temper became.

Now he was gnawing at one of their last strips of jerky, the Armalite lying across his lap. Abe was stretched out on the dry turf, massaging his belly, trying to get some relief from the raking claws that were working his guts.

"How long to dark, Trader?"

"Your eyes failed, Abe?"

"No. But the sun's gone behind some cloud. I figure it must be—" he thought about it "—I figure that dusk'll be in about another three hours."

Trader didn't even reply.

"We got any water left?" Abe asked.

"Yeah. But you don't get any. Looks like we'll be going down again after we top this ridge. Could be more streams or rivers down yonder. Drink then."

It was a river. A big river.

ALL OF THE PINE TREES vanished once they were over the far side of the hill, replaced by shrunken bushes and outcrops of bare, ferrous rock.

The sides of the gorge were the steepest that they'd come across since fleeing the squalid settlement. The path almost disappeared, with tumbled boulders and shale blocking it in several places.

There were blotches of sickly green lichen dappling the stones and the long-dead trunks of trees, blighted about a century earlier. Abe wished that they'd had rad counters like Ryan Cawdor and J. B. Dix carried, so that they could watch out that they didn't get trapped in any potential hot spots.

"You sure we can get out of here, Trader?"

"Why?"

"Steep."

"And?"

"River looks much wider."

"So what?"

Abe was concentrating on trying to hear what Trader was saying, so he slipped and nearly went cascading down to the bottom of the path.

"So, I don't see any sign of a trail going up the other side of the canyon."

"Bound to be a way out."

"Hut of some sort down there." Abe pointed to the roof of a small building that had just come into view, a little way above the cresting white water. On the ground alongside the cabin was a large rubberized, inflatable raft.

"Take that boat and run the rapids," Trader said, having to raise his voice to a full shout now that they were close to the noise of the river.

"Great," Abe muttered. Swimming had never been one of his favorite activities, and the thought of going down the dark-shadowed gorge wasn't that appealing.

It also worried him, as it had earlier, that they wouldn't hear above the rumbling of the frothing water the dogs, or the men, trailing them. They could be coldcocked and not even know it—not until they found themselves on their backs, looking up at the sky through fading eyes.

As THEY EMERGED from the bottom of the path, about fifty yards from the hut, Abe wondered if it had started to rain. But he realized that there was just a fine drizzle, spraying from the river as it pounded over the boulders.

Trader paused a moment, glancing behind them at the flank of the ravine, checking for any sign of pursuit. "Seems good to me," he said. "Let's go boating, Ches. I mean, Abe."

"Smoke from the chimney of the hut."

"Yeah. I see it. Get your blaster out. We'll try words first. Then bullets if we need them."

Abe eased the Colt Python in its holster, sighing at the prospect of more chilling. During the time that he'd traveled with Ryan and the others, there'd been plenty of death. But it had somehow seemed unavoidable.

Whereas with Trader, it was always first choice.

Trader grabbed at Abe and pressed his mouth to his ear. "Play the cards lucky, and we can get that raft into the river and be away 'fore anyone sees us."

At that moment the door swung open and a man stepped out, holding a long-barreled musket, staring straight at them. They were less than thirty yards away from him.

"Single shot," Trader said. "Means he can only chill one of us. The other'll get him."

Abe had spotted the torn curtain across the square window of the hut twitch as though someone were peering out. "Think there's at least one more inside," he said.

"Damn!"

The man with the musket had a long beard, flecked with white. His blue shirt had been crudely patched around the collar and cuffs with some flowered pink material.

"Help you, outlanders?" The muzzle of the musket was steady in their direction. The little window creaked partly open, and the barrel of another blaster poked through, instantly confirming Abe's suspicion.

"Hire your boat to go downriver a spell?" Trader shouted, the Armalite swinging loose in his right hand, pointedly not threatening anyone.

"Nope. Not for hire."

The voice was hard and inflexible, not the kind of voice that you wanted to waste time arguing with. Trader reached that conclusion immediately.

"I'll take out the one hiding in the building, behind the curtain," he whispered to Abe, at his shoulder. "You get the one with the musket."

"He could waste one of us first."

"You chicken-shit little bastard. I'm opening fire on the count of three, and if you don't back me then we both likely get chilled."

"What you whispering about, mister?" Suspicion grew with each word.

"One," Trader said.

"Shit," Abe whispered, wishing that his hand wasn't so wet and slippery.

"Means trouble, Carl!" the man yelled to whoever lurked inside the cabin.

"Two and three," Trader spit.

Abe had been right to worry. As he snatched the Colt Python from the damp leather of the holster, it slipped through his fingers, clattering on the stones by his feet. He started to stoop to grab at it, wincing at the uncertainty of a ball through his skull. Trader had begun shooting, and Abe heard the tinkling of broken glass and a yelp of pain.

As his hand finally found the reassuring weight of the Magnum, he glanced up, seeing the man with the musket seemed frozen, shocked into indecision, torn between the eruption of lead from the Armalite, and the sight of the small man with the limp mustache dropping a big handblaster in the dirt.

Before he could make up his mind, and before Abe could squeeze the trigger, Trader drilled him twice through the middle of his chest.

"'He who hesitates is lost,'" Abe said, quoting something he'd once heard Doc Tanner say.

"Hey, I like that." Trader grinned. "Wish I'd said that, Abe. I do."

"You probably will, Trader," Abe replied, covering his own panic attack with a broad smile. "Shouldn't we see to whoever's inside the cabin?"

"Got him. No way he can take three rounds from this—" he patted the Armalite "—and carry on living."

The man with the musket lay still on his back, arms spread, eyes wide open, a dark stain at the crotch of his pants leaking into the dirt.

Trader stalked past him and into the hut. Abe looked behind them, wondering if he'd spotted a flicker of movement high on the ridge.

"Yeah. Smacked him through the mouth and throat," Trader shouted. "There's some food in here, Abe. Come and stock up and then we'll raft off."

"Could be after us," the little gunner called, holstering his unfired piece.

"Not yet. We'll be twenty miles downstream before those dipshit hicks get here."

Abe looked again, but the sun was well behind the top of the cliffs and it was impossible to make out any details in the splashes of black shadows.

He wandered over to look at the raft, his heart sinking at the thought of riding it along the murderous river. Downstream the walls of the gorge were glistening with silvery spray. It was impossible to see whether the run was navigable at all. Even the short stretch that Abe could see was a frothing maelstrom of saw-toothed boulders.

Trader emerged from the door of the cabin, holding a wicker basket. "Got some eggs, bread and potatoes," he called. "Last us a couple of days."

Abe was hardly listening, as he looked farther up the ravine. A frail, rusting bridge crossed over the river a little way upstream, and he could just make out what might have been another path climbing up the opposite wall of rock. He shook his head, unable to decide which was the most frightening. Certainly the raft offered the best hope of escape. Once aboard it, if they didn't drown in the first hundred yards, there was no possible way the posse could catch up with them.

But the vital word was "hope."

And that hope seemed to have shrunk from small to invisible, just in those racing minutes that Abe looked at the river.

"How about crossing and going up the other side, Trader?" he shouted.

"Why?"

"Safer."

"No way, Abe. Once rode one of these white-water beauties, when I was sixteen or so. Colorado River. And I fought the Snake and licked it, a few years later. I'm looking forward to going on this one."

Abe looked disconsolately down at the swollen, green rubber raft, seeing the flimsy paddles, feeling a sense of deep hopelessness.

He heard a loud hissing, as the material punctured and ripped.

Then the sound of the rifles.

Chapter Sixteen

It was like seeing something out of the midnight darkness of a bad dream, something that really happened with appalling speed, yet seemed, at the same time, to be happening with slow-motion crystal clarity.

The sequence began with the scar-faced man's brutal act of stubbing out his glowing cigar on the tender flesh beneath Rajah's tail.

Ryan's hand was actually on the cool metal of the SIG-Sauer's butt. By the time he'd drawn it from the oiled holster, the buffalo hunter was already down in the dirt and done for.

Despite his increasing senescence and physical weakness, the tiger reacted to the painful affront to its dignity with dazzling speed and ferocity.

Its head came around, jerking the chain out of Ellie's fingers, and it reared up, one of the big front paws scything at the man's grinning face. For a moment there was a bizarre resemblance to a reveler at Norleans Mardie ripping off his own grinning carnival mask.

The unsheathed claws stripped the entire scarred front off the buffalo hunter's skull. The naked frightened eyes glowered for a second from their brimming caverns of bright blood, and the remaining teeth gleamed like pink coral. The veined nose disappeared, leaving a snuffling orifice in the center of the face that welled with scarlet.

The man tried to stand, breath bubbling from his throat, but Rajah wasn't going to be so easily satisfied. The tiger dug the remains of its fangs into the hunter's shoulder and pulled him to the ground, embracing him like a lost lover, then bringing up the enormously powerful rear legs. The tiger gutted the helpless man with a single thrusting upward kick, opening up the stomach, gouging meat and muscle off the raw hipbones, spilling the blue-gray intestines in the dirt.

"Fireblast!" Ryan breathed.

"Dark night!" J.B. echoed, bracing the Uzi ready at his hip.

"Here we go," Nell yelped, letting go of the chain that held Balthazar, releasing the lion to play its part in the screaming carnage.

Rosa sprang forward after her mate, head thrown back, jaws open in a terrifying roar.

The panic among the crowd of spectators had become absolute and total.

Julie slapped at Ryan and J.B. to attract their attention. "Stay here!" she shouted. "Just don't move and don't shoot unless you have to."

PARTS OF THE ORCHARD were awash with fresh blood, the ground sticky beneath the apple tree. There were nine corpses.

One was a little boy, less than two years old, his neck broken by someone trampling on him in the panic rush.

Ryan walked through the carnage, while the Kissoon girls struggled to return the excited lions to their cages. Rajah lay on his side, bleeding from three bullet wounds to his chest and back. Ellie was kneeling by him, cradling the great bristling head in her lap.

She was crying.

"Bastards," she said. "Those drunk bastards. Deserved what they got."

J.B. was looking at the backs of the buildings of the main street of Wetherill Springs. "Won't be long before they recover their courage and come out here. And blow away you, your daughters and the animals." He paused. "And probably me and Ryan. Best move fast."

Ryan nodded. "Armorer's right, Ellie. The tiger's finished. You can see that. No reason to lose the other animals as well. Never mind the risk to all of us. Come on."

Nell shouted from the barred wag as she slammed home the iron bolt to lock in Balthazar and Rosa. Both animals were slobbered with blood. "Move it, Ma!"

There were already blowflies gorging themselves on the flayed, disemboweled body of the big buffalo hunter who'd started the massacre.

Ryan noticed that the bald barkeep was among the dead, lying facedown in a pool of crimsoned mud. Unlike most of the other corpses, he didn't seem to have been raggled and torn by the wild beasts.

The metal jackbox was missing, and he guessed that someone in the screaming mob must have picked it up and taken it into the Shangri-La for safekeeping. He was slightly surprised that anyone would have had so much presence of mind in the face of the ravening big cats.

His eye was caught by something on the back of the man's black vest and he stooped to look at it. A thread of bright turquoise silk was caught in a deep, narrow cut, below the barkeep's left shoulder. The wound didn't look much like a claw or a bite. Much more as though the man had been stabbed.

But that wasn't Ryan's business.

His business was simply keeping himself and J.B. alive, in a situation that was threatening to become positively terminal at any moment.

"We're getting our wag," he said to the kneeling woman. "Got to go."

"Do it for me, Ryan." she said, lifting her tear-stained face to his. "Please."

"Rajah?"

"Do it."

J.B. was already moving out of the orchard of death, toward where they'd parked the LAV. "Move it, Ryan. They're goin' to be pissing steam when they come out."

"Please," Ellie begged. "Then we can go."

"All right."

The three daughters were waiting. The engines of their wags were fired up, exhausts smoking.

Ryan stood over the dying tiger and pressed the barrel of the SIG-Sauer against the side of its skull, just behind the right ear. "Best move," he said to the woman. "Full-metal jacket could easily go clean through and into you, Ellie."

She kissed the tiger on the forehead, lowering it gently to the floor. "Goodbye, Rajah."

"Now?" Ryan asked.

"Now."

The blaster had its own built-in baffle silencer, developed during the arms races of the late nineties. But extended use meant it didn't work quite as efficiently as it once had. Even so, the fur and flesh of the tiger acted to muffle the noise of the explosion as Ryan squeezed the trigger.

There was a tiny flicker of pale fire as the muzzle-flash ignited the golden fur. To Ryan's alarm, the effect of the 9 mm round was spectacular.

Rajah gave a coughing roar and exploded into the air, one of his rear paws knocking Ryan flat in the dirt. The tiger's powerful body tensed in midair, as taut as a bowstring, its muscular neck arched, blood gouting from its open jaws. A rainbow of rank urine jetted from the big cat.

By the time it dropped to earth, it was quite dead.

Ellie managed a half smile for Ryan. "Thanks." She sniffled and wiped her nose on her brocaded sleeve. "Meet ten miles north of town, if you want," she said.

J.B. HAD THE six-cylinder turbocharged engine warmed up as Ryan ran toward it. Someone had screamed incoherent abuse at him as he passed along an alley behind the saloon, but he hadn't been able to catch what had been said.

Now he was only a few yards from the wag, ready to vault on top and slide into the safety of the turret.

He never heard the blaster. Dirt and pebbles exploded by his boots, followed by the dying whine of a ricochet bouncing off the armor. Ryan saw the bright splash of lead, just above the second set of wheels.

J.B. had heard the bullet pinging against the outside of the wag, and he revved the throttle hard. He'd been able to glimpse Ryan running toward him through one of the viewers, giving him three-sixty vision from the driver's seat.

Ryan jinked left, then left again, seeing more bullets hitting the packed earth to his right. He was so close to the wag that it wasn't worth trying to draw the SIG-Sauer and return the fire. His instinctive guess was that the shooting was probably coming from the upper stories of the buildings, while the first-floor doors were blockaded against the threat of the merciless carnivores of Mistress Satana.

The Armorer put the LAV-25 into first gear and started to swing it around to the left, trying to give his comrade cover from the shooting. He also brought the Bushmaster cannon to bear on the ramshackle houses, offering a realistic threat to the band of hidden snipers, even though they were completely out of ammo for the huge blaster. But the enraged inhabitants of Wetherill Springs didn't know that.

Ryan cut back right again, jumping for the body of the wag, feeling his hands slip, leaving his legs dangling, brushing against the ribbed tread of one of the tires. He fought for a grip, speeded up by a bullet hitting the metal less than two inches from his scrabbling fingers.

He was looking back over his shoulder as he battled to heave himself up, finally reaching the side of the turret, where the swinging barrel of the blaster nearly knocked him back off again.

"Shit." He slid under the muzzle, feeling like the target in a crazy shooting gallery. Now he could hear the blasters, see bursts of powder smoke from what looked like every window of every building in the pesthole ville.

Ryan glimpsed the wags of the Kissoon family in the distance, moving at a steady rate toward the north, keeping clear of the main drag of the ville. As far as he could see, nobody was firing in their direction, reserving all their bullets for him.

"Get in, Ryan!" J.B.'s voice cracked with the tension.

"I'm trying!" He rested a hand on the open hatch and slid down without his feet touching the rungs of the ladder.

It was like being inside a metal drum while a lunatic banged an irregular beat on the outside with a baseball bat. Ryan reached up and closed the hatch, swinging across the locking latch and picking up the phones and throat mike.

"I'm in."

"Hit?"

"No."

"Hatch?"

"Shut. Let's get out this place, J.B., before some bright son of a bitch has the idea of putting a blockade around us and then lighting a big bonfire."

The rotation had stopped, and Ryan heard the Armorer selecting a higher gear. They began to move forward. The ob slit in front of Ryan showed a tall, unpainted fence, which crashed over as they collided with it.

Eventually the firing faded away, and there was only the sound of the thirsty engine and the wheels, rumbling over the blacktop north.

THEY FOUND THEMSELVES behind the traveling animal show after only a mile or so. J.B. throttled back so that they could act as rearguard if anyone came out of Wetherill Springs after them. Ryan had opened up the hatch again, relishing the fresh afternoon sunshine and the smell of the pines around them. He kept a careful look behind, but there was no sign of any pursuit.

After nearly half an hour, the wags ahead of them signaled they were turning off into a scenic overlook and the LAV followed them.

Chapter Seventeen

"We owe you two."

"What for?" Ryan asked.

Ellie stood in front of him and J.B., her face still pale from the recent ordeal and the shock of Rajah's death.

"You helped us."

"We didn't even pull a trigger once." J.B. wiped road dirt off his glasses.

"Didn't need to," Nell said. "Just by being there you gave us support."

"It was the lions and the tiger that saved your bacon." Ryan whistled between his teeth. "I suggest you don't ever go within a hundred miles of Wetherill Springs again."

"And keep away from buffalo hunters," the Armorer added. "Some of them got long memories."

"And long guns," Katie said.

"Uncle of mine was a buffalo hunter," Ellie told them. "Trained animals, some of the time. Used to go after those big white bears up north."

"Polar bears." Ryan nodded. "Seen some of them. Swift and evil bastards."

"Big, huh? Uncle Jack used to trek north, way up past the Canada line. Spent most of his life there. Died up there. Damnedest thing."

"How?" Ryan asked.

"Let's crack open a bottle of vino pinko I been saving, and I'll tell you."

"Better keep a lookout behind," J.B. warned. "Least from here we can see miles south. No sign yet of anyone driving out after us."

Nell was picking at a loose thread of pretty silk on the hilt of one of her knives. "I reckon that they had too many chilled to be eager to come running after us."

Ryan disagreed. "Not sure about that. I've known a posse of fifty men chase for five hundred miles over a misunderstanding about a woman's honor. There were a lot of corpses to be buried back in the ville."

They sat in a circle, and Ellie passed the bottle around. The wine was the most delicate shade of pink, much closer to being clear than to red, with a subtle taste of sunlight on a summer meadow.

"Your Uncle Jack?" J.B. prompted. "Said he died strange up north."

She wiped her mouth, licking her full lips and smiling directly at Ryan "Yeah. Unlucky, you could say."

JACK KISSOON HAD BEEN hunting with a partner, which was where the first part of the story came from. They'd been after a big white bear, a loner with an old shoulder wound that gave him distinctive tracks as well as a vile temper. The animal had taken refuge from the two men in the ruins of an old copper mine, up in the Canadian tundra, in the middle of winter.

Jack had been ill. Some kind of fever that was making him sweat, his body literally steaming in the biting cold of fifty below, the kind of cold where the line between living and dying was thinner than in most places. Illness wasn't that uncommon up there. There were plenty of triple-red hot spots from a radar defense line before skydark.

The two men had agreed to split up while tracking the bear, which was where the rest of the tale turned into supposition and deduction.

"Frank Tunstall, Uncle Jack's partner, skirted around the edge of the old workings, trying to head the animal off before he went clean on through and vanished into the badlands beyond. It started to snow and turned into a full whiteout in less than five minutes. Frank and Jack were both old hands and knew that you didn't last long at that sort of temperature in the middle of a blizzard. There was no time to light a fire."

Frank had found shelter in a hut that had once stored dynamite. Thick walls and a stout roof and a solid door. No windows to let the chill factor in.

He'd curled up to wait out the storm.

It had taken the rest of the day and the whole night and right through past noon the following day.

"Frank finally opened the door. Not easy with a lot of snow piled against it. No sign of the bear, and no sign of Uncle Jack, either. So he started to scout around. Plenty of places that his hunting partner might have tucked up against the blizzard. It took nearly three hours before he found him. He was dead."

Frank found that Jack had crawled into a narrow drainage pipe with a constricted opening. It was just large enough to contain his body if he stretched out, but it kept off the murderous wind and the heavy fall of snow.

What Jack hadn't reckoned on was what would happen when his sweat began to condense on the cold plastic of the pipe's interior. It formed a layer of ice, which grew thicker as the storm raged on when Jack had most likely fallen asleep.

His breath and his perspiration made the pipe grow ever tighter and tighter as the sheathing of clear ice became thicker and thicker.

"When Frank Tunstall found him, spotting his boots sticking out, Uncle Jack had been sealed and suffocated in a tomb of ice. Of his own making."

The ghoulish story and the bottle of wine finished at the same time.

IT WAS an uncomfortable and stilted parting. The four women pressed Ryan and J.B. *very* strongly to remain with them.

"At least for a few days," Ellie said. "We can move along the same trail as you. We don't have anyplace special to go. Be company for each other. Find another, bigger pesthole to put on another show."

Ryan shook his head. "Sorry, but we have to move on. We can make better speed than your wags."

"Long as we don't run out of gas," J.B. said. "Can't keep going for too much longer."

"There's some powerful villes lying along your route toward the Cascades." Katie glanced behind her as Balthazar suddenly threw back his maned head and roared. "What's gotten into him? Could be he scents something."

J.B. climbed quickly onto the top of the turret of the LAV-25, shading his eyes against the bright afternoon sunlight. He stared along the winding length of the blacktop, all the way back toward the faint blur that was Wetherill Springs. "No," he said. "Nothing at all."

"We got plenty of jack."

"Nell!" her mother said angrily, her eyes narrowing. "You got no right to say that."

"Why the fuck not, Ma? I reckon I've got the best right on this. After all, I was the one who..." The sentence trailed off into the stillness.

"Since when did you get plenty of jack?" J.B. asked curiously.

Ryan broke the silence. "Nell's the one closest to the answer. Her and those short-bladed knives she carries."

The Armorer sat on the body of the wag, his eyes crinkling with puzzlement behind the lenses of his spectacles. "I don't get..." His face cleared. "Course. The barkeep. Never saw the tiger or the lions take him out, but he was dead, wasn't he? And that jackbox was missing." He looked at the nineteen-year-old and whistled in admiration. "You are one hell of a family, aren't you? Dark night! You don't need anyone to ride shotgun for you. Do the job yourselves."

"Well, the offer's there. For both of you." Ellie grinned, suddenly looking no older than Julie. "You guys just don't know what you're turning down. Do they, daughters? Losing a chance with the four lovely ladies of life, like some old poet once said. Still, if you gotta go, then you gotta go." She shook hands with Ryan, the palm dry and callused, her grip firm. "Best of luck to you on your quest north. And to you, J.B., as well."

One by one the young women came and kissed both men on the cheeks.

It was Ryan's turn to drive and he clambered into the armored wag, with a last wave of the hand and a shout of good luck. J.B. followed him, sitting comfortably inside the main hatch, the Uzi in his lap.

The engine rumbled into life and Ryan kicked her into low gear, carrying on along the winding blacktop toward Durango.

THEY DROVE THREE MILES up an unmarked farm road, past a mountain of rusting relics of predark automobiles, jumbled together at the entrance to a quarry. Ryan slowed, wondering whether this might possibly presage some kind of wag works or gas seller. But there was nothing at all. Just the overgrown remains of a scrap-bean farm.

J.B. spoke into the mike. "Haven't seen any sign of life since we came off the highway. Nothing wheeled or hoofed or booted. Could be a safe enough place to park for the night."

Ryan brought the wag down from walking pace to a full stop. "Still some daylight left."

"Gas?"

Ryan's voice crackled in the cans. "Be lucky to get past noon tomorrow."

"Then we should stop now and economize as much as we can. Start fresh tomorrow and go hunting for fuel."

"Sure," Ryan agreed.

Chapter Eighteen

Krysty came awake with a sharp intake of gasping breath and a feeling of bitter cold. It was an hour after midnight, and the bedroom on the western side of the Lauren spread was chilly. As she slid from under the beautiful Amish quilt, she found her feet shrinking from contact with the old linoleum. The patterned coil rug beneath the window was softer and warmer as she stood and stared out across the New Mexico desert. The stars gleamed mistily through a bank of high, watery cloud.

There had been a disturbing bad dream, but the shock of being jerked from sleep had driven the details away from her mind. Krysty folded her arms across the thin cotton shirt that she had been wearing to bed.

They were still there. She could see the ruby-gold flicker of their camp fires, less than a half mile away.

This was the second night they'd been there.

The first warning of their arrival had come from Doc, heeling the recalcitrant Judas onward, his feet sticking out either side of the rangy mule as he careered erratically toward the spread.

He'd reported seeing movement of a group of people, out across the dusty gray wilderness toward the north. But he hadn't been able to give any details or approximate numbers. Jak's immediate response had been to wonder whether the LAV-25 might have broken down and this could be Ryan and J.B. plodding their way homeward.

But it wasn't.

They'd stayed out in the desert for that night. Dean had wanted to go out and spy on them, find out how many there were and who they were. But the grownups had all agreed that the game wasn't worth it. If they had evil motives and captured the boy, then the result would be catastrophic.

"If mean harm know soon," Jak said. "If not come in morning. See then."

But he also insisted that they work a shift system of sentries for the night. Two at a time, four hours on, one inside the house and the other one outside, but moving no more than a dozen feet from the walls.

Nothing had happened.

And in the morning, the group of travelers had approached the ranch, right out in the open, hands showing, without a blaster in sight.

Jak had everyone organized to greet them.

Dean watched the rear of the building from an attic window, with a Remington 580 hunting rifle that fired a .22-caliber round. The boy was under orders to also move at random intervals to the two flanks and make sure that no intruder tried to creep around on the blind side.

"Don't play games, kid," Jak said.

"I really do wish you'd stop calling me that," Dean replied wearily.

The albino ignored the boy's complaint. "If you think only small risk, put bullet in dirt two feet in front. If big, then chill them."

Krysty and Doc were positioned out of sight behind the lace curtains over the windows to either side of the main door of the house. The sliding casements were open about six inches. Doc had his Le Mat, in the event they tried to charge the place. Krysty relied on her double-action Smith & Wesson 640, chambered for five .38 rounds.

Jak had quickly become aware that Mildred was much the best shot of them all. It wasn't altogether fanciful to claim that the stocky black woman might very well be the finest shot in the whole of Deathlands.

She sat on the bench on the veranda, beside the swing seat, with a piece of embroidery on her lap. Her Czech tàrget revolver, the ZKR 551, was hidden beneath it.

The front door had been kept open in case anyone had to get inside or out in a hurry.

Jak stood at the front of the porch, his left hand leaning against the sun-warmed wood. The right rested easily on the butt of the .357 Colt Python with the big six-inch barrel. The jagged scar on the teenager's left cheek tugged up the corner of his mouth in what might have been a smile of welcome. But wasn't.

The strangers were all male. Fourteen of them were grouped together, except for one who was some distance behind, dragging along an enormous wooden cross, large enough to hang a man on.

The leader was extremely tall and thin, naked above the waist, his body darkened and seamed like a storm-blasted poplar. As they came closer, Jak blinked his pink eyes into the sunlight, trying to make out more details.

There was no sign of any weapons, though most of the group carried short whips, their tips caked and clotted with dried blood. Jak also noticed that most of the men had been cruelly beaten, their flesh embossed with scars and cicatrices, a few of them so fresh that they were leaking watery blood over the cotton pants.

It didn't look like any of them had been close to a barber in the past five years, with filthy hair trailing over their shoulders and straggling, matted beards.

They were one of the ugliest bunches of human beings that the teenager had ever seen.

Having lived for some recent time in the arid and ageless Southwest, Jak also knew well enough what kind of people they were.

The group was twenty yards off. "Hold there," he said, standing comfortably in the shade, partly hidden from their sight. "Let's talk some before closer."

The obvious leader carried a wooden staff, polished from long use, as tall as himself, bearing the twisted figure of a silver tortured Christ.

He flourished it toward the house.

"Hallelujah, brethren!" His voice sounded as if it had been dragged protesting over red-hot sand.

"What's business?" Jak asked. His keen hearing caught the sound of Doc thumbing back on the hammer of the massive Le Mat, knowing that the blaster was adjusted to the 18-gauge scattergun round.

"Business of the Almighty, young man."

"You penitentes?"

"Some call us that."

The man with the cross had finally joined them, laying his burden carefully on the dusty earth. He knelt beside it and picked at a scab on his shoulder.

"What call yourselves?"

"We are the Slaves of Sin. And my name is the Apostle Simon, leader of this brotherhood. We have many masters and mistresses. Dolores, our lady of pain, is but one of them. But their name is legion."

"You heading through?" Jak asked.

"We move always. Now we are bound for the Gulf where we shall find a vessel to transport us to India."

"India?" Mildred repeated, shaken out of her silence by the absurdity of the idea.

"Yeah, verily, woman of Africa, that is our plan. Do you not approve?"

"Firstly I come from Lincoln, Nebraska, not Africa. And second it doesn't matter to you whether I approve of your plan or not, does it?"

"No."

She nodded, laying aside the embroidery and standing, the revolver in her right hand. "So don't fuck around with wasted words, Apostle Simon."

There was a muttering of anger from some of the group of flagellants, one of them slapping his whip sharply against his own leg.

The leader turned to quiet them, lifting his staff. "The words of a foolish woman are but the rattling of pebbles in an empty vessel, brothers."

Mildred grinned. "And the uses of men are less than those of a fish upon a bicycle, brother."

Jak turned to Mildred. "Quietly."

"Sure."

"We need water and food."

"Need?"

"We demand it as our right, for we live upon the land and pray for all men."

Jak sniffed. "Don't live my land, mister."

Krysty leaned on a pillow placed on the windowsill, concealed from the Slaves of Sin by the lacy curtain. She had been studying the fourteen men, noting the dreadful self-imposed wounds on their emaciated bodies.

Doc stood nearby. "What do you make of these sickly visitors, Krysty?"

"Sick is the word. 'Fladgies' is what we used to call them when I was a little girl back in Harmony ville. Couple of bunches of them came visiting us once, but the menfolk made sure they didn't linger long."

She could just make out the figure of Doc, kneeling uncomfortably on the other side of the front door, the filtered sunlight glinting off the gold engraving on the commemorative handblaster.

"I once saw a very old black-and-white video," he said, keeping an eye on what was happening outside. "It was set in the Middle Ages, and included a knight and the figure of Death himself, his face like a white moon. And a quartet of flagellants." He shuddered. "They were offensive enough in the video, but these men here..."

"Least they don't normally hurt anyone else, except themselves, Doc."

"Did I hear the word 'normally' pass your enchanting cupid's-bow lips, my dear Krysty? I hardly think that is the right description to apply to such depraved and miserable specimens of humanity."

Krysty didn't carry on the conversation, stopping to listen to what was going on between the self-styled Apostle Simon and Jak Lauren.

"You refuse us food and drink?"

"Water in well. Take what need. No food."

"Why?"

"Get what deserve in life, not what ask for. Just askin' doesn't mean gettin'."

The religious madman stamped the butt of his staff in the dirt, raising a tiny cloud of sandy dust that instantly vanished in the wind.

"We are many and you are few."

Dean's voice came from one of the attic windows. "We come cheaper by the dozen."

Simon looked up, seeming aware for the first time of the curtains flapping over the partly open casements. "How many of you? How many? Not so many as us."

"Enough," Mildred said.

"We deal in the word of the Almighty and cruel Lord and will punish the graceless at his command."

Jak sighed. "And we deal in lead." He stepped out into the light, his blaster drawn.

The sun blazed off his pure-white hair, flaring like a magnesium grenade, catching the ruby glint in the eyes and revealing the long pallor of the tomb in his cheeks.

Three of the Slaves of Sin dropped to their knees, crossing themselves and beginning to patter a furious litany of prayer. Even the Apostle Simon was startled enough to take three stumbling steps backward.

"God protect us," he gasped, holding the staff toward the albino teenager as though it would hold some nameless and blasphemous entity at bay.

"Take water and go," Jak said.

"You are the promised Antichrist!" Simon turned to his thirteen followers. "It is written that he shall have eyes of fire and a halo of silver light, and he shall come to Earth to destroy all that is pure and holy."

Mildred laughed. "You shit for brains bastard! My daddy was a minister and he'd have had you slung out of any church he ever preached in for this crap."

"And his concubine shall have skin of ebony," the leader of the flagellants screeched.

The black woman shook her head, the beaded plaits tinkling against one another. "Put a bullet through his knees, Jak. Get the sickos out of here."

"Heard lady." Jak gestured with the cannon-mouthed Python. "Off my land by noon."

Simon went through a sudden and total change of personality. He lowered the staff and smiled at Jak. "I should not have spoken as I did. Foolish pride and prick-powered anger. The goat of Mendes entered my brain and stole my tongue. Dialogue is a two-way street, is it not?"

Jak's expression didn't shift. "Waste of time buttering steak after it's eaten. Take water and go. Noon."

"Could we camp out yonder for one more night, friend? We are greatly fatigued and we fear that we might meet the horned beast whose name may not be whispered. And us weakened and unready to defeat it."

"Dawn tomorrow. Find you on land after that and blood gets spilled."

The flaggelants' leader bowed so low that his matted hair tumbled over his face, hiding his eyes and mouth from the watchers in the house. "Kindness such as this shall be rewarded. Oh, truly shall it be rewarded."

Mildred spoke quietly to Jak, a few paces away from her on the porch. "Trust him just about as far as I could kick his skinny ass."

"I know it."

"Why not scoot them off now?"

"Ryan said talk beats chilling."

Mildred smiled. "That sounds more like one of the notorious sayings of good old Trader."

"Could be."

The Apostle Simon had been staring intently at them during the whispered exchange. It crossed Mildred's mind that the man might have the gift of reading lips. Unaccountably, in the warmth of the sun, she shuddered.

Now he banged the end of his staff into the earth, three times. "We are sent away hungered, brothers. Vengeance belongs to the Master of us all, He who orders us to punish and purge and cleanse our own flesh through mortification. We have been lax, brothers. Through the rest of this day we shall scourge one another, turn and turn about, until the blood flows over our ankles. Then, He will show us the true path."

Without another word or glance at Jak, Mildred or the house, Simon turned about and led his little band of fanatics back into the desert. The one who had been carrying the cross fought to lift it again, dragging it behind him, gouging a great furrow in the dry dirt.

"Be gone at dawn," Jak said.

Mildred nodded. "Hope so."

Chapter Nineteen

"End of the day, the gas gauge's going to be down to the red line, Ryan."

"Figures. We've done well so far." They were taking a break in the late morning, allowing the overheating engine a chance to cool.

"Sure. Long ways to go."

Ryan nodded. "Yeah. Too far to foot it."

The Armorer picked at his teeth with the needle point of his knife. "Bit of gristle from that ham the ladies gave us," he explained.

"Weren't they something?" Both men laughed quietly. "What would Trader've said about them?"

J.B. considered the question. "Never quite comfortable around powerful women, was he? Hunaker was one of the only people riding the war wags that he didn't scream at. Not often. Reckon he was afraid that she'd have crawled up on him in the night and sent him to live with the geldings."

"That'd be the day, pilgrim," Ryan said, imitating the Trader's voice.

J.B. stood, pushing the fedora back on his head. "Guess we might as well move on."

The land they'd reached was high plains country, flat acres and plateaux of good pasture, riven by steep, wooded valleys. Tree-lined mountains, dappled with all-season snow, rose all around them.

"Good country," Ryan said, getting up off the cropped turf, breathing in deeply. "I guess that this was always real good country."

"Yeah. Grazing and water. Shelter in the low places for the winter."

"Thinking of retiring here, J.B., to raise cattle? Get a decent spread, you and Mildred. Few little ones to carry on the dynasty. How's it sound?"

His oldest friend had been just about to climb aboard the LAV-25, but he paused and turned to stare at Ryan, his face unusually solemn.

"My thoughts a thousand times, Ryan. And yours, too. That's right, isn't it?"

"Yeah. I remember Doc quoting some old Chinese proverb about how difficult it is for a man riding a tiger to ever dismount safely."

"God himself must've lost count of all of the men and women and children that you and I have personally sent across the black river, Ryan."

"Fill a decent-sized ville, I reckon." He hesitated. "Or a big graveyard."

"And all of them was some mother's son or daughter. Every damned one."

Ryan knew precisely what J.B. was driving at. Deathlands wasn't anywhere near a big enough place to hide in. Not when there was as much old blood on your hands as there was for the Armorer and himself.

"Doesn't stop you wanting," he said.

A long pause. "No."

THE WAG WAS SHOWING ominous signs of mechanical deterioration, which wasn't surprising considering that the eight-wheeler was the better part of a hundred years old.

Ryan had taken over the driving controls, discovering that the brakes were sticking and the gears had started to get sloppy, like stirring a bowl of watery grits. Several of the main comp repeaters on the dash had malfunctioned, meaning that they'd lost important sections of information.

"Looks like a serious chem storm." The Armorer's voice whispered into Ryan's ears through the phones. "High thunderheads, northeast."

There was a radar scanner on the armawag, but it was one of the pieces of equipment that had gone down.

"Do I need a look?"

"No point. Reckon it's about an hour away. When it gets closer, Ryan, we should think about finding a good place to park. Keep out of the bottoms of dry rivers."

Ten minutes later J.B. had called through that he could see dust, rising up to their right, from the far side of a tall bluff. They were driving slowly across a rough, boulder-strewed spur of land, where a major quake had taken out the highway.

Ryan slowed and then put on the hydraulic brakes, the LAV halting with a hiss of compressed air. J.B. shouted for him to turn off the engine.

"Hear thunder, but the storm's still some way off."

Ryan switched off the ignition, sitting for a few moments in the welcome stillness. But he narrowed his eye, almost instantly aware of the noise that J.B. had mentioned, distant rumbling that made the big wag vibrate.

He picked his way to the turret, finding that his companion had already climbed out on top. Ryan joined him, looking toward the east, seeing a pillar of dust swirling a thousand feet high. And the sound was swelling, so deep that it felt as though it were dissolving the marrow of the bones.

"Earth moving?" he asked.

J.B. considered that. "No. I can feel the shaking, but it's going on for too long. Biggest quake I ever knew only lasted about a minute or so."

"Then what?"

Both men stood together, one on either side of the big gun barrel, staring toward the dust and the noise.

It was Ryan who solved the mystery, a second before J.B. also realized what was coming their way.

"Buffalo," he said.

It was only possible to make out the animals leading the stampede, all of the others invisible within the impenetrable blanket of reddish dust. They were big animals, full-grown, running at a full gallop, heads down, their hooves pounding the dirt behind them to fine powder.

As they swept around the lowest part of the bluff to the right, the herd was around six hundred yards away, heading straight toward the parked wag, with nowhere else to go, along the narrow spit of land.

Ryan's combat-honed brain made the calculations before he'd even begun to think consciously about the enormous danger that he and J.B. were facing—at least thirty miles an hour, around one-third of a mile in around...

"Forty seconds!" he yelled above the swelling thunder of the buffalo.

To drop into the driver's seat and start up the engine would take at least fifteen of those seconds, then to get the wag moving at even walking speed would be another ten to fifteen seconds. To reach forty miles an hour and keep ahead of the stampede would be close on a minute.

"No time," shouted J.B., who'd just reached the same conclusion.

"Inside and lock everything." Ryan led the way into the turret, hesitating a moment as his holster snagged on the rim of the steel hatch.

J.B. was so close behind that his boots clipped Ryan's fingers. "Closing down," the Armorer shouted, the hatch dropping with a resonant clanging noise.

For a moment there was the illusion that the threat from the stampeding herd was over, the sound of the hooves muffled by the armasteel walls. But the vibration was stronger, growing with every second.

"I'll seal the ob slits as well," Ryan said. "Strap yourself in."

He slid the chromed tongue of the safety belt into the waiting mouth, feeling the click. All of the ob slits had closed, with the exception of the one directly in front of him, facing the oncoming herd. Ryan had left that on manual override, hand on the control, ready to shut it at the last moment. He wanted to watch the rushing wave of animals for as long as possible. The inside of the LAV-25 was almost completely dark.

His brain had been mentally ticking away the seconds, reaching beyond thirty.

"Ten to go," he said.

"Ready as I'll ever be," J.B. responded quietly.

The LAV-25, partly loaded for combat, weighed in around the eleven-ton mark.

A big mutie buffalo, full-grown, topped the ton.

It was beyond calculation how many animals there were in the galloping herd, but Ryan's instant guess had put them well over one thousand, perhaps ten times that number.

One of his last sentient thoughts before the first jarring impact was to wonder whether, given enough time, Doc's mathematical brain could have worked out details like momentum, inertia and deceleration, and what the odds were against their surviving.

He slammed shut the last opening of the armawag and braced himself.

In a bar in a gaudy just near the western foothills of the Sierras, Ryan had once been coldcocked by a sec man swinging a two-by-four at the back of his head.

The sensation of everything coming loose inside his skull was almost identical to being in the wag when the first wave of the buffalo hit.

Ryan's good eye shuddered in its socket, and every one of his remaining teeth seemed to become loose in his jaws.

All of the vital organs of his body were on the move, liver, lungs, bowels and heart.

The back of the seat rapped him smartly across the head and consciousness slipped beyond Ryan's control for a few moments.

When he blinked his eye open again, the world was pitchy black and he was upside down, supported by the straps. For a moment he thought that he'd been making a jump from a gateway and something had gone drastically wrong.

The cosmos was filled with noise.

The wag was moving, constantly buffeted by collisions with the maddened animals.

Ryan cracked his head again and he fell into the blackness. This time the LAV was the right way up when he came around, and the bedlam seemed a little less.

"J.B.?" His voice was a croak.

"Yo. Been around and around like a leaf in a twister. Feels like it's easing."

Now there was only an occasional jarring thud on the outside, and the ground was no longer vibrating.

"Just hope we haven't lost a tire or anything," Ryan said. He cautiously leaned forward in his seat, feeling a muscular pain across his ribs from being tossed around, and opened the ob slit in front of him. A whirling cloud of dust filtered in, and he closed it again.

Now the stampede was over.

He could hear J.B. unlocking his safety belt and he followed suit. He opened the ob slit again and peered out, seeing that the turf had been churned and trampled by thousands of pounding hooves.

The hatch was thrown back and the Armorer sucked in a great gulp of air. "Dark night! Surely do detest being locked away in a steel coffin like that. Doesn't do a damned thing for my claustrophobia."

J.B. wasn't joking. Though he often appeared to be a man without any weakness, the one thing that he couldn't handle was being closed away in a confined space.

"Can't see any immediate damage."

Ryan climbed into the open, looking immediately to see the last limping stragglers of the huge buffalo herd picking their way past the wag.

"Wish I could've watched that from a safe hillside," he said. "Must've been something to see."

J.B. had hopped down onto the ground, going around to check all the wheels. "Seems okay," he said. "Watch the stampede? Sure. I read old books that talked about the prairies in the early days of white men."

Ryan sat on the side of the LAV and kicked his feet against one of the tires. "Yeah. I read that, too. Man could lie down on a bluff and watch the buffalo pass.

Hundreds across and moving slowly on by from sunrise to dusk.''

J.B. fanned flies away from his face with his fedora. "Used to be an old song. 'Show me a home where the buffalo roam, and I'll show you a house full of shit.' Like it?''

"Not a lot." He jumped down, looking away toward where the herd had vanished into a broad valley, an almost biblical pillar of dust marking their progress.

"Storm's coming closer," J.B. commented, wiping smudges of dirt off his glasses.

Ryan had been so preoccupied with the stampede that he hadn't even bothered to look up at the sky to check the progress of the chem storm.

The sky was blackening, with streaks of purplepink-silver lightning lacing it.

"Coming our way," he said.

J.B. had walked quickly around the wag, and Ryan followed him. Considering that the armasteel was designed to keep the occupants safe against the direct hit of an armor-piercing 7.62 mm round, it was staggering how much damage the rampaging buffalo had done.

Superficially it looked as though the LAV had been dragged backward through hedges and fields, upside down into swamps and middens.

There was mud, grass and leaves covering the outside, with several dents and gouges. One of the wheels looked as if it had been knocked slightly off-center, and the barrel of the cannon was totally blocked with dirt.

"Good job we don't have any ammo for that," J.B. said, climbing back up for a closer look. "Blow ourselves into the middle of the next century."

The distant thunder of the storm was nearer, sweeping in toward them over the Colorado mountains.

"Big one." Ryan instinctively hunched his shoulders. "Think we could find a better place to park this wreck and face the chem storm? Narrow spur like this could flood in no time."

"Higher ground," J.B. agreed. "How about straight ahead and up there? Seems like a trail."

Ryan looked, aware that the wind was suddenly starting to rise with startling speed, a sure sign that the approaching tempest was going to be triple bad.

"Could be. Means heading right into the heart of the chem storm."

"Can't outrun it, anyway."

"True. Least the rain'll clean the wag up some. Let's go. I'm driving."

Chapter Twenty

"Think this is God trying to send us a message, Ryan?" The tinny voice of the Armorer crackled faintly in his ears through the intercom.

"How's that?"

"He's decided that He doesn't want us to go to this meet with Trader."

The rain pounding on the outside of the LAV-25 was deafening, the thunder from the heart of the chem storm a constant sullen threnody.

Ryan laughed. "You mean that if He's all-powerful, then how come He doesn't come and tell us outright? A letter written in the dirt by some infinite and eternal moving finger."

"Right. 'Dear Ryan and J.B., don't go to meet Trader. Lots of love and all good things, God.' That kind of message. Why doesn't He do that?"

"Instead of double-crazy women and lions and stampeding buffalo and now the grandfather of all bastard chem storms? Give us a straight-out message."

They'd managed to get across the slender strip of open ground, where a flash flood could've done them some serious harm. Ryan peered through the ob slit, under the darkening sky, picking a path toward the trail that wound up the flank of the mountain ahead of them.

Just before the rain hit, Ryan checked the condition of the pavement ahead, seeing the marks of wheeled vehicles on it. He warned J.B. that there might be some kind of human habitation farther up the trail. But the weather washed out all thoughts of that, the storm so powerful that Ryan had to close all of the vents and ob slits on the wag.

EVEN WITH ALL the precautions, the air inside the LAV began to taste damp.

"Acid," J.B. commented, having removed the cans now that the engine was turned off.

"Yeah." Ryan nodded, aware of the futility of the gesture in total darkness. The Armorer was correct. There was the unmistakable taint of acid rain, a bitter, nitrous flavor, unlike anything else in Deathlands.

It was overlaid by the flat odor of ozone, from the electricity that cracked and hissed outside.

There was no serious threat to either of the men, as long as they stayed snug inside the armawag. The large wheels, with their rubber-compound tires, would keep them safely earthed. Even so, Ryan was aware of the short hairs on his arms, and his nape, prickling with static.

"Rad counter's showing yellow," J.B. said.

Ryan glanced down at the tiny instrument in his lapel, seeing that the usual green glow had been replaced by a pale golden light, an indication that the acid water that was vomiting out of the heart of the vicious chem storm had been contaminated from one of the skydark rad spots.

The thunder seemed a little fainter, the pounding of the rain slightly less hard.

"Passing?" Ryan asked.

"Guess so."

THEY BOTH TOOK the chance to get some fresh air. The last few leaden spots of rain were still dripping off the overhanging branches of the larches that lined the road on the right. To the left was the misty expanse of the valley, the trampled turf streaming with a river, two feet deep.

"Wonder if God has any more of his cryptic messages waiting for us," Ryan said. In the aftermath of the chem storm, the temperature had dropped by twenty degrees and his breath feathered out in front of him.

J.B. was on the brink of the drop, looking down. "That was one bastard of a storm, Ryan. Reckon we were lucky to make it through the last couple of hours."

"Trader used to say that a man who claimed to be lucky was one of two things."

The Armorer turned to him, smiling. "Right. Said he was either triple stupe . . . or he really was lucky."

Once back inside, J.B. took over driving, while Ryan sat perched on damp top of the big wag, locking his feet on the rungs of the steel ladder to hold himself steady. The Steyr SSG-70 rifle was within easy reach, in case the tracks he'd spotted earlier turned into real trouble.

"Gas is double low, Ryan."

"How about the steering?"

"Why?"

"Seemed to me that the buffalo might've affected the tracking of one of the pairs of wheels. Steering didn't seem quite on the line."

"Trail's rough."

Ryan looked ahead of them. Decades of rain had gouged great furrows from the packed dirt, and the wag was shuddering from side to side.

"True."

"Wait until we get it on the flat."

"Reckon there's probably a small ville up there. Or the remains of one."

"Could be. Got to go someplace. Loads of old mining camps around here."

The dirt track wound back and forth, sometimes with trees pressing in on both sides. Muddy water streamed down and, in places, there was barely enough room for the seven-foot width of the wag.

J.B. had dropped down to one of the lowest gears, the engine laboring, struggling for adhesion on the sharp bends. The smoke from the exhaust seemed to be thicker, leaving gray coils behind them. Ryan was beginning to worry about the noise, audible to anyone within a dozen miles.

They'd managed to make good time so far, but at least three-quarters of the trip remained. With reliable transport it would be a matter of less than a week. On foot they'd not even be close to the rendezvous within their five-week schedule.

They drove past the remains of a sign, leaning at a drunken angle over the edge of the drop. With the storm's passing, the sun had peeked through the skein of high, thin clouds, illuminating the faded letters. Ryan heard J.B.'s laughter as he read the sign through the driver's ob slit—"Steep Grade—Take Extra Care."

After one more rough section, the beat-up track began to level out, the bends becoming much less sharp, the trees starting to thin to scrubby brush.

A shack, the walls weathered and split, appeared on the right. Ryan had eased himself a little lower in the turret, leaving just his head and shoulders protruding. The Steyr was in the cabin, and he held the SIG-Sauer cocked and ready.

Now the engine of the wag sounded better and the exhaust fumes were markedly less. But J.B. had called back that the gas was almost gone.

"Looks like a ghost town," Ryan shouted. "No sign of any life."

It was difficult trying to get hold of quality gasoline in Deathlands. Generally it was only the barons of powerful villes that had their hands on reasonable quantities, and they weren't going to part with it that easily or cheaply. They always had sec men guarding their fuel dumps, so stealing was also a high-risk option.

But the smaller villes and frontier pestholes rarely had more than minimal supplies of anything.

The ghost town that they were entering looked like it was high on rotting, worm-eaten wood and tumbleweed, and very low on anything else.

"Reckon we should stop now," J.B. said, braking to a halt, allowing the engine to idle. "Looks like it might be a dead end farther up. Get ourselves stuck there and we might never move out of the place."

"Yeah." Ryan climbed down onto the damp earth, scanning the line of abandoned houses.

The Armorer switched off the LAV, the silence surging in around them.

He joined Ryan, wiping oil sweat from his forehead, replacing his time-worn fedora. "Reckon we have enough gas now to turn around and run for a quarter mile."

"I don't see a Mobilgas station," Ryan commented.

"A what?"

"Krysty showed me a picture in an old magazine. From the second of the world wars. Painting by a man called...Hopper. I remember that it was a gas station. A Mobilgas station. Lovely feel to it. Sort of amazing atmosphere."

"I don't see any sort of store. Or any sort of school or church. Or eatery or gaudy. Dark night, Ryan! There's nothing here at all."

THE FIRST FEW BUILDINGS that they entered had obviously been deserted from well before skydark. What glass remained was crazed by the sun and covered in a patina of spiderwebs. Doors hung crookedly from their hinges, and not a single roof was in place.

Nor was there much evidence of anyone living there after the long winters.

The recent heavy rain had destroyed any tracks that the main street might have held, though Ryan spotted what looked like muddy boot marks on the splintered boardwalk.

"Sheltered like that, they could have been made anytime in the last hundred years or so," J.B. said. "Still, there were the tire treads coming up the trail."

Caution was second nature to the two old friends.

Having decided to explore a little farther, they made sure that the wag was safely locked and all of the ob slits secure. Despite its power and armasteel, a quart of gas poured through an ob slit and ignited would quickly reduce the LAV to a glowing heap of twisted metal.

Ryan slung the Steyr across his shoulder, keeping the automatic in his hand. J.B. had the scattergun at his hip, the Uzi strapped over his back.

"Sure you want to do this, Ryan?"

"What?" The one-eyed man was genuinely surprised at the question.

"Something I don't like here."

Ryan looked at his companion, knowing better than to mock him. "We haven't seen anything dangerous."

"I know that."

Ryan nodded. "Look, J.B., if you want to get back in the wag and see how far it'll take us, then I'll go along with you. You know that."

"If Krysty was here she could 'feel' if there was anyone living around here."

The main street bent around to the right, continuing toward the top of the hill, where it looked like it probably dead-ended.

"Been empty so long there's no signs on the stores or anything." It was as dead a small ville as it was possible to imagine. But after the Armorer's concern, Ryan found himself starting to feel the familiar prickling at his nape. He glanced behind him, making sure that the wag was still safe where they'd left it.

They turned the corner, so that the rest of the settlement opened before them.

"Fireblast!" Ryan whistled softly between his teeth. "You were right," he said. "Something triple strange going down here."

It was as if there were two separate villes, one behind the other. The desiccated timbers of the old town, whitened by age, were replaced by a row of fresh-painted houses, about six of them, with a saloon, a couple of stores, a barbershop and a law office. There was even a small school, with its bell swinging in the wind, its clapper barely making contact with the faintest whisper of sound.

But still no sign of life.

The two men spread out automatically, without a word being said by either of them. The Armorer took the left side, keeping close to the shadows of the buildings.

Ryan came first to the barber's store, a bright red-and-white-striped pole mounted outside the door. The paint was sparkling new, and the windows shone as if they'd just been polished.

Ryan paused, his finger on the trigger of the blaster. The doubts that J.B. had mentioned earlier were now firmly in the center of his mind. He glanced across, above the Armorer, checking that there was no movement at any of the curtains at the second-story windows.

J.B. was doing the same for him, the barrel of the M-4000 Smith & Wesson raking along the row of buildings.

"Nothing, Ryan," he said. "Not a breath of life."

"Got to be somewhere. Can't just've upped and walked away leaving this place. I swear the boardwalk along here was swept this morning."

"Same this side. You going in?"

"Can't hear anything."

The Armorer darted across the rain-smeared mud of the street, flattening himself against the wall of the barber's. "I'll cover you," he whispered.

A large crow, yellow-beaked, flapped down the street and perched on the roof of the school, head on one side, watching the pair of intruders.

Ryan eased himself toward the half-open door, wincing as the boards creaked beneath his boots. There was still no sign of any danger, from norms or muties.

He pushed at the door with the barrel of the SIG-Sauer, so that it swung silently back, revealing the shadowy interior of the building.

"Going in," he said.

J.B. waited, his eyes scanning the rest of the deserted township, all of his combat-sharp senses ready for trouble. He started, the muzzle of the shotgun jerking upward, reacting to the sudden movement of the carrion crow, flying heavily away. There had been no sound from inside the hairdresser's.

"Ryan?"

The door opened wider and the one-eyed man walked out, his face puzzled.

"Anyone in there?" J.B. asked.

"Yes. And no."

Chapter Twenty-One

Abe was on the move. The deflating raft at his heels sounded like a posse of angered cottonmouths. Bullets whipped into the mud around him, the noise of the rifles from the flank of the hill behind them almost drowned out by the thunderous roaring of the river.

"Make for the bridge!" Trader shouted, his long legs taking him ahead of Abe, who didn't actually need the suggestion of heading upstream toward their only chance of safety.

The two men that they'd killed had obviously been part of a larger group. Hunters, perhaps, or trappers.

And their companions had returned.

The bridge was covered in a glistening patina of bright red rust, the strongest color in the dark, damp gorge. It was suspended across the torrent on slack cables, weakened by age. The center of the bridge drooped so low that it was only a foot or less above the frothing surface of the river.

Trader had the wicker basket of stolen food slung over his left arm, and gripped the Armalite in his right. Both men knew that there was no point in trying to stand and fight. The little cabin would keep them safe for a short while, but it would inexorably prove to be a death trap, with nowhere to run, leaving them help-less, like a pair of bottled spiders. To try to return fire against their unknown assailants would be plain tri-ple stupe. They had no cover, and the men with the long blasters would have the advantage of numbers and height and plenty of places for them to hide among the rocks and stunted trees.

A bullet gouged a furrow in the sodden turf a few inches to the right of Abe's feet. From the size of the hole it looked like a large-caliber musket ball.

"Cover me while I cross, Abe!" Trader flung the words over his shoulder.

Another round whined past the little gunner's ear, almost trimming the end of his straggling mustache, smashing into the basket carried by Trader.

The container exploded in a mess of burst eggs and mildewed potatoes that spilled all over Trader's pants and boots, leaving him, for a moment, holding the curved, splintered handle and nothing else.

"Fuck it!"

There was shouting behind them, angry, ragged sounds that bounced back off the cliffs opposite. The spray from the falls was so dense that it drifted like fog, making it almost impossible to see anything clearly on the other side of the river. But Abe was sure he'd spotted a path of sorts.

He *hoped* there was a path over the swaying, ram-shackle bridge, just ahead of them.

"Let 'em have it!" Trader shouted. "I'll cover you from the far side."

Abe found, to his surprise, that he was still holding his .357 Colt Python, the stainless-steel metal gleaming with tiny drops of water.

Fighting to control his breathing, he dropped to his knees, looking, for the first time, behind him. For a few lung-bursting moments he couldn't see any sign of the enemy that was shooting down at them. Then there was a muzzle-flash and a burst of white powder smoke. And another. And a third.

Trader was on the bridge, the wire stays singing and groaning at his weight.

Abe gripped the butt of the big Magnum in his right hand, steadying his aim with his left, pointing up into the swirling clouds. He fired one round, brought the four-inch barrel back onto the target, waited a moment, then shot again.

He risked another glance behind him, seeing that Trader's gaunt figure was almost across, his pants wet above the knees where the bridge sagged at its center.

A bullet struck the earth right in front of Abe, showering him with mud and tiny, sharp splinters of stone, making him gasp with shock and wince at the sudden stinging pain.

"Shit a fuckin' brick!" He fired the last rounds from the Colt, spraying the cliffs opposite without even bothering to aim.

He holstered the warm gun and started to scramble back toward the bridge, jinking from side to side, boots slipping in the cropped, sodden turf, aware that the attackers would eventually get the range right.

To Abe's great relief he heard the flat crack of Trader's rifle.

It was almost impossible to be sure, above the leaden roar of the river, but he thought he heard a high-pitched scream from across the valley.

Abe's main preoccupation was with readying himself to tackle the rusted bridge.

For a moment he hesitated.

"Move, you shit-for-brains little fucker!"

The familiar rasping bark of Trader's voice, from behind the ruins of a small stone hut on the far side, prompted him to start moving.

Immediately he felt sick, the bitterness of yellow bile rising into his throat, into his mouth. Abe spit out, blinking to try to clear his vision. He didn't think he'd ever been so frightened in his entire life.

He gripped the two narrow ropes of plaited wire on either side, realizing that the actual walkway of the bridge was a number of rotted planks, set crosswise, and that more than half of them had vanished, leaving gaps of varying width where the river frothed and raged just below.

A bullet pinged off the cable, scant inches from his left hand, sending up a shower of red dust. His weight was making the bridge buck and sway, the middle section already dipping below the surface of the icy water.

Through the paralyzing terror, the knowledge came faintly to Abe that he was going to die. If he moved forward, then the whole structure would collapse and tumble him into the nameless river. And if he stayed where he was, then he would inevitably be shot, his body falling into the rapids.

He saw another burst of fire from the Armalite and a frantic wave of the hand from Trader.

Abe knew that his old leader was quite capable of shooting him if he didn't do like he'd been told, and it was that chilling certainty, more than any other gut-rending fear, that made him begin the crossing.

The swaying redoubled, until he feared the bridge was going to swing completely upside down. Gray stone, white water and pewter sky all rolled and merged. But he gritted his teeth and battled onward, a careful step at a time, his knuckles white with the strain.

A freezing sensation around the ankles made Abe yelp in fear, until he realized he was nearing the center, where the water boiled over the missing slats. If the enemy were still shooting at him, then he was no longer aware of it.

Did he hear the cry of "Blood for blood" that had been haunting them since the killing in the hamlet in the hills? Was it still the posse?

Time had ceased to exist for Abe.

He remembered that one of the slats had parted like a whisper and he'd dropped through the gap, one hand slipping, skin tearing from his fingers, blood dripping, watery, down his wrist. He hauled himself up by the other hand, soaked above the waist, trembling with shock.

He reached the middle, where the tug of the river was like a fierce embrace, trying to suck him down into the gray-green pools. It reached to his groin, chilling Abe to the heart, while he hauled himself along the cutting wires, feeling for a footing below him.

He glimpsed Trader, crouched behind the tumbled walls of the hut, keeping up covering fire, pinning down their attackers if any of them showed themselves.

Abe didn't even realize that he was crying, and the soaking from the tumbling meltwater concealed the fact that he'd pissed himself.

Then he was across.

"RECKON THEY'LL TAKE their time coming down after us," Trader said.

Abe was flat on his back, cold and wet, fumbling with his clawed and frozen fingers as he tried to reload the Colt Python, dropping shells in the dirt.

"Can't we wreck the bridge?"

"No."

"Why?"

"Checked it as I came over."

"And?"

Trader straightened and the Armalite snapped again. "Missed the son of a bitch! This fucking spray makes it bastard difficult to shoot well."

"The bridge?" Abe prompted.

"What the ... Oh, yeah. Middle part's rotted to shitland and back again. But the main stays are better than they look. If we had some plas-ex, we could blow it."

"We could wait here, Trader."

"Why?" The lined face turned toward him, genuine puzzlement in the deep-set eyes.

"Hold the ridge. Chill them when they come down after us. What do you reckon?"

Trader shook his head. "Short-term thinking, partner. Man who looks five minutes ahead gets wasted by the man who looks an hour ahead."

"Seems a good idea." The ex-gunner was aggrieved by the dismissal of his plan, though he was real pleased with the unexpected "partner" from Trader.

"We're shitting in their backyard, Ryan. I mean, Abe. They know this place and we don't. Could be a back-double around the top of that canyon. Bring some of them down on top of us while the rest hold us here."

"So?" The reloading of the big .357 blaster was finally completed.

"I'll be hung, quartered and dried for the crows! I swear I never met anyone with so many fuck-stupe questions as you, Abe. We go up, of course."

The moment of delight in the "partner" hadn't lasted very long for Abe.

THE WEATHER GREW WORSE, with the sky darkening as though it were about to unleash a storm of biblical proportions. The wind rose, lashing the foaming water to a greater turmoil, while clouds of misty spray rose to fill the gorge.

As soon as Abe had recovered his breath and his nerve from the crossing of the bridge, Trader urged him to his feet and began to lead the way up the narrow rain-furrowed path that clung to the face of the cliff.

There was still an occasional shot fired in their general direction, but none of the bullets came within fifty yards of them.

"Wasting lead," Trader grunted, not bothering to return the futile fire.

"You said they'd stop chasing us," Abe panted as they paused for a few moments at one of the break-backed turns in the steep trail.

"Thought they would. These could be compadres of the couple by the hut."

"Then again, they could be that bastard posse on our asses from back yonder."

Trader didn't bother to reply, striding onward and upward with the vigor of a man a third of his age.

Gradually the ceaseless roaring from the turbulent stretch of the falls began to fade away beneath them.

Abe felt the muscles at the back of his calves beginning to tweak with the remorseless pace that Trader was setting and he leaned forward, pushing with his hands on his thighs to try to help himself over the worst parts.

His heart pounded and the breath rasped in his chest. Abe licked his lips, tasting salt and cold iron. A tight band was squeezing around his temples, and he felt a sudden urge to stop and throw up.

The track was so old and faint that earth slips had washed it away in several places, necessitating a muddy and slippery clamber up over a dangerous detour across bare dirt and rock.

Finally the shooting had stopped.

The track wound away from the river, cutting toward the east, up a side canyon.

"Once we get over the ridge we'll have an ace on the line to get away," Trader said.

"Long as they haven't second-guessed us," Abe panted, but he wasn't sure that Trader had heard him. Truth was, he hoped that the man hadn't.

IT WAS RAINING, a steady downpour, lancing vertically from the dark clouds, seeking out every gap in their clothes. Abe had it running down his nose and inside his collar, both at the back and the front. There didn't seem an inch of his body that wasn't sopping wet. It had also become colder.

Trader was moving ahead, the gap between the two of them widening. Every time there was a sharp bend in the trail, the older man vanished for almost half a minute.

Abe had heard about the cold sickness. Something that insinuated itself into the marrow of your bones and froze your blood and dulled your mind. He knew that one of the first signs of that was fatigue. A terrible weariness that dragged at your feet and made every step seem like ten.

"Trader." The word carried away on the rising wind. "Hey, Trader!"

But the gray man didn't hesitate or check for a moment, striding on, around the next turn in the track.

"Get a fire going," Abe said. "What I need most. Dry myself and get warm. Be fine then. Fucking fine with a good blaze to heat me up."

A small carved sign, under an overhang, protected from the elements, read: Quarter Mile To Hotel.

"Sounds good," Abe said.

Around the next bend, Trader was so far ahead of him that he wasn't even in sight.

For the first time, dimly against the skyline, Abe thought he could make out the tumbled ruins of a building, presumably the hotel that the sign referred to.

He slogged on, face down against the driving rain, stumbling in the deep ruts that crisscrossed the trail, hoping that Trader would be in sight when he reached the top.

But he wasn't.

Abe was greeted instead by a small group of bedraggled men with muskets. "Blood for blood, you bastard," one of them said. "You're a fucking dead man."

Chapter Twenty-Two

"Dark night!"

"Yeah," Ryan agreed. "If that's not one of the damnedest things you ever did see."

The barbershop was brightly painted, all of the wooden surfaces varnished and polished. The mirrors gleamed, and the floor was clean enough to eat off.

"See what you meant," J.B. said.

"What?"

"About there sort of being someone in here. I see what you mean."

There were nine figures in the single long room. Three were dressed as barbers, in blue-and-white-striped aprons. Three were customers, sitting in each of the mahogany-and-brass chairs. The other three sat or lounged on the padded bench that ran the length of the shop.

They were all dead.

"KNEW WHAT HE WAS DOING. Or she was doing," Ryan commented, touching a wondering finger to the cheek of the stoutest of the barbers. It felt cool and waxen to the touch, like artificial fruit. The glass eyes twinkled with a convincing jollity, and the mustache had a spiky elegance.

"Seen plenty of stuffed animals." J.B. lifted the arm of a young man on the bench seat, testing it for weight and movement. "Real light," he said.

Ryan shook his head. "Damnedest thing," he repeated. "Yeah, I've seen fishes and birds and moose heads and cougar and bear. Every kind of embalmed and stuffed creature in the world. But never human beings."

The place was immaculate. Everything gleamed and sparkled, all dust and dirt banished.

There was a beautiful sampler on the wall, above the bench, in a hand-turned beechwood frame. The date at the bottom was the eighth day of the eighth month in the Year of Our Lord, 1888, with the name of the person responsible for the embroidery—Jemima Auster—and her hometown of Pawtucket.

The sampler was a quote that Ryan knew related to the Great War between the States from the middle of the nineteenth century. "Grant stood by me when I was crazy and I stood by him when he was drunk. Now we stand by each other, always."

J.B. had taken off his glasses to read it out loud. "Double-weird thing for a girl to sew," he said.

"Look at this." Ryan had seen a plastic box fixed to the wall beyond the second of the swivel chairs. A sign nearby read: Turn This Handel Fifty Times And Youl Heer Whats On Our Minds.

"Go on then," the Armorer said.

"Could be boobied."

J.B. laughed. "Anyone takes this much trouble to set up these dummies isn't going to want them blown apart. Go ahead, Ryan, turn it."

There was a resistance, which he guessed came from it being used to generate some small flow of electricity, dutifully counting up to fifty turns.

There was a red button on the side of the box, and Ryan pressed it.

After a few moments of hissing and crackling, what he figured was a loop tape began to play through concealed speakers around the barbershop. They heard the clicking of scissors and the humming of clippers, overlaid with the voices, supposedly, of the trio of men standing frozen behind each of the chairs.

Different accents. One from the bayous and one, more terse, from New England. The third with the Texas drawl. The words were overlaid and overlapped.

"Blue Jays came back, top of the sixth, last night..."

"So the priest looks at it and sprinkles holy water over the hood..."

"Should've gone to the wide receiver on that third and long call..."

"Bases loaded when he comes in and trips over the dugout steps and breaks his ankle..."

"Buddhist holy man lights twenty sticks of incense and waves them around the outside of the auto..."

"Little bit more off over the ears, sir? I couldn't agree more. Change comes from the top, not the guys doing the business on the line..."

There was a click as the hidden tape wound through to its ending.

Though the recreation had been done with considerable skill, the overall effect was undeniably creepy. The skins had been cleverly preserved, and it was only when you looked real close that you saw the tiny network of fine lines and cracks that revealed the embalmer's artifice. Ryan noticed that one of the customers had tiny flecks of sawdust leaking out from a fault where the right hand joined the wrist.

"Think the rest of these painted buildings are going to be filled with these...these things?" J.B. pushed back the fedora and shook his head.

"One way to find out."

"Yeah."

They shut the door behind them, just as the tape started to play through again. "Blue Jays came back..."

Ryan paused, fingers on the brass handle. "You notice something about those three voices?"

"No."

"Reckon they're all the same person. Just disguising himself by using different accents."

"Could be."

EACH OF THE REDECORATED buildings had its own macabre inhabitants, and each one had its own recorded tapes that could be played by turning the handle on the little generator fixed discreetly to the walls.

The lawyer's office had a tall, stately old man in a high wing collar, with long white hair and a snowy beard, his hands clasped piously in front of him dictating to his prim, gray-haired secretary.

"The message and other elements of the hereditament can be included, inter alia, as in the abovementioned paragraph, which shall be interpreted as at the vendor's discretion for all purposes and uses. Notwithstanding per ardua ad astra and nemo me impune lacessit whereby..."

Ryan and J.B. left at that point, but the thin, prissy little Connecticut voice kept droning on behind them in the walnut-and-oak office.

"Triple crazy," the Armorer said.

"Can't argue with you."

They wandered through the largest house, decorated in the white Victorian Gothic style that they'd seen in other parts of Deathlands, but rarely in such wonderful condition as here.

There were embalmed corpses in most of the rooms, all placed with infinite care into pseudolifelike poses. Everything had been done with an astonishing eye for detail: a grandmother in a mobcap, fringed with stiff white lace, perched in a rocking chair with an armful of knitting, a stuffed Pekingese dog by her slippered feet; father, reading a book, in a comfortable armchair in the parlour, a luxuriant mustache, each hair carefully glued into place by the mysterious master craftsman, a monocle gleaming in his right eye. Mother was in the kitchen at the back of the house, surrounded by shining copper pots and pans. There was the makings of a meal on the table, with a mid-

dle-aged cook, rosy-cheeked, up to her elbows in flour.
J.B. checked out the meat and vegetables that lay
scattered artistically around.

"False," he said. "Made out of clay or something
like that. Looks good enough to eat."

There was another of the black plastic generator
boxes on the wall, with another misspelled notice at its
side, identical to the one in the barbershop.

Ryan turned the handle and waited.

The voice that floated out of the speakers was high
and strained, giving the instant suspicion that it was a
man attempting to impersonate a woman.

"Now make sure you get the bread baked, May, and
you know that the master must have his gentleman's
relish with his rarebit. The stew goes on in forty minutes, and remember to mix in the sassafras and
moonlight."

J.B. walked out into the shadowed hall, pushing at
a half-open door, brushing past a tinkling curtain of
beautiful colored crystal beads.

"Fancy some music, Ryan?"

The one-eyed man followed his friend, hearing the
plaintive, bossy little voice fading behind him in the
kitchen. He looked into the room where J.B. stood by
the window, beneath the elegant golden drapes.

"Notice the smell?" he asked.

The Armorer sniffed. "Yeah. Sort of bitter chemi-
cal kind of a scent."

"What the embalming was done with."

"And there's death."

Ryan nodded. It was true. Every room of every building that they'd been in contained that unmistakable odor, the sour-sweet taint of life departed.

Whoever had constructed this bizarre series of *tableaux morts* had obviously been aware of the problem. There were bowls of dried flowers and dishes of scented potpourri in each building. But their faded, dusty scents could do little to overcome the grisly reality of what stood and sat in all the chambers.

J.B. wound away at the handle that was set alongside a walnut harmonium. A young woman sat with her hands resting on the black and white keys, her head on one side, an attempt at a smile on her painted lips, a smile that resembled a rictus of horror at what had come to pass.

Ryan stood close behind her, and he pointed at a mark on the back of the neck, almost hidden by the tightly wound chignon of straw-colored hair.

"Bullet hole," he commented.

At that moment the music began, wheezing and slow, with a thin little voice trilling out the words.

"'Shall we gather at the river, the beautiful, the beautiful river? Shall we gather at the river that flows by the throne of God...of God...God...God... God...'" The repetitive click got louder, the music also halting and repeating the phrase. There was a faint grinding noise, like gears failing to mesh, and the silence returned.

The friends went back outside, Ryan holding the SIG-Sauer cocked and ready, the Armorer with his Uzi cradled in his arms. But there was nobody in sight.

It was late afternoon, the sun already slipping out of sight behind the range of mountains to the west. The township was still and silent.

Suddenly up beyond the school, they both heard the noise of a generator firing up, and the fragile evening breeze brought the odor of gasoline. All around them, lights began to flicker into life in the newly painted buildings.

Ryan instinctively crouched behind a tub of flowers—artificial flowers, he noticed. J.B. flattened against the wall of the house.

"Might get to meet the creator of all this," Ryan whispered. "Not sure how I feel about that."

"Me neither."

"Notice something?" the Armorer asked quietly.

"What?"

"No children."

It was true. Even in the big mansion with the harmonium, where you would have expected to see little ones, in the nursery or in the living rooms, there had been no sign of any.

"School?" Ryan said.

"Could be."

They moved up the street toward the crest of the hill, where the small white school stood. The rhythmic thudding of the generator was somewhere beyond it, just out of sight. They overlapped each other, in classic urban skirmish style—Ryan going ahead while J.B. covered him, then the Armorer moving past, while Ryan kept watch with his blaster.

The church was on their right, the doors open, and a freshly printed poster pinned to the noticeboard outside: Faith In The Lord Doesn't Determine Who Goes Right Ahead—Just Who Gets Left Behind.

"Yeah," said Ryan, to himself.

It was possible to make out several silent figures sitting in pews in the incense-scented pools of darkness inside the church. There was no need to go in and find out whether they were embalmed corpses.

They reached the school, looking at the gently swinging bell, listening to the sound of the gas generator.

"Up the hill?" J.B. asked.

"School first. You want to wait outside and keep watch or come in?"

"Guess I'll come in with you."

The grisly ville of the dead was getting to Ryan, his discomfort heightened by the memory of the puckered bullet scar in the tanned skin of the dead young woman at the keyboard of the harmonium.

The hinges of the entrance door had been recently oiled, and it opened without a sound.

"The children," J.B. said. "Black dust, Ryan! There's a triple-crazy mind working here."

It was like an illustration from an old predark magazine. Ryan remembered Doc had mentioned the name of an artist who specialized in portraying everyday life in the United States before it became Deathlands.

"Rockwell," he said.

There were rows of little figures, their straight backs toward the two men, faces toward the blackboard and the rigid statue of the teacher.

He was a very tall, skinny man, in his mid-thirties, with gold-rimmed pince-nez perched on the end of his beaky nose. His hand was folded around a creased book of grammar, and there was a whippy cane on the desk behind him. Ryan saw yet again the incredible attention to detail that the mysterious embalmer used. There was a faint dusting of chalk on the cuffs of the faded blue pin-striped suit, and a pottery apple rested on a table in the corner, by a globe of the planet.

There were about eighteen children in the classroom, all of them wearing antique clothes, making them look like visitants from Victorian times. All of them, boys and girls alike, wore cotton caps on their heads.

Ryan turned the handle on the box on the wall, by a poster showing the location of the centers of the wheat belt across the Midwest.

After a few seconds of hissing static, piping voices, overlaid, chanted their number tables. "Eight sevens are fifty-six and nine sevens are sixty-three and ten sevens are seventy."

J.B. walked slowly to the front, his boots squeaking on the waxed and polished floor. He turned and looked at the children, hesitated and peered more closely.

"Ryan..." He gestured with the muzzle of the Uzi. "See what I see?"

"The kids?" He joined his friend. "Oh, fire-blast!"

At a first glance, all of the eighteen children looked roughly the same size and age, roughly ten years old. But that wasn't the reality. Now that he could see beneath the caps, Ryan realized the truth. Only four or five of the class were actually human. The rest of them were...

"Dogs," J.B. said, unable to conceal his disbelief and disgust.

All of the other corpses that they'd seen had been skillfully preserved, arranged with great cunning into acceptable facsimiles of normal behavior. But the embalmer had been less successful with the dog-children.

You could see where vulpine jaws had been pushed back and muzzles extended, bristling hair shaved off and the sharp teeth filed and drilled. The peaked ears were hidden under the caps, but some of the silent rows of creatures showed mutilated paws, resting on pencils and primers.

And the clothes had been clumsily pinned and sewn together to try to fit around the misshaped bodies of the variety of canine breeds.

In the background, the tape was still grinding on. "Six eights are forty-eight. Seven eights are fifty-six. Nine eights are seventy-two."

"Let's get the fuck out of here," J.B. said. "Place is a nightmare."

"I'll go with that."

Ryan was ready to go. Before leaving he glanced up at the blackboard. There was a line and a half of roughly scrawled writing chalked on it, that simply ended, as though the person had lost interest.

Once upon a midnite dreery, while I pondered week and weery,
Over many a...

"What's it mean?" J.B. asked. "Looks like some sort of a poem."

"Rings a kind of bell with me. But the spelling's all up the creek."

They both felt the slightest breath of air as the door opened behind them. They started to turn, aware that they were going to be too slow and too late.

The voice was mild and gentle. "I fear that spelling was always my weak point."

Chapter Twenty-Three

"Sure looks good," Ryan said, returning from washing his hands at the pump out back.

J.B. was just behind him, wiping his fingers on the leg of his pants. "Surely does."

Malachi Gribble smiled at them from his seat at the head of the table. "If only it was real, gentlemen. But I fear the bread and the venison alone are fit to be eaten. The rest are the products of my humble skill."

"You're greasing our wheels," Ryan said. "You mean all that other stuff is faked?"

"Sorry." He smiled thinly, the eyes staring at them, magnified by the enormously thick lenses of his spectacles. "Like I said in the schoolroom, I have talents in that line. Though spelling has, sadly, never been among them. As a child I was whipped by my father for that failing. I can read well enough. Always could. But when I try and scratch the black marks on the page, they become muddled and jumbled."

"We noticed that," J.B. said, sitting where Gribble indicated.

"That was why I abandoned my attempt to copy Mr. Poe's wonderful verses about the raven onto the board. I knew things had run away from me."

Ryan sat down and looked at the groaning table, hardly able to believe that so little of it was real. Until he spotted that imperfection meant reality.

The bread was burned on one side and looked underbaked in its heart. The bowl of venison was thick with grease, a clotted scum floating on its top.

Everything else was flawless.

The salmon, freshly caught, with its scales shining like a thousand rainbows, was dry and dull to the touch. The quail, every feather vibrant with life, was long dead. The pile of fruit—peaches, a mango, oranges, bananas, a pineapple and some unskinned lychees—was made from clay, glazed and fired.

"Did all that myself," Gribble said. "Like I say. God gave me a real talent for that. Got my own kiln out back by the generator. Drives the electrics. And for the embalming. In return, He made words and letters go into a corkscrew dive when I come anyplace near to them."

J.B. ladled some of the venison stew onto a cracked dish, hacking off a slice of the bread. He sniffed suspiciously at the food, looking up at their host.

"Yeah..." Gribble said sorrowfully. "Cooking isn't a skill I possess, either. Sorry."

During the next half hour Ryan and the Armorer learned most of what there was to know about Malachi Gribble.

He'd been born on the edges of old Denver, fifty-three years ago, when there were plenty of serious hot spots around Colorado. His parents died of rad sickness when he was eleven, and he headed for the hills, lived in a ville near Telluride and learned all about taxidermy from an old-timer.

"Had a store. Did some hair-cutting. Claimed to do manicures, though I never saw him do that. And embalming. Called his place 'Buff 'em, Fluff 'em and Stuff 'em.' Honest. Left him. Married. Had a couple of kids. All died. Cholera. Found this place about four years ago. Going to call it Gribbleville once it's done."

The little blue eyes, behind the dense, magnifying lenses, really came alive when Malachi talked about his dreams and ambitions. He wore a three-piece suit that looked like it came from the same era as the clothes of the children in the schoolhouse. As he talked he slurped stew all over the vest and dropped crumbs in his lap. But he seemed oblivious to the mess.

"I want to have this place looking so real you can kind of squint and believe it. Did all the voices myself. Never have guessed that, would you?"

Both J.B. and Ryan shook their heads, battling with the rotten food.

"Moving onto smaller animals."

"Like dogs?"

Gribble blushed at Ryan's words. For a moment there seemed a fiery glimmer of real anger behind the glasses, but if it had ever been there it was swiftly gone.

"They're a mistake, aren't they? Come on, now. Admit it. Mistake. Error city. Failure avenue. Lapse of taste. On a scale of one to a hundred, the dogs rate a flat zero. I know that. But it's hard to get hold of children."

Ryan couldn't eat any more. His stomach was already revolting at the greasy mess. "Where do you find your..."

"Specimens?"

"That'll do for a name. Yeah."

Gribble was helping himself to the last of the venison, shreds of gristle and sinew plopping into his dish. "Oh, here and there."

"They dead when you get them?"

"Of course, Mr. Dix." A vacuous smile of dubious morality pasted itself onto the pallid cheeks.

"Where?"

"Here and there. Plenty of small villes around. Sometimes I go as far as Denver. Plenty of cold ones there."

"What did you chill the deer with?" J.B. asked. "What kind of blasters you got up here?"

"Oh, just a long-barrel musket. Nothing else. With my sight I'm not a good shot. I was hunting when you arrived. Or I'd have seen you or heard you coming. I always come and welcome strangers. Gets lonely. Not many visitors this far off the trails. But I can always go and talk to my friends in the houses and the church and the school and all."

Malachi Gribble smiled again. He stood and pushed back his chair.

Ryan and J.B. also stood. "You said you'd got a bed for us for the night, Malachi?" Ryan asked.

"Indeed I do. Best in the house. Sure you don't want to bring up your wag for safety?"

"Safe where it is, thanks." J.B. wiped his mouth on his sleeve. "If you just show us..."

Gribble's own house was little more than a shotgun shack. But he had proudly showed them his workshop out back, near the gas generator. It was wonderfully equipped with all manner of tools, and was spotlessly clean. And was more than twice as big as the actual house.

"Keep your gas in that green tank?" J.B. had asked.

"Yeah. Trade some of my stuffed animals around for it. Folks like them. Specially barons. Some times they bring me bears and wolves and muties they've chilled and get me to render them more lifelike than the living. That's my motto."

"Muties?"

"Oh, mutie *animals* only. I keep the... well, special ones to come and be my friends here. There's always space for more friends, in life, isn't there? In the mansion of Malachi Gribble there are many rooms."

THE ROOM HE SHOWED to Ryan and J.B. had two narrow beds in it, each piled high with ragged and filthy blankets.

After the little man had left them, they looked at each other, grinning.

"Crazier than a shithouse rat," the Armorer commented.

"Agreed. Still, beats sleeping in the armawag. Can always wash off the fleas in the morning." He paused, lowering his voice. "And help ourselves to some of his gas."

The door was sturdy with a good strong bolt on it, and J.B. threw it across.

"There. Still, if he's only got a black-powder musket, I guess there's not much to fear."

Ryan thought for a moment about the bullet wound in the back of the young woman's neck. It had looked like a high-velocity round had done the damage.

J.B. laid the 12-gauge Smith & Wesson against the side of his bed, placing the Uzi on the floor, within easy reach of his hand. He didn't bother to pull off his combat boots. "Anywhere to piss in the night?"

"Window." Ryan looked around the room and saw a low cupboard in one corner. He opened the door and spotted the gleam of white porcelain. "Thunder pot in here," he said.

To try to wash down the noxious meal, Ryan had drunk a lot of water from the chipped glass jug, and he suspected that he might not make it through the night. But he laid down his weapons and eased himself under the blankets on the bed nearest the undraped window, wincing at the stench.

"He been wrapping dead bear guts in these?"

"Kind of ripe," J.B. agreed.

Both men were tired and, feeling secure behind the stout bolted door, they quickly fell asleep.

THERE WAS a bright moon.

Ryan lay still for a few moments, his eye taking in his surroundings. Something had disturbed him, and he wasn't quite sure what it was.

One of the first things you learned about survival in
Deathlands was that being awakened in the night, in
a strange environment, could be profoundly hazard-
ous. But that didn't mean you leaped into instant,
clumsy life. Better to take a dozen heartbeats and wait
and watch, without giving a clue to anyone that you
had actually returned from sleep.

The square of the window was brilliantly lighted,
throwing a block of silver across the room, showing
the door, still securely locked and bolted.

Ryan was aware of pressure on his bladder from
drinking so much water over supper, and concluded
that it could easily have been this that had eased him
awake. He could have taken the SIG-Sauer and gone
outside, but there was something about the short-
sighted Malachi Gribble that he didn't quite trust.

The second option was to piss out of the window.

Ryan recalled staying in a dormitory block in a ville
down in the bayous, not all that long after he'd joined
Trader and the pair of war wags.

The local baron had been having trouble with
stickies, having burned out a nest of the ferocious
muties only a week earlier. Ryan and the others in the
crews had been warned about going beyond the pa-
trolled walls, particularly at night when stickies were
likely to be out hunting.

The man had been a map reader and maker on War
Wag One, a tall, silent man with a hooked nose named
Jerzy Wajda. He'd been one of the tiny number of
people who'd fled the Old World of Europe during the
long winters and survived the almost impossible

crossing of the Lantic to make a fresh start in Death-lands.

Jerzy was suffering from what one of the war wags' medics said was a prostate problem, which meant he had to get up to take a leak several times during every night. He couldn't be bothered to go all the way to the johns in the eastern section of the ville. He just opened the window, without waking anyone, and stuck his cock out.

Where a stickie was waiting. It reached up with the lethal sucking pads on palms and fingers and ripped Jerzy's genitals off his body. Shock and blood loss chilled him within eighty seconds of the attack.

Ryan decided not to risk taking a piss out of the window of the shack. There hadn't been any sign of stickies—or any other muties—in the region. And Gribble claimed that his only weapon was a ponder-ous black-powder musket. So there wasn't that much danger around.

He swung his long legs out of the bed, pushing back the mound of noisome blankets. It was cold, and Ryan could see his breath feathering out in a white mist, drifting into the area of bright moonlight.

J.B. moved a little, the faint disturbance from Ryan reaching him through the layers of sleep, but not quite enough to wake him properly. He lay on his back, hands folded across his chest like a statue on a medi-eval tomb.

Ryan stooped toward the cupboard where he'd seen the chamber pot, opened the door and took it out. He unbuttoned himself and held the pot in his left hand, controlling the amber stream with his right hand.

When he'd finished he placed the pot on the floor and buttoned his pants again.

The floorboards creaked as they shrank in the chill of the night.

Ryan bent down and carefully put the receptacle back into the cupboard, closing the door and straightening again, ready to climb back into the warm nest of the blankets.

When he hesitated.

"What?" he whispered.

There'd been something glinting in the moonlight, underneath the small cupboard.

Ryan knelt again, reaching his right hand underneath the legs, feeling for what had caught his eye. His fingertips brushed the coldness of metal.

He withdrew it and held it up to his eye to see it clearly, realizing immediately that it was a full-metal jacket, 9 mm round of ammo—a bullet for the sort of blaster that Malachi Gribble had denied owning.

At that moment, Ryan's attention was caught by something else in the room. A section of the wall, behind the beds, was swinging silently backward on oiled hinges, revealing Gribble himself, holding an old Luger automatic in his right hand.

Chapter Twenty-Four

Dean had persuaded Doc to go out with him from the safety of the house, leaving quietly an hour after supper was finished, to creep across the night coolness of the desert toward the camp fires of the Slaves of Sin.

"Are you certain that young Master Lauren and Mistress Wroth have given their permission for this shadowy enterprise, my dear boy?"

"Sure, Doc."

"What precisely is the point of this nocturnal expedition, if I may make so bold as to ask?"

The boy had stopped and grinned at him, as they paused by the fence that separated the old orchard from the pasture. "Sometimes you speak even odder than other times, Doc. Point is to go and take a look-see, see?"

"I suppose so."

"We can loop around the arroyo to the north. Bring us close to where they are without them spotting us."

"Unless the flagellants have taken the elementary precautions of placing sentries."

"Yeah. I mean, no. Triple crazies like that need both hands to find their assholes, Doc."

"If you say so, my gilded bird of youth." Doc sighed. "If you say so."

THE WILDERNESS SEETHED with nocturnal life.

Dean led the way, moving at a fast crouch, followed by Doc, stumbling over the uneven terrain, knees creaking like muffled pistol shots.

An unidentifiable mutie snake, twenty feet long, its skin black as jet with streaks of silver, slithered away from them, looping up and over the brim of the narrow draw, hissing in anger.

A pair of coyotes suddenly appeared ahead of them, eyes glinting in the moonlight like burned rubies. Dean halted, waving his Browning Hi-Power at the scavengers. For several long beats of the heart the animals didn't move, crouching, bellies down, tails stiff. Their slightly open jaws dripped threads of pearly saliva into the dry sand.

"Move," the boy whispered, and the coyotes spun and loped off toward the north.

Doc ducked as a hunting owl swooped low over his head, its great skull face as white as parchment, claws raking at the air just above him.

"By the Three Kennedys!" He wiped perspiration from his temples with the swallow's-eye kerchief. Dean had persuaded him to leave the silver-headed cane behind at the house, but the commemoration Le Mat was snugly holstered at his waist, the hammer set over the single shotgun round.

"Keep it down," the eleven-year-old ordered. "Can't be more than three hundred yards from their camp." He sniffed at the night air. "Taste their fires."

Doc tasted the air, nodding as he identified the familiar scent of burning wood.

In the early days of his marriage, he and his young wife, Emily, had taken pleasure in going camping, an activity that most of their friends in 1890s Omaha regarded as being suspiciously bohemian.

The smell of the fires brought back those happy times: the small two-person tent, its ridge throwing sharp shadows across the box canyon where they'd pitched it; a pot of fresh coffee brewed over the flames; their empty plates waiting to be washed in the nearby stream; the curved meerschaum pipe that Doc had favored in those far-off days, sending out plumes of smoke, keeping the invasive midges at bay.

And he remembered Emily, her formal hiking clothes disarrayed, the collar of the silk blouse open, revealing the beginnings of the soft swell of her breasts, the roll of hair, unpinned, tumbling about her shoulders, the ankle boots unlaced, her skirt pulled up to her knees as she relaxed.

"Doc?"

He saw the tenderness in her eyes and the pouting smile, half teasing him, both of them knowing that the evening was nearly done, soon they'd be snug in their tent, bundled together, gently exploring each other's bodies.

"Doc? Come on."

"What is that?"

"Quiet." Dean grabbed him by the arm, his fingers digging in hard. "You dropped off into a dream, Doc."

"My sincere apologies, Dean. I shall do better and concentrate more. I promise you that."

THE OLD MAN FOLLOWED the boy as he crawled the last few yards, cautiously sticking his head above the top of the arroyo.

"Shit!"

Doc joined him, moving more slowly, looking out the camp of the group of religious crazies, now less than fifty yards away from them.

"My sweet Lord," he breathed. "It's like something from the fevered imagination of Bosch, the inner circles of hell! How can they..."

There had been fourteen of the Slaves of Sin, including their leader, the Apostle Simon. Thirteen of them paced slowly around the large cross that had been dragged up to the house. Now it was set upright in the sand, in front of the largest fire.

And it had a tenant.

The fourteenth member of the group was crucified upon it, dark blood showing black in the moonlight at the center of both palms and through the center of the crossed ankles.

A crown of rusty barbed wire had been jammed over the man's head, leaving worms of blood to inch down over the agonized face. And someone had stabbed him in the side, under the ribs. Not hard enough to kill him, but enough to leave a gaping wound with glistening lips.

The wretched man's mouth sagged open, but if he was making any sound, it was drowned out by the slow, rhythmic chanting of the rest of the sect.

Led by Simon, banging his staff into the dirt, each scourged the back of the man in front, in a circle, so that every man received an equal whipping.

After the initial shock and revulsion had worn off a little, Doc found that he could actually make out the words of their obscene hymn.

"Dear Lord of Pain aid us. Blessed Virgin of Suffering, weep tears of blood that will blind our enemies. Dolores, our lady of agony, tear at our worthless flesh with your many-thonged lash of silver nails. Accept the sacrifice of our own humble spots of fallen crimson and give us help."

"These people are in serious need of advanced and prolonged psychiatric counseling," Doc whispered.

"They're just sick stupes," Dean replied.

"Perhaps we should return to the ranch now. I hardly think that they would welcome the knowledge that they were being watched in their disgusting practices."

Dean was lost, staring at the tableau of horror so close to them. The man on the cross writhed in agony, head moving from side to side, more blood flowing over his eyes and face. The nails hammered through both his palms held the arms rigid, and his whole body strained forward at an unnatural angle that put an immense strain on his lungs.

Doc closed his eyes, sickened at the sight. He had read of crucifixions in learned textbooks, tomes that spoke of the bodies of the thousands of losers in the revolt of Spartacus, exhibited all along the endless miles of the Appian Way. Most had eventually died of suffocation, their chests constricted, each breath that little bit smaller and more painful than the one before. The executioners, bribed by despairing relatives, would remove support from the feet, making the final passing of the anguished victims that much swifter.

He had never, in his worst laudanum-tainted nightmares, imagined that he would one day be a witness to this barbaric method of execution.

"Butchery," he whispered.

The steady pacing in the circle had ceased, and the twelve acolytes of the brotherhood were standing looking toward their skinny leader.

He had lifted the staff with the tortured Christ on its head, pointing with it away to the south, toward Jak's homestead.

"Those who are not for the Slaves of Sin are against them. Those who are not believers are blasphemers. Those who will not help us on our chosen journey to the Indies shall die. Yea, verily, they shall die. Die one and die all!"

"Should warn Jak," Dean breathed.

Doc shook his silver mane of hair. "He heard Simon say this kind of arrant nonsense-babble earlier, did he not? Empty words. For all her manifold faults, Dr. Wyeth is a good hand with a pistol. She would be able to cleanse the planet of all of them before they closed to within fifty yards of her."

"Yeah . . ." The boy sounded doubtful.

Doc patted Dean on the shoulder. "They seem to have no weapons, except for an occasional knife. I believe they could do precious little harm to us or our friends."

"I guess not."

The Apostle Simon had turned toward the man on the cross, the rest of the followers silent. The tortured victim moaned softly. His head had fallen forward on his breast, and it seemed as though he'd already slipped into semiconsciousness.

"The sacrifice is seemly." Simon fumbled with the head of his staff, and Doc and Dean heard a metallic click. A long slender blade of steel had shot out of the head of the Christ figure, glinting brightly in the moonlight.

"I suggest you look away, dear boy," Doc said, his mouth close to Dean's ear.

"Seen plenty of chilling, thanks."

"Very well."

The Apostle Simon stood below the crucified man, stared at him, then reached slowly up toward the exposed throat with the concealed dagger.

"Take this life for all our lives. Take our blood for their blood. In return, for our humble self-abasement, give us divine vengeance. Give us that, dear Lord. Let us crush all those who mocked and derided us. We have truly scourged ourselves clean of pride, Lord."

Doc was beginning to feel physically sick from the acrid stench of their unwashed, tortured bodies and the bitterness of fresh blood.

"We have made of ourselves a seemly sacrifice. The sands of the desert are red with blood."

The movement was quicker than a striking rattler, the pilgrim's staff that had become a spear darting at the neck of the helpless victim.

Blood jetted from the severed artery, the pattering sound as it fell into the thirsty earth clearly audible to the pair of hidden spectators. Simon moved swiftly to one side, retracting the blade from the head of his staff, showing all the skill and balance of an expert knife fighter, avoiding both the blood and the urine that fountained from the dying man.

"Take our blood and give us vengeance!" chorused the thirteen members of the cult.

"Let's go," Doc said, pulling insistently at Dean's jacket. "Now."

"Wait."

"I see no... Ah, should we not warn them of the danger ahead?"

"Too late. Don't worry, Doc. They won't let this mess of triple-stupe crazies catch them."

One of the most ill-matched couples in all Deathlands, Jak Lauren and Mildred Wyeth, were walking casually across the desert toward the camp and its bright fires, following the dusty track, making no attempt to conceal themselves from the Slaves of Sin.

The albino teenager, his white hair blazing like a brilliant torch, carried a hunting rifle, with his big .357

blaster at his hip. Mildred had her .38-caliber Czech target revolver holstered at her belt. Neither of them looked at all apprehensive.

Simon saw the two strangers coming and gave swift orders, snapping them out in an undertone. In less then a dozen seconds the cross and its dead victim had been struck to the ground and laid flat. A few ragged blankets were heaped over it.

Dean knew that seeing at night was often difficult and misleading, guessing that the combination of bright moonlight and the flames of the fires would have made it hard for their two friends to make out much inside the camp.

"No," Dean said, sensing that the man at his side was about to shout some sort of warning. "Make things worse, Doc."

"But—"

"You and me got short-range weapons. Wouldn't do much chilling. Chances are the crazies don't mean any real harm to Jak and Mildred. Be too scared of us."

"Hope you're right, son."

Dean was wrong.

JAK AND MILDRED WALKED unsuspectingly in among the fladgies.

"See kid and old man?" Jak asked.

"No," Apostle Simon replied, not bothering to conceal the sneer in his voice. "You mean your precious party? Haven't seen anyone since you refused us water and food. Not a living soul. Gone missing, have they?''

Mildred, sensing that something was off-kilter, dropped her right hand to the butt of the blaster and stared at the raggedy man with a growing anger.

''You seen them or not?''

''Not.''

Jak looked around, seeing that something was hidden under the pile of rags. ''What's that?'' He started to draw his Colt Python.

Simon swung the staff, with its lead-loaded butt, in a vicious circle, striking the teenager across the side of the head, just behind the left ear, felling him like a poleaxed steer.

Mildred started to turn, the pistol in her hand. ''What the fuck are . . .''

She was too slow. Three of the brotherhood of pain flung themselves at her, wrestling away the blaster, punching Mildred quickly into unconsciousness.

It was all over and done with in less than five seconds. The Slaves of Sin had a rifle and two handblasters, as well as two prisoners, both out cold.

Dean and Doc watched in helpless silence. The boy looked at the old man, eyes wide in the moonlight. Suddenly Dean seemed no more than a frightened child.

''If Dad was . . .'' he began uncertainly.

''He's not,'' Doc whispered. ''Best we can do is get back along the draw to the house and warn Krysty.''

''Then?''

''I don't know, Dean. I just don't know!''

Chapter Twenty-Five

Most men would have tried to keep still and very silent, and hope for one lucky chance to surprise and attack the murderous little man with the bottle-glass lenses and the 9 mm Luger pistol.

And most men would have died.

Seeing the hidden door opening soundlessly, and Malachi Gribble poised to open fire at J.B.'s sleeping figure, Ryan didn't hesitate. He sucked in a quick breath, then shouted at the top of his voice, simultaneously powering himself upward and sideways, directly at the killer.

There wasn't a moment to think about going for his own blaster, or trying to reach the panga with its honed eighteen inches of steel, only the single moment for his combat reflexes to take over and act for him.

The deafening bellow of anger, followed by the powerful shadow looming up at him from the corner of the room, nearly paralyzed Gribble. His finger tightened on the broad trigger of the old German blaster, totally beyond his control. The gun fired, the bullet burying itself in the wall, three feet above J.B.'s pillow.

Gribble tried to scream, but his fleshy throat was being squeezed shut between the iron fingers of Ryan's right hand. The left hand gripped the thin wrist of the little man, steering the Luger away.

It was no contest between Ryan's six feet two and two hundred pounds of bone and muscle against the small, near-blind Malachi. To stop the frantic struggling, the one-eyed man brought his right knee up hard into Gribble's groin, crushing his balls against the unforgiving ridge of pubic bone at the front of his pelvis. There was a squeak of pain, and the blaster clattered to the floorboards. The body went instantly limp.

"Got him covered, if you need it," J.B. said, standing by the side of his bed, the Uzi cocked at his hip. "But I see that you don't."

"Reckon not."

"How did he get through the bolted door without... Oh, I get it. Second door. Should've looked for that, brother. Nice trick to play."

"Yeah." Ryan hardly breathed any faster than usual, moving to the bed to connect with his weapons, glancing once at the whey-faced, unconscious figure on the floor by the cupboard. "Live and learn, like Trader says."

Ryan took Gribble outside and tied him to a fence, a thin cord around his thumbs and another around his neck, holding him upright, leaving a finite decision on him until the dawning.

Then he and the Armorer went back to sleep.

"I WAS GOING TO HAVE a special tableau," Gribble stammered. "Bring folks from miles. Gunfighters. Like in old westy vids and stuff. And you two would be wonderful." He paused ruefully. "Would've been wonderful, I guess I mean."

Ryan was munching a hunk of the ill-cooked bread, J.B. at his side. It was a beautiful morning, with the bright sun hovering over the eastern range. The paint on Gribble's hobby town glinted, and the windows shone.

"You both got real mean and ornery killers' eyes. Cold as cold can be. Dress you in black, Ryan, and you in white, Mr. Dix. I got a pair of Peacemakers."

The gas generator out back was silent. The Armorer had spent an hour, just after dawn, helped by Ryan, draining off fuel and transferring it to the LAV-25, which he'd driven up the narrow street and parked outside the schoolhouse. Now they were gassed up and ready to go another thousand miles or so.

"Didn't mean any harm."

"How many you chilled altogether?"

Gribble blinked nervously at Ryan. His thick-lensed spectacles had been broken during the attack of the previous night and he seemed almost blind, his eyes wide and vulnerable.

"Don't recall."

"Try."

"Not everyone you see in my portraits of old-time life. Most, I guess. But there was a couple died natural."

"Twenty? Thirty? Come on," J.B. prompted. "Must be that many in the town here."

Gribble licked his lips, his tongue like a feeble slug crawling over his mouth. "Well... You have to understand that they didn't all work out properly. Made some mistakes. Specially early. Had to reject some specimens."

Ryan glanced over at his friend. Time was passing, and they had a pressing appointment up in the Northwest with Abe and the Trader.

"One last time, Malachi," he said. "How many folk have you chilled?"

"I could tell you if I referred to my books. I kept an accounting, you see. How old and dates and clothes and weapons, and with the woman, whether I had—" He stopped abruptly as he realized he'd gone a step further than he'd intended.

"You fucked the corpses?" J.B. asked, incredulous.

The little man trembled, tied upright to the fence, his head turning from side to side as if he were seeking a light. "Not kind of... Not with... Altogether there was around seventy or eighty. But I could never get enough children. What I wanted most was to have children... really loved children and—"

Ryan shot him once, between the eyes, with the SIG-Sauer, holstering the blaster as the corpse slumped down, blood and brains gushing from the shattered rear of the skull, dripping off the posts of the fence.

"Waste of a bullet. We should have left the sick little fuck for the rats."

THE VIOLENT CHEM STORM of the previous day had done a lot of harm to the highways and trails of the region, slowing their progress, some of the time to a crawl, sometimes slower.

Streams had become rivers, and many of those rivers had burst banks, leading to detours of several miles to find a safe fording place.

It took them three days to get clear of Colorado and across the old state line and up into the San Rafael Valley of Utah. The wag was running much better than it had before their run-in with Malachi Gribble, and the damaged wheel from the buffalo stampede didn't seem to give them any trouble, as long as they kept the speed down below forty.

"Into the second week," Ryan said as they lay on warm grass and chewed the roasted flesh off a wild turkey that J.B. had shot with the Steyr the previous evening.

"Yeah. Making good time, though."

"Been this way before?"

The Armorer thought about it. He'd taken off his glasses, leaving them on the sun-dried turf at his side, his fedora next to them.

"Not for a while."

"I remember a ville, west of here. Could be a ways north as well."

J.B. threw the gnawed bone against the slender willow tree that stood near a narrow stream, hitting it smack in the middle of the delicate trunk.

"I think I was off with War Wag Two at the time. Was it a baron who collected firearms?"

"Yeah, but not in a big way. Not modern stuff. His interest was flintlocks, wheel locks, percussion caps, muskets, dueling pistols. Old blasters. Can't remember his name. Baron... Something to do with numbers. Tenbos? Yeah, that was it. Baron Tenbos."

"Don't remember," J.B. said. "Like I said, I don't think I ever been here. Trader sent me off on some fly-swatting trip. Little place near the Grandee. I'm nearly sure that's what happened. It was a long time ago."

"I'm sure that was the name. Baron Tenbos."

"BARON TENBOS," the sec man said.

Ryan was in the driver's seat of the LAV-25, with J.B. poised in the turret, ready to slam down the top at the least sign of any threat.

"All right if we pass through?"

The man wore a dusty uniform of maroon and black, with a nondescript postdark rifle remake slung over his shoulders. He stood by a long striped pole that rested across the highway. Ryan thought that he had to be one of the least threatening sec men that he'd ever seen.

"Baron'll like to meet you. All outlanders interest him. Specially when they come driving along the blacktop in an armawag like that."

Ryan had the ob slit a little way open and he nodded, then realized that the man couldn't see the gesture. "Sure. Any chance of food and a bed for the night?"

It was a little after five in the late afternoon, with a cold wind springing up from the east.

"Yep."

"What do we do?"

"Keep right along until the fork by the lake with a boulder sticking up out of the middle. Hang a left there. Up a hill, and you'll see another sec post. Stop there and let 'em clear you on through. Straight ahead and over the bridge, and you're in the ville. Just like that. Can't miss Baron Tenbos's place."

"Thanks."

"Welcome. That sure is a pretty wag. Cannon work, do it? Blow the shit out of a mutie army, that would."

"Sure would," Ryan agreed, careful not to answer the question about the 25 mm Bushmaster for which they had no ammo.

Trader used to say that a man who told his enemy his weaknesses deserved to buy the farm.

"Just two of you's in there?"

"Right."

"Go ahead." He lifted the counterbalanced pole and waved them through.

"WASN'T TROUBLE in this ville, was there, Ryan?" J.B. asked his friend. "Not riding into a blood feud, are we?"

"No," the one-eyed man replied confidently.

"Sure?"

"Course." He sounded just a little less confident.

Ryan had a vague memory of Tenbos as a chunky man, broad-shouldered, with the tanned face of an outdoor person, with a free and easy smile. He was in his late thirties, or early forties.

Married? Ryan thought for a while as he steered the wag past the lake and up to the next sec barrier. No, he decided, he wasn't.

THE VILLE WAS a collection of scattered buildings of the type that had once been called condominiums. There had been a lot of climbing and snow sport in the area before the nuke holocaust, and small settlements had sprung up all across Colorado and the adjoining states, catering to the influx of tourists.

Now the area around Tenbos's demesne was mainly farming land. Raising horses was a staple, along with hog ranches and some cattle on the open range to the north.

Most of the expensive apartment buildings were built from local wood, dark-stained, but the years had taken their toll. Nearly a hundred years of wind, rain, bitter frosts and scorching summers had rotted many of the buildings, levering out windows and splitting doors, stripping fragile shingles off roofs and flooding basements.

But there were still enough habitable for the occupants of the ville, which one of the sec men estimated at around two hundred and fifty souls.

Baron Hamish Tenbos lived in a strange circular tower that had probably been used as an observation deck and revolving restaurant in the predark days. Now there was a drinker at the bottom of the building, where Ryan and J.B. sat and waited to meet the ruler of the ville.

Half a dozen other men lounged around in the gloom, all of them members of the sec force. Despite their casual approach, the two outlanders had been impressed with their laid-back professionalism.

"Don't need flash uniforms and pretty blasters and marching around like a gaudy slut in a tantrum to run a tight ville," J.B. commented.

The wag had been locked and secured in a vehicle park to the flank of the hundred-foot tower. Ryan had made sure all the ob slits were safely sealed.

Just in case.

"Why do so many barons like big, tall towers for their own headquarters?" Ryan said musingly. "Some sort of delusions of power?"

"Could be."

The man behind the bar was around five feet tall, with a pencil-thin mustache and a pallor that made it look like he didn't get to meet much sunlight. A tattoo of a butterfly was just visible inside the collar of his pale yellow denim shirt.

"How about another sipper?" he called across to Ryan and the Armorer.

"On the baron," one of the sec men said. "Tenbos looks after guests. Not like the cock-cutting sons of bitches you get in some of the villes."

"Have a beer." Ryan glanced across at J.B. and got the nod. "Make that two beers."

"Coming right up, Captain." The foxy eyes watched them closely in the mirror at the rear of the bar. "Sure you wouldn't both like a spotioti?"

"Dark night!" J.B. pulled a face of revulsion. "Run a hundred miles in the opposite direction rather than drink that vile stuff."

Ryan looked puzzled. "Spotioti? Name rings a bell, but... What is it?"

The barkeep smiled, showing that he'd had his front teeth filed to points. "It's the nectar of the gods, Colonel. Brings a glimpse of paradise."

"Glimpse of the bottom of a bucket of cold puke," J.B. said with a sneer.

"Fine muscat wine, mixed with some good home-brewed whiskey. That's spotioti. Sure I can't tempt either of you with a glass? On the house?"

"No." The Armorer pulled a face. "I had some once. Kansas. My twenty-fifth birthday. Crew bought me a quart, ready-mixed. I tell you, Ryan, I don't think I've ever, *ever* felt so sick in my life when I woke up next morning. Headache, right across my forehead so that even opening my eyes was like razor-wire, heated white. I started to throw up in just fifteen seconds, and I was still doing it eight hours later."

The barkeep brought over their beers, smiling as he listened to J.B.'s recollection of spotioti. "Can lie a little sickly on the stomach if you aren't used to it."

Ryan nodded. "I remember some mix of fruit juice and honey and brandy and beef-fat with crushed bananas that brought on the dreaded rainbow yawns."

"Nothing as bad as spotioti," J.B. said, taking off his glasses to polish them. "I got to know the inside of that bucket better than the inside of my own blaster.

Twisted my guts so bad I kept expecting to see my ass drop out of my mouth!''

"J.B.! That's disgusting."

"Yeah, Ryan, I know."

The Armorer turned to one of the laughing sec men. "Baron Tenbos still collect blasters?"

"Only old stuff."

"Not ready for a rebellion, then?" Ryan rarely encountered a baron who didn't have contingency plans for a revolt against his or her authority. Not all that many barons eventually died in their beds.

"No. Doesn't even have much ammo for them. Too much trouble to cast. Most things are—" He stopped suddenly.

The barkeep straightened, picking up a cloth and starting to polish one of the row of goblets in front of him. Ryan caught the hasty gesture and guessed that they were about to meet Baron Hamish Tenbos.

Chapter Twenty-Six

As they sat and drank with Baron Tenbos, Ryan thought a lot about age and the passing of time. It was partly the excellent home-brewed beer that brought on the process of ruminative melancholy, and partly the shock of seeing what the passage of the years had done to the baron.

The memory of the ruddy, tanned figure with broad shoulders and deep chest, rushing about his ville, hearty and perpetually busy, was rudely dispelled by the man who walked slowly into the bar, leaning heavily on an ivory-handled cane.

Hamish Tenbos was probably still in his fifties, but he had the appearance of someone twenty years older. His back was stooped and he dragged one leg behind him, the worn boot scuffing on the flagstones. A few fronds of lank white hair straggled down both sides of his lined face, held in place with a neatly knotted ribbon of black velvet. One eye drooped, and a corner of the mouth was pulled down, giving Tenbos a look of permanent dissatisfaction.

"Stroke" was Ryan's immediate reaction to the radical changes he saw in the baron, a reaction that was quickly proved to be correct.

"Mr. Ryan Cawdor, the number-one lieutenant of the hardest of the hard. How is Trader now? I heard he had been chilled in a skirmish with some renegade Cheyenne or some *comancheros,* down near Mazatlán. True?" He waved a clawed hand. "Doesn't matter. Nothing much matters. You look well, Cawdor."

Ryan had introduced J.B., explaining briefly the purpose of their quest to the Northwest. Tenbos listened quietly, once clicking the fingers of his good hand to attract the attention of the barkeep, who immediately brought a tray with three foaming glasses of beer.

"Pleasure to meet you, Mr. Dix. Heard of you. Best man on blasters in all of Deathlands. I must show you my own collection." The ravaged face clouded suddenly. "What remains of it. Like their owner, my guns have suffered much over the past few years."

"Mainly flintlocks and muzzle-loaders, I hear, Baron," the Armorer said. "Nothing much after the middle part of the nineteenth century."

"Correct. I used to strip and clean every gun at least once a month. But since my...my 'accident'..." He touched his drooped eye with the withered hand. "Since this, I have rather lost my interest." He paused, smiling wryly. "I figure that I've lost most of my interests."

"Still be pleased to look at them."

"Good." The baron drained the glass, spilling a fair part of it over his black jerkin.

"All right with you, Baron, if we stay the night here?" Ryan asked.

Tenbos tilted his head a little to one side, as though his hearing were poor. "Stay the night? Of course. I have a fond memory of the Trader. I had heard that he had been chilled down..." He tutted to himself. "Stupe! You told me that you and Dix here were planning to resume contact with him. Near Seattle, wasn't it? My memory is failing me now, the last part of my wretched body that survived unscarred from my stroke."

"When?"

"Two years back, come Thanksgiving. Found my wife in bed with one of her sons. Chilled them both. Fell down. Woke up fucked like this."

That short piece of quietly spoken dialogue contained such a surfeit of dreadful information that Ryan and J.B. sat silent, looking at each other, both hugging their half-empty schooners of beer.

Tenbos laughed, a short, bitter, barking sound. "Generally takes strangers that way."

"Don't remember you as a married man." Ryan wiped a streak of white froth from his upper lip. "Not when I rode through your ville with Trader."

"Wasn't."

J.B. had steepled his fingers together, a sure sign he was doing some kind of mental calculation. "Reckon it wasn't *that* many years ago Trader was here. You weren't married then. Had your attack around two years ago. Your wife was screwing with your son. How old was he?"

Tenbos beckoned to the barkeep for another round. "No, you got the mule by the tail, Mr. Dix. Her son. Not my son. Her son. He was twenty-four. She had three boys. Other two live here now, both waiting for me to die. Getting less patient every day."

The baron turned to the sec men, all of whom had sat like embalmed statues since his arrival. "Right, isn't it, lads?" He put on a thin, whining voice. "I never believed that the old man would have stayed alive for so long." Then he reverted to his own tones. "Miserable little sons of bitches! Time was I could've taken all..."

The barkeep arrived. Tenbos was sitting with both eyes shut tight, head dropping forward, his breathing heavy and regular. "Baron has these turns," he said. "Gets himself angered up about Robby and Teddy. Twenty-six and twenty-three now. Mother was Janine Emms. Dead boy was Damian." He wiped the table with his apron's hem. "You'll see them both if you stay the night here in the ville. They'll be at dinner."

THEY HAD BEEN GIVEN a room on the third floor of the tower. Unusually Baron Tenbos lived on the bottom story, in a small suite of rooms. There were sec men on the second level, and the two stepsons on the fourth. Then nothing up to the very top, where, so Ryan and J.B. were told, the baron kept his diminished firearms collection.

Ryan stood by the window, gazing out over the pastures and orchards while J.B. sat on one of the pair of single beds, cleaning the Uzi. A small can of oil was balanced against a length of white rag.

"Lovely place," Ryan commented.

"Yeah. Change to find a ville where the folks seem happy. The sec men are doing a fair job in a fair way, and the baron doesn't want to chill every outlander that steps across the borders of his domain."

Ryan stretched. "Promised us a bath. Beds seem comfortable. Good food. Tenbos said we could take some dried meat and fruit with us when we go tomorrow. Eggs and cheese and stuff. Mebbe make a leisurely start, for once. I reckon this is going to be the best part of this rad-blasted journey. Just for once, we can relax. Just a little."

A SEC MAN KNOCKED on the door at seven-thirty, telling them to go down to the ground floor and follow the old, faded signs to the Portofino Diner.

The corridors were dark, and the carpet on the stairs was worn and threadbare. A pair of doors stood open and Ryan walked in, J.B. at his heels. The Uzi was across the Armorer's shoulders and Ryan's SIG-Sauer was safely holstered.

There was nobody in the room.

Nor were there any windows. Oil lamps stood on broad ledges, casting a warm glow over the room. The dining table was twenty feet in length, set with a good linen cloth and a mixed and mismatched assortment of china, glass and cutlery. Five dining chairs were ranged around it—one at the head, a pair on each side, quite close, and then another pair, farther down, close to the bottom of the table.

"We the first?" Ryan said.

"Looks like it. Hey, take in those swords up there, over the fireplace."

It was a fine array, the points all driving toward the center, the hilts equidistant from one another, golden tassels dangling beneath.

"Two different kinds," Ryan observed. "Why's that, J.B.? Whole shape... and the hilts aren't the same."

J.B. stared up at them. "Kind of dusty and dirty, aren't they? Could do with a polish. Different, Ryan? Not sure. Edged weapons aren't my specialty. I think those that are slightly less curved with the bigger guard are for cavalry officers from the Civil War. So, the other kind is probably infantry."

"Nice try, Mr. Dix, and half-right." The baron reached up with the tip of his stick. "That is indeed a Model 35, the cavalry saber. Regulation weapon. This other one, this is a Number 24 light artillery saber."

Neither of them had heard Baron Tenbos enter the room.

J.B. nodded, not even turning around. "Yeah. Course. I should've been able to work that out for myself. Like I said, blasters are my love."

"Then we'll have a look at them before you leave. If you want to stay a few days, rest up, you'd be welcome. Don't often get outlanders passing through who rode with Trader. Toughest man I ever met. Not many pleasures left to a man in my sorry condition, and talking over old times, not worth the forgetting, would be good for me."

Ryan answered for both of them. "Thanks, but no thanks, Baron. Things we have to do."

Tenbos sat down at the head of the table, wincing with pain, trying to disguise it. "Things that a man can't ride around, Cawdor? I understand that." He gestured to the pair of seats nearest to him. "Please..."

"Your sons?"

"They prefer not to be too close to a man with the taint of death about him. All they wish is that I take the ride with the dark ferryman as speedily as possible. None of us have any doubt that they would help me across the river if they could find some scheme that would enable them to get away with it. Ah, speaking of the devils, here they come."

J.B. and Ryan had only just sat down, and they both looked curiously at the pair of young men who walked in through the double doors.

At a first glance, it was quite difficult to tell the brothers apart. Both were stocky, powerfully built, with the tanned faces of young farmers, both with black curly hair that hung low across their napes and both had a single gold stud glittering in their right ears.

"Robby and Teddy," Tenbos said in the sort of voice that might describe something stuck to the bottom of your boots. "Robby is the one slouching on the left, the one who is wearing my wife's wedding ring."

"My mother's wedding ring, Baron," the young man replied, his voice quiet and unemotional.

"As you like, as you like. Sit down. These guests are Ryan Cawdor and—"

"J. B. Dix," Teddy finished. "We know, Father." He managed to make "father" sound like something very disagreeable. "Two old killers from Trader's gang."

Ryan smiled at them, concealing the sudden red mist of anger that flooded over his mind at the studied rudeness. "There are those who have said that over the years. But Trader had no enemies, young man."

"No enemies?" Robby mocked.

"None alive," J.B. said.

THE FOOD WAS PLAIN and adequate, without any fancy sauces or herbs and spices.

The sons and Ryan and J.B. had a soup of vegetables, followed by a plain trout with a green salad and then slices of rare roast beef with whipped potatoes and thin-sliced carrots. The dessert was a sponge pudding with honey and thick cream. Beer accompanied the meal.

Baron Tenbos sipped at his soup, picked at some of the tender flesh of the fish and barely touched the main course. Twice he had a coughing fit, dabbing hurriedly at his mouth with a white napkin. Ryan noticed that it came away from the pale lips flecked with spots of scarlet.

"My apologies to all."

"Should you go and lie down and rest, Father?" his oldest stepson asked.

Teddy whispered something in his brother's ear at that, making him grin.

Tenbos sipped at a mug of water. "I shall be lying down soon enough."

"Sooner the better, Father, dear," Robby said in an extremely audible undertone.

THE MEAL ENDED early.

The brothers stood with an uncanny synchronicity and bowed stiffly to the baron, turned on their heels, one to the right and one to the left, and marched to the doors and out of the room, the sound of their boot heels ringing in unison along the corridor.

Tenbos threw his napkin to the floor and reached for his stick. "There are many days that I think deeply about following my slut wife into the long blackness."

"Life's better than no life," Ryan said, finishing his last glass of beer.

"Shit it is!" Tenbos was on his feet, moving clumsily and slowly. "Don't peddle your homespun bullshit at me, Cawdor. It insults me and demeans yourself. Life has become a grinding journey that I wish to leave. My doctor says that the road is measured in weeks now. And I'm glad of that."

"Your collection of blasters?" J.B. said, seeking to change the subject. "Can we see them now, Baron?"

"No." The baron closed his good eye wearily. "No, Dix, not tonight. First thing in the morning, if you are early risers. And I figure you are."

The two friends watched him limp out, his one leg dragging behind him.

"Shame," J. B. commented. "Think we should do something about those sullen, silent little bastards?"

Ryan pursed his lips. "Can't say it didn't cross my mind. What do you reckon?"

"Tenbos seems a nice guy. For a baron."

"Sec men like him. Can't say I got the vibes they like the boys."

The Armorer nodded. "Agreed. So?"

"No." Ryan stretched his shoulders, easing the blaster in its holster. "Tempting, but I think not."

"Trader would've cleansed them, Ryan."

"Sure. He's not me and I'm not him. Can't wipe up everyone's spilled blood."

THE HEAVY MEAL and the beer combined to make them ready for their beds at an unusually early hour.

Ryan slipped easily into sleep.

He woke just before dawn, watching the first light edging over the hills, seeping into their room, unaware that the next three hours would bring violent deaths.

Chapter Twenty-Seven

Abe came around from the beating, unable at first to decide whether the vigilantes had blinded him.

He was in so much pain that he couldn't even begin to decide what hurt most. Every inch of his body was throbbing and bruised, and his head felt like someone had levered open the skull and poured in boiling battery acid.

His tongue was swollen, his lips cracked and dry. Abe tried to lift a hand to touch what he guessed were some broken and missing teeth, but nothing happened. He got the same result when he tried to bend his legs to a less uncomfortable position.

Slowly his brain began to function again, remembering.

The rain was still pouring, but it had become full dark. Squinting through his puffy eyelids, Abe was just able to make out the sheen of the water on bare rock, feel it on his upturned face.

He remembered the chillings that had taken place, the man in the store and the posse pursuing him and Trader over the hills and down dark valleys. Then they had met by the cabin near the flooded river.

"Bullets had burst the fucking raft," Abe muttered, hardly hearing himself. He swallowed hard and tasted the bitter iron of his own blood.

He felt cold, though it was impossible to try to work out which bits were numb with cold and which were numb from the savage beating.

The Trader had gone on ahead, clutching the battered Armalite, his long legs eating up the steep trail, vanishing while Abe was still laboring, chest bursting, two or three hundred yards behind him.

They'd been waiting by the ruins of some predark building.

Abe struggled for the memory, a sign that he'd spotted. "Hotel," he mumbled.

They'd greeted the hapless, soaked, breathless figure of the gunner. "Blood for blood, you bastard," one of them said. "You're a fucking dead man."

Abe hadn't bothered to try to draw his Colt Python. There were eight blasters cocked and aimed at him, from less than twenty feet.

It seemed like they'd tied him up and then started the brutal battering. But there might have been some punches and kicks even before the rawhide cord was knotted viciously tight around wrists and ankles, then looped around the rusting iron bars that protruded from a massive block of fallen concrete. A fourth piece of cord ran from his neck to a tumbled fence behind him, holding him stretched out and helpless.

Abe sniffed, spitting out a lump of congealed blood, feeling that there was more trickling down his throat from his gums and torn lips. It made him feel sick, adding to the nausea from the boots to his groin.

Now he remembered a little more.

The beating had definitely commenced as soon as they had him in their power, once they'd taken away the blaster, before and during the tying up.

It had still been light then, because Abe could recall the milling figures, jostling around him. He'd gone down quickly, and the silhouettes had loomed over him, pushing and screaming at one another as they fought to get at him.

They'd cursed and threatened, reminding him of the deaths on his hands, asking what had happened to his companion, the old fucker. Where had he gone? Did they have a camp nearby?

Did they?

"No," Abe breathed.

No, they didn't.

IT WAS ALARMING the way that he kept drifting in and out of consciousness.

When you'd been tied by a vengeful enemy, unable to move more than an inch or so in any direction, without garroting yourself, then it was difficult to try to carry out a check on how badly you were injured.

But Abe did his best.

Trader used to give occasional talks to all of the crews of the two war wags, picking a wide variety of relevant topics, almost all of them based on his own experiences. Or sometimes asking J. B. Dix to lecture on certain types of weaponry, or Ryan Cawdor on back-country survival.

Abe remembered that one of them had been centered on the idea of self-diagnosis of injuries and wounds. Where precisely had you been shot? What blaster? Had the bullet penetrated clean through or lodged somewhere? Broken any bones? Sliced into lungs or any other vital organs?

Same with knife or spear injuries. Burns and scalds. Drowning and hanging.

And beating.

Trader had given some excellent advice on what to do if you were recovering from a good kicking. The only trouble was that the kicking he'd received had driven all of it clean out of Abe's befuddled skull.

But he did recall that it was important to try to deduce how badly you'd been hurt.

Just that would do for a starter.

"Head?"

Some teeth damaged and cuts inside his cheeks and lips. He very slowly moved his jaw, wincing at the stabbing pain beneath the right ear. Could be that the bone there was cracked. Abe couldn't feel his nose at all, but he had been in enough gaudy brawls to be fairly certain that it would definitely have been one of the first things to get pulped.

Still, it wasn't the first time.

And it probably wouldn't be the last.

He shrugged. Collarbones were also vulnerable. Abe had lost count of the times he'd had one or the other—or both—broken. His fingers were still and numb, but that could be the tightness of the cords that held him helpless.

As soon as the fists and boots began to thud in, Abe had gone down and curled himself up into the approved fetal position, knees up to save his genitals, elbows pressed in tight over his stomach and groin. Face buried in his hands.

He'd screamed a lot.

That had been one of the tips that Trader had passed along to them.

"Nothing to be shamed of," he'd said. "My experience is that a crowd attacking will be deterred if you scream and scream and keep on screaming. Top of your fucking voice. Shatter crystal at a hundred paces. Make them think they're doing a lot more damage than they are. Good chance it might make them stop just a little while sooner."

Abe hadn't the slightest idea whether screaming had helped or not. Unconsciousness had come slinking along and swallowed him into its velvet maw.

Then nothing.

His attempt to take stock of his injuries hadn't really been all that successful. There was only one thing that Abe was positively, definitely certain about.

He was soon going to die.

They'd made that clear to him.

He remembered that he'd recovered once, a little earlier. It hadn't been full dark, and the rain had eased.

Abe had opened his eyes, blinking and choking, liquid splashing in his upturned face, into his open mouth. It was bitter, salty and warm.

"What the fuck?"

"Just a start, you little bastard!" said a voice, anger overlaying the soft country drawl.

Three men stood around him, the last of them buttoning up his pants. Abe couldn't see their faces, but he didn't need to. He could still remember what they looked like from the tumbledown store in the backwood ville.

They took delight in telling him what was going to happen to him. The details didn't matter all that much. The end result was going to be death, and it was going to come as slowly and painfully as their ingenuity could manage.

"Knives..."

"Fire..."

"Needles..."

"Razors..."

"Gasoline..."

"Hammers..."

"Suffocating, hanging, drowning, burning, shooting, stabbing, castrating, slicing, crushing, breaking and gouging..."

It was a litany of hatred and pain that quickly lost all sense of meaning for the helpless little man.

One of them had squatted astride him, sitting on his chest, muddy boots holding Abe's head still, while he leaned forward and gripped him by the throat. Fingers and thumbs ground into the front of the neck, cartilage creaking at the pressure, shutting off Abe's breath, holding him as he wriggled and squirmed, choking him until blackness swam up and myriad tiny silver spots swirled inside Abe's skull.

The same man had laughed as he'd finally let him go, standing up, looming over Abe.

"Got you and we'll get your murderin' friend. Start after him after dawn. He won't get far. Others of us out and around the hills, on the watch. Lots of us was kin to Luke. Don't figure on just walkin' away and lettin' go. Blood for blood's what we say."

Abe hadn't even seen the work boot that struck him with savage accuracy, just behind the right ear, tossing him back into the darkness.

AROUND MIDNIGHT, Abe became aware that the wind had veered more southerly, taking the rain away with it on a bank of low cloud. The skies cleared and the stars broke through, pinpoints of diamond light staring down impassively at his suffering.

It became much colder and he found himself shivering. Once or twice it crossed his mind to call out and beg for mercy. Even if it were only the dubious mercy of a bullet through the back of the head.

But yet another of Trader's thoughts came to him. "If you think begging might save your life, then you should just get down on your knees and start licking the boots. But this isn't going to be true more than one time in mebbe a hundred thousand. So you might as well keep your mouth clamped shut and look to die with a shred or two of dignity."

Now that the wind had dropped, Abe could hear the gang of men who'd captured him with such ease, smell the smoke of their cooking fire and the flavor of some sort of meat being scorched over the flames.

His mouth began to water, and he realized that he was also extremely thirsty. But his previous experience with his captors made him realize that asking for something to drink wasn't likely to be a very good idea.

The men were singing a crude song about a gaudy slut and her experiences with a beaver trapper. Every now and then Abe heard bellows of raucous laughter.

The only thing that seemed likely was that they weren't going to chill him during the night.

This was the best hope he had to hang on to.

It gave Trader a little time.

Chapter Twenty-Eight

"One of the few times in my life that I've ever felt reasonably safe in the middle of a ville."

Ryan grinned at his companion's words. But there was some truth in what the Armorer had said. Tenbos, despite his obvious serious illness, seemed to be on top of things, including his two unpleasant and threatening stepsons. There was no evidence of evil or cruelty, and the sec men simply went about their work without bullying or sadism.

"Yeah," he said. "If we weren't in a hurry to meet up again with Trader, I wouldn't mind taking up the baron's offer and staying here awhile longer."

"Me too. Hope he's well enough to show us his weapon collection this morning."

"Main thing I want is to get some more decent food under my belt. See me through the next few hundred spine-rattling miles in the armawag."

There was a discreet knock on the door of their room. Both of them reached instinctively for their blasters, hesitating, both laughing.

"Death doesn't often let you know he's coming," J.B. said.

He raised his voice. "Yeah?"

"It's Edward Tenbos, gentlemen. The baron wonders if you would like to visit him on the top floor of the tower to view his firearms? And then to the first floor for breakfast?" The voice was calm and very deliberately neutral.

"Thanks a lot," Ryan replied. "Tell him that the answer to both of his invitations is 'Yes,' and we'll be with him in about five minutes."

They heard steps moving away. J.B. turned to face Ryan. "Only thing that worries me is those two boys. Something seriously creepy about them. Mebbe it's that everyone knows they're just waiting for dead man's boots."

"Mebbe. I know what you mean. Wish Krysty was here. Could do with her 'feeling' about them."

"Taking your blasters?"

Ryan looked at the Steyr rifle and the SIG-Sauer automatic. "I don't know. You?"

"Don't really want to hump the Uzi and the scattergun up and down stairs."

"Doesn't seem dangerous."

"True."

"Fireblast! Look, I'll just take along the SIG-Sauer. Should be more than enough for any piss-ant problem that might blow up in our faces."

THE STAIRS WERE DARK, curling around and around, with only an occasional slit casement to let some filtered light through. One of the great problems of windows in Deathlands was the amount of ordinary glass from predark days, a century back, that had become crazed and dulled by the harsh elements.

There was a pair of sec men on the landing below the arms collection. By the time that Ryan and J.B. had reached them, the two guards had tensed, recognized them, then relaxed, waving them through.

"Baron's been there for an hour or more. Got a half dozen of us to try to do some cleaning and dusting."

The other sec man nodded. "Even had his shitbag sons—pardon my speech—up here. Truth is, since his illness and the business with the slut-whore wife, well, the baron sort of lost interest in his blasters."

"You'll be the first ones—first outlanders—up these stairs for months and months. Still, best go on ahead. Don't keep him waiting."

J.B. ran his finger along the curving balustrade, brushing his hands together. "Filthy," he commented.

THE LIGHT WAS FAR BETTER at the top of the old tower, with windows on every side. There were a few padded seats remaining around the periphery of the large circular room, left over from its use as a revolving restaurant.

Baron Tenbos was sitting on one of them, his head leaning back, motionless.

Ryan stopped at the top of the stairs, holding up a warning hand to J.B.

"Chilled?" the Armorer whispered.

"Far from it, Mr. Dix." The voice was weak, but the piercing eyes under the hooded lids were still keen.

"Forgive my not rising, but I found the climb rather more steep than I remembered it. A real bastard becoming feeble when once you were so strong. Do come on in, gentlemen."

The air of neglect was palpable.

The room smelled of disinfectant and polish, and they could both see the evident signs of some hasty and halfhearted cleaning. But cobwebs still clung to the corners, by the old mock chandeliers. The carpet was dirty, with spots of oil and grease marking the delicate floral pattern.

Tenbos waved a hand. "A sorry thing these days, but mine own. Feel free to wander and look at anything."

"They been fired lately?" J.B. asked, picking up a poor German replica of a Genoan wheel-lock pistol.

"No. I haven't..." The words trickling away. "I did once but...there is no ammunition now kept up here."

"Why?" Ryan asked, squinting along the chased barrel of a superb saw-handled dueling pistol, still carrying the maker's gold cartouche on the breech plug. "Parker?" he said.

J.B. joined him, taking the blaster with an almost religious awe. "Beautiful," he breathed. "William Parker of 233 High Holborn, London, England. 'Massive magnificence,' someone called it. Walnut stock. Nine-inch smooth-bore octagonal barrel. There's the sighting groove out into the tang of the false breech." He pointed with his index finger. "There. Look at the lovely plates, silver, here, protecting the stock by the barrel cross bolt. Single set trigger."

Ryan watched and listened in silence. J.B. wasn't the most talkative of men, and to hear him whisper this eulogy of the gun maker's art was extraordinary. Baron Tenbos was also transfixed, standing and making his slow and painful way around the room to join them.

"Must date from around 1812. Possibly a year or so later." He tested the action. "See, there's no adjustment for 'let-off' on the trigger. Wonderful swan's-neck lock. Bit fragile if you're in a touch-and-go firefight. Safety catch here behind the cock. Bolts the tumbler. See. Ramrod beneath."

"I swear that you must know more about firearms than any man living, Mr. Dix," the baron said. "Would you not like to remain here for a month or so and put my guns back into shape? Categorize and label them all."

"No. I've made a promise to a friend, and that is worth more than all the blasters in all of Deathlands."

Ryan had known his companion for long enough to be fully aware what that cost J.B.

The Armorer laid the pistol down on its rack. "This is a wonderful weapon. But that cheapjack German copy of the wheel lock is total shit. Why?"

"Why both in the same room?"

"Yes."

Tenbos sighed. "Because I became lazy, Mr. Dix. A wretched reason, but the truth. Though my lack of health was something of a factor in this. Perhaps you might give me the incentive to begin again.''

''Worth it, for the good stuff.''

''Why no ammo?'' Ryan asked again.

''No ammo means no risk to me.''

''I would've said you had some good men in your sec force. Where's the threat?''

Tenbos took a long, slow breath. ''By now the poison will have begun to seep into the ears of my people. Two strangers in the ville. Perhaps their intention is to chill our beloved stepfather, the honored baron, and usurp his rightful successors. That has started already.''

Ryan didn't say anything for a moment. He looked at the Parker flintlock, its stained copper powder horn below it in the glass-topped display case. ''Why not simply remove the problem?'' he said finally.

''Not my way, Cawdor. I did what I did to their mother and brother in a bloody rage.''

''You had cause,'' J.B. protested.

''Perhaps. But that dodges the bullet, doesn't it? That night, when I visited the two cold corpses in our small chapel, I swore I would not take another human life. I have managed to cleave to that oath.''

J.B. had turned and picked up the pistol again. ''You said there was no ammo.''

''Ah.'' The baron's fragile smile was back in place. ''I couldn't fool a gunsman like yourself. Some of the weapons carry a single charge. Most do not. That Parker is one of the loaded guns. But let us make the most of our small time together, outlanders. Let me show you around.''

The whole collection was much as J.B. had spotted, a strange mixture of rubbish and wonders, an occasional gold nugget glittering among the coal.

Cheap cast replicas of Second World War Brownings and Mausers and Walthers lay alongside an immaculate, cased, five-chambered flintlock revolver, made by Collier over two hundred and fifty years earlier.

''The Civil War blasters are the nicest,'' the Armorer commented. ''Why not ditch the crap and keep those?''

The baron had been forced to sit down, fighting for breath. He looked up, nodding. ''Should. Mebbe I will. I started collecting that period.''

J.B. walked slowly past the rows of weapons, mainly handblasters. ''Eighteen forty Colt Army. Forty-four caliber. Colt Navy next to it. Eighteen sixty-one. Thirty-six. I reckon one of the finest, best-balanced blasters anybody ever made. Anyplace. Anytime. Lovely gun. Nice .44 Remington New Model Army. Thirty-six caliber Savage. Some English blasters. Beaumont-Adams.'' He showed it to Ryan. ''This was the first of the genuinely manufactured double-action revolvers. Double-trigger Tranter, eighty bore. Dark night, Baron! Man could lose himself up here.''

''Delighted you . . . you like them, Mr. Dix. If only you and Cawdor would . . .''

Ryan shook his head. ''What we said still holds. We have to be up north and time's passing.''

"I understand."

There was a circular display of muskets, similar to that of the swords, and Ryan stood and stared at it. The stocks were dusty and dull, and some of the metal parts showed rust and verdigris, signs of shameful neglect.

"I think I need to rest," Tenbos said, tearing them away from the display of firearms. "I slept badly and rose too early. I think some morphine might make me a more presentable human being. Why don't you two go down to the first floor and have some food. It'll be ready by now."

"We can help you down," Ryan offered.

"No, no. Ask one of the sec men to bring the small brown vial from my bedside table."

"Sure?"

Tenbos nodded, then turned toward J.B. "And you have given me a new heart, my friend. If I may call you that. Pass this way again in a month or so, perhaps if you return toward your homes. And you will see everything as sparkling and clean as a new-minted bullet. I promise you that."

"Might take you up on that, Baron."

They left the lofty chamber, winding their ways down the stairs, pausing to pass on the message from Tenbos about the morphine to one of the armed guards. He nodded. "Baron gets this way. More and more often these days. Least you got him up and moving. More than those ass-shafting little bastards ever try and do for him." He called after them.

"Watch your backs, outlanders. Best advice I can give you."

Ryan waved a hand. "Thanks."

SLICED HAM, smoked above hickory, with eggs over easy and some fried bread, made a good breakfast. The cook came and asked if they wanted anything to take on their journey and promised to make up a pack of food as well as filling up their canteens and tanks with fresh water from the ville's own well.

As Ryan and J.B. had walked into the rather gloomy dining room, Teddy and Robby had been eating at the far end of the table, heads close together, talking animatedly. As soon as they saw the two outlanders, they'd risen hurriedly and left. Both remembered to paste bright smiles on their sullen faces.

Ryan and J.B. ignored them, concentrating on their own meal, charging up their batteries ready to continue their odyssey to the Northwest.

One of the sec men had warned them of travelers' reports of unseasonable falls of snow in that direction, though the climate in Deathlands had been irretrievably altered by the massive nukings of skydark and nobody could rely on finding the weather that they expected.

"More to drink or eat?" the cook asked, wiping his large red hands on his greasy apron. "Baron said to give you all the best we had."

"I'm stuffed," Ryan said. "Thanks, though. Know where Baron Tenbos is?"

"Don't believe that he's come down from the gun collection yet. He hasn't been up there at the top of the tower for such a long while." He turned to go. "Saw the two boys going up the stairs," he added.

THEY QUICKLY GOT everything ready for their departure.

"Best say our goodbyes to the baron," J.B. said. "Leave our blasters here."

"Yeah."

Surprisingly the staircase was deserted, without a single sec man on duty. But neither of them thought anything about that. The air of relaxed competence that ran through the ville meant that it seemed as secure as anywhere.

They were near the top of the stairs.

"Quiet." J.B. halted a few steps from the open chamber. "Very quiet."

"Could be that he's sleeping. Looked like he needed it earlier."

The Armorer moved more slowly, his head turning from side to side, glasses glinting in the spears of dusty light. "Something's wrong, Ryan," he whispered, as the baseball bat from the shadows came hissing around in a lethal arc and struck him across the side of the head, knocking him to the floor.

Chapter Twenty-Nine

At the same moment, Ryan was aware of someone moving fast and silent behind him, up the stairs. He started to turn, reaching for the hilt of his panga, half drawing it, when the bulky figure hit at him with another polished baseball bat. It caught the panga across the steel blade with a loud ringing sound, sending it tumbling down the steps, out of reach.

There was no time to stop to wonder what was happening.

"To wonder is to begin to die," Trader often said.

The bat swung toward Ryan and he ducked, vaulting onto the open landing, glimpsing a second shadow, poised ready to swing at him.

"Outland bastard!"

He dived and rolled under the blow, feeling it brush against his ribs, cracking into the floor. There was no time to worry about J.B., who was down and out of it.

Out of the corner of his good eye, Ryan caught a glimpse of the baron, who looked almost as if he were sleeping.

Almost.

Once you've seen the overwhelming stillness of death, you can never mistake it for anything else.

There was a splinter of frozen time for Ryan to see the unnatural angle of the head on the neck, where the body lay against one of the padded chairs, and the dark grinning mouth that had been ripped open below the line of the baron's jaw.

As he scuttled across the large room, ducking and weaving, he heard the characteristic light crack of a high-velocity, low-caliber handblaster being fired. There was a hot, whining sound, and the bullet smacked into one of the supporting pillars.

"Get him, Robby?"

"Don't think so, Teddy. You chilled the little prick with the glasses?"

"Think so, Robby. I'll give him another good one for luck."

"Best get one-eye first, Teddy."

Ryan was pinned down behind a chair, safe for the moment. But he could assume that the brothers, having butchered their stepfather, would each have a blaster. All they had to do was move around the top floor in opposite directions and he was dead meat. He looked behind him, seeing that the only case of blasters anywhere near him contained the single-shot Parker dueling pistol that J.B. had talked about with such enthusiasm.

The baron had said that it was one of the blasters that was actually charged with powder and ball. But if he could reach it and manage a shot at one of the brothers, then there wouldn't possibly be any time for the complex procedure of loading a flintlock pistol. He would be helpless and exposed for the other brother to gun him down.

"Come and give yourself up, one-eye!"

"He thinks that if he stays in hiding, then a big, brave sec man'll magic himself up here and save his skin, doesn't he, Teddy?"

"He does, Robby."

They were starting to move closer. Ryan could tell because they were so double stupe and arrogant that they continued talking to him.

"But they won't will they, Teddy?"

"No, they won't. Because we sent them away and said that our beloved stepfather was tired and didn't want to be disturbed by anyone."

"Very tired, Teddy."

"Very tired, Robby." Both of them giggled.

"Then we'll chill one-eye and little glasses man, and show everyone what they did to Baron Hamish Tenbos and how we tried to save him, Teddy."

"Just too late, Robby. Just in time to avenge his bloody murder."

They were already nearly a quarter of the way around the big circular chamber.

There was no point in waiting.

Ryan suddenly screamed and erupted from the shadows, heaving the heavy chair in the general direction of the stairs, bisecting the approaching brothers. Both of them yelped in shock, both firing twice at the fast-moving figure.

One bullet smashed into the stock of a Kentucky musket on the wall, inches from Ryan's head. But he was too quick. His hand darted into the glass display case and grabbed the saw-handled pistol, plucking up the flask of black powder as he dodged away again.

"Missed him, Teddy."

"And I did, Robby."

"Why did he do that?"

"He got a blaster, Robby."

"Does he know it's not loaded, Teddy?"

He raised his voice. "Stepfather never loaded his guns up here, one-eye. So it won't do you any good."

Ryan eased back the hammer, hoping that the powder and charge were fresh enough. All he needed now was a flash in the pan to see him into eternity.

"Time to finish this, Robby." There was a new sense of urgency in the voice, with the awareness that someone might hear the sound of the shooting and come to investigate.

"Agreed, brother."

Ryan was crouched behind another of the soft, metal-framed chairs, the gun cocked and ready. He peered around and saw that the brothers, thinking themselves safe, had come out into the open. Teddy— Ryan thought it was Teddy—was perfectly silhouetted against one of the floor-to-ceiling windows, about forty feet away from him.

"Please," he breathed, sighting along the elegant barrel and gently squeezing the trigger.

Ryan hadn't fired a flintlock blaster for a long, long time, and he was taken a little by surprise by the tiny puff of smoke and flash as the hammer dropped, the flint igniting the powder in the pan, which was followed almost immediately by the main charge firing. The gun bucked in his hand. The sound of the explosion, so much softer than more modern firearms, drifted into the room.

Teddy Tenbos staggered three steps backward, dropping his own Saturday-night special, and clutched at his chest. "I'm fucking shot, Robby," he said, dismay rising above anger or pain in his quiet voice.

"What?"

"Gun was loaded after... Chilled me, Robby."

"He might chill me, Teddy."

The younger brother suddenly sank to his knees, as though some mighty prelate had entered the top chamber. "No. Sure about it, Robby. Get him for..."

He fell forward, like a man sliding headfirst off a breakwater into shallow waves.

"Teddy? Teddy!"

Ryan had considered charging at the surviving brother, while he was still in shock. But he was too far away for the gambit to have much hope of success.

"I'm reloading, Robby," Ryan said, snapping back the hammer and carefully priming the beautiful Parker pistol with the powder horn.

"You lying bastard." The voice was taut with an icy rage.

"Putting the ball in now." Ryan removed the ramrod and pushed it down the nine-inch, smooth-bore octagonal barrel. "Nearly done."

Robby was totally confident, stepping slowly toward Ryan's crouching figure. He passed the blood-sodden corpse of his stepfather without a single sideways glance, the chromed revolver in his hand.

"Wasting your time, outlander."

"Keep coming," said Ryan.

Robby stopped and sniggered, standing still, less than twenty feet away from Ryan, his blaster steady in his right hand. Behind him, Teddy's death-rattle told that his race was run.

"You did me a favor, one-eye. Our plan was to share the barony between us. Blame you and your companion for the murder of poor Hamish. Chill you both. Now it's even better. I'm the sole baron, with a dead brother to add weight to my tale of woe. Thank you, outlander." He laughed again as Ryan leveled the dueling pistol at him. "An empty gun frightens nobody," he said.

Ryan pulled the trigger and the powder fired, shooting the ramrod at Robby. It struck him in the throat, smashing through his windpipe and severing the spinal cord, protruding three inches from the back of his neck.

There was a choking, gargling sound from the mortally wounded man. He fired his own gun once, the bullet disintegrating one of the tall windows of the tower.

As Robby stumbled backward, drowning in his own blood, he tripped over his brother's corpse and fell dead on top of him.

Chapter Thirty

J.B. lay facedown, blood seeping from his right ear, nose and mouth, forming a small puddle on the dusty carpet. His glasses had fallen off and were glinting a couple of feet away from him, close to his fedora.

Ryan checked first that the two brothers were indeed chilled, pressing a finger to the arteries in the neck. In the case of Robby Tenbos there wasn't very much artery left.

Then he knelt by J.B., doing the same, finding a slow but steady pulse. The blow with the baseball bat had been ferocious, but it now looked like the Armorer might have spotted it coming at the very last second and just managed to dodge enough to deflect the worst of the impact.

Ryan rolled his friend onto his side, making sure he hadn't swallowed his tongue, picking up the glasses and the hat. Below him he caught the sound of boots mounting the staircase toward the top of the tower.

Not wanting to get chilled by a trigger-happy sec man, Ryan called out.

"You can come ahead. But there's a lot of death up here. Baron and both his stepsons caught the last train west. My friend's injured."

"Who did the chilling and the injuring up there, you?"

"Brothers wasted the baron. One of them decked J.B. I chilled the brothers."

"Both?"

"Both."

"You got a blaster up there?"

"Not of my own. I used a flintlock pistol. It's empty now. There's a panga of mine down the stairs someplace. Look out for it."

"How bad's your friend, outlander?"

"Knocked out. Needs some care."

There was a muttered discussion. "We're coming up. Just stand by one of the windows and keep your hands where we can see them and don't make any sudden movements."

"You believe me?" Ryan shouted.

A pause. "Yeah. I guess we do, all right. This has been coming for a long time."

"I'm waiting for you," Ryan said, moving to look out through the shattered window, breathing in the cool, fresh air of the morning.

THERE WERE six men in the sec team, moving through the carnage with an exaggerated care, trying to pick their way around the sticky blood, and the shards of splintered glass, shaking their heads over their dead leader. One of them spit into Robby Tenbos's open eyes.

"Bastards. They were sack-jack bastards, Cawdor. You done real good here. Shame is that the baron had to get himself snuffed as well."

"Can you get help for J.B., here, before you start shifting the bodies? They can wait. He can't."

The local medical help turned out to be a wise woman from one of the wrecked condominium buildings nearby. But, by the time she came fussing into the bedroom where J.B. had been carried, the Armorer had recovered a sort of consciousness.

Ryan called for a large bowl of clean water and some linen rags, bathing away the crusted blood from his friend's face, gently probing the duck-egg swelling on the side of his narrow skull. The wound felt hard, without the unmistakable softness that meant a fracture.

Touching the spot brought J.B. around, his eyes blinking open, trying to focus on the figure looming over him. "That you, Ryan?"

"Yeah. Lie still."

"What happened? Can't remember."

"Got whacked."

"Who by?"

"Terrible twosome. Robby and Teddy Tenbos."

"Really?"

"Yeah. Don't move, while I try and bathe some of this blood out of your hair."

"Ouch! They hit me? What with? Feels like they used an implode gren on my head."

"Baseball bat. They were waiting for us at the top of the tower. By the time we got up there, they'd already slit the throat of the baron."

"Who had?" Ryan noticed that the Armorer's voice was peculiarly flat and toneless, and that his eyes were struggling to come into focus.

"Robby and Teddy. The stepsons. How's your head feeling? Or is that a stupe question?"

"Stupe question. So, what happened to me?"

The repetition made Ryan certain that his friend was suffering from concussion.

"Robby and Teddy knocked you out."

"Where's the baron?"

"Dead."

"Where are those two? They escape? Did you say they were the ones who hit me, Ryan?"

"Yeah. I chilled them both. But I'll tell you about it later, when you feel better."

"Don't feel too bad, considering what happened to me." He paused for a long moment, his face puzzled. "Can you just tell me again, Ryan, what happened to me?"

"ALL YOU HAVE TO DO, my dear, is not to do any worrying. Have no fear, Mystical Meg is here." The wise woman was stout and jolly and had a large wicker basket filled with the herbs and unguents of her art.

"Don't worry," J.B. said confusedly. "My own words to myself, ten thousand times a day."

"What are you going to do?" Ryan asked, watching as the woman took out a large jar that seemed to be stuffed with ragged leaves of some sort.

"Bleed him," she replied. "Got some of the finest leeches this side of the Pecos."

"No," Ryan and J.B. said in unison.

"Stuff and nonsense. You go away, with your ugly great patch scaring the daylights out of poor little Johnny Dix here. And I'll apply a few of these big tom leeches of mine about his body. Soon have him up and about, won't we? Then, if it's needful, I can always cup him."

"No, you fucking well won't," the Armorer grated with a rare venture into profanity.

"No leeches," Ryan warned. "Mebbe some broth or a poultice. But no leeches."

The jolly face creased with disappointment, the corners of her mouth turning down. "Now, you don't catch me coming along and trying to tell you how to go about your own killing trade, do you? You do not."

Ryan had been looking out of the bedroom window. Now he spun on his heel and walked around the bottom of the Armorer's bed, stepping in close to her. He leaned down so that his face was on a level with hers.

She recoiled at his cold anger, nearly dropping her jar of leeches. "Oh, don't hit me, Master!"

"I won't."

"Send her away, Ryan," J.B. said, shaking his head, then wincing at the distress that it caused him. "Only a knock on the skull. Soon be better."

"I can help," the wise woman protested. "But it has to be my way."

"Or?"

"Or not at all," she said smugly.

"Agreed," Ryan replied. "So it's not at all."

J.B.'S RECOVERY from the murderous blow to his head took longer than either he or Ryan had guessed. The concussion lingered for three more days, with blurring of vision and voracious, sickly pains across the side of his skull that made him throw up a dozen times.

It was an additional two days before they both felt that the Armorer was fit enough to face the rigors of long hours on the road inside the LAV-25.

During that time, the mourning ville seemed to be frozen in a vacuum around them, like a fly trapped helplessly in a block of cooling amber.

The death of a baron can often result in a period of limbo before his successor appeared.

But there was no clear claimant in the ville.

The parricides were dead, tipped together into an unmarked grave in the depths of the forest of pines to the east of the ville. No tears were shed for them.

The funeral of Baron Hamish Tenbos was a splendid affair. A cortege wound through the ville, following the oak coffin on the back of a flatbed truck. Men, women and children, many of them weeping, all in their best dark clothing, trudged through the sleet that fell that afternoon. Most of them cast curious sideways stares at the tall, one-eyed outlander who strode among the sec men.

It had been a deputation of the senior sec men who had come to visit Ryan and J.B. in their bedroom, the evening before the interment of their last master. Five of them stood uncomfortably around the walls, blast-

ers holstered, none of them wanting to be the one who
started to speak to the dangerous outlanders.

In the end it was the oldest of them, his long gray
hair streaked with white, who put the suggestion.

After he finished speaking, his nervous words
gathering pace and tripping over one another, Ryan
and J.B. were silent for fifty beats of the heart, glancing at each other.

Finally it was Ryan who broke the stillness.

"We're flattered, aren't we, J.B., by what you've
said. We've both been around Deathlands all of our
lives, and there've been times we've had some good
offers. But I don't think we've ever been offered everything. Not to be the barons of what seems to be a
thriving, contented ville. Takes the breath away a little. But that isn't the way."

"We don't want some wolf's-head strangers coming in and snatching power," said the oldest of the sec
men, "mongrels that hear of a house empty and come
crawling in to try and fill it themselves. Not that."

J.B. eased himself up on his pillows. "Ryan's right.
We're strangers, passing through. And that's what
we'll be doing in a day or so."

"Nothing magical about being a baron," Ryan said.
"Be strong and be fair. Only two rules that really signify." He looked at the sec man. "Why not you?"

"Me." His jaw dropped. "Me?"

"Why not, Jethro?" asked one of the others.
"Compared to those dead bastards, you're a real
prince. We'll back you, and I can't think of a living

soul in the whole ville and lands around who'd stand against you.''

Ryan could see that this was far too cataclysmic an idea for them all to get their brains around. When the five left the bedroom, it was obvious that a great deal of talking still needed to be done.

But with fundamental decency on all sides and a fair share of goodwill, there was no real reason to think that the idea might not work.

FINALLY, WITH THE THRONE still vacant, it came time for J.B., almost fully recovered, and Ryan to be on their way northward once more.

They left early in the morning, having made their farewells the previous evening. It was much colder, with a dusting of snow over the armasteel of the wag, the exhaust belching blue-gray smoke into the dawn.

Ryan drove, steering them north toward Oregon and then on to the ghost-haunted ruins of Seattle.

And Trader.

Chapter Thirty-One

"Go on ahead, my swift-footed Mercury. Leave this laggard cripple to follow at his own poor pace."

Doc was doubled over, hands on knees, fighting for breath. A worm of white spittle dangled from his open mouth, swinging in the watery moonlight.

Dean danced from foot to foot, burning in his eagerness to return to the safety of the farmhouse and warn Krysty of the lethal treachery on the part of the Apostle Simon and his Slaves of Sin.

"We're almost there, Doc."

"And I am almost done, dear boy. Please, go on and I'll be there as fast as I can."

"Sure you'll be okay, Doc?"

"Of course. I have my equalizer here." He patted the butt of the Le Mat. "And it will support me against those evildoers that trouble me."

Dean squatted on his heels, his face sheened with sweat. "Doc?"

The old man read the unspoken question. "Of course they'll be all right. Now go ahead and warn Krysty. Tell her I'll be there in two shakes of a gnat's tail."

The boy vanished, his dark clothing quickly merging into the desert.

Doc straightened, waiting for the tightness of the steel band around his temples to loosen its grip, trying to slow his breathing and pulse, the way Krysty had sought to teach him. But worry over Mildred and Jak swamped his mind and he found himself on the brink of tears.

He folded his gnarled hands together and peered for a moment into the star-spangled firmament above him. "Listen a moment to a silly old fool, Lord," he whispered, clearing his throat. "I know that I've been things I don't take pride in. And I don't recall the last time I asked for help. But if you can aid me and the woman and the boy against those... They take your name in vain and abuse the ideas you stand for, Lord." His breathing was easing and he felt able to go on toward the ranch. "Anyway, just do what you can and lend a lick to what's right, Lord." He paused. "Amen."

KRYSTY HAD BEEN STANDING on the porch, staring out into the blackness, when she spotted the small figure of Ryan's son panting his way toward her.

Before he'd even said a word, she called out to him. "I know."

"What? How?" He wanted to lie down and recover from the cross-country dash, but he wouldn't let himself show any weakness in front of the tall redheaded woman.

"Felt it. Where's Doc?"

"Following. Couldn't keep up."

Even in that moment of extreme tension, Krysty managed a smile. "Well, he is around two hundred years older than you, Dean. Come in and sit down and have a drink of buttermilk and tell me what happened."

Doc arrived less than ten minutes later, having fallen a couple of times as he picked his way through the arroyo. Part of him simply wanted the security of the front door of the house being slammed and bolted behind him. Another part of him kept hearing steps following him, and his back twitched at the expectation of a steel blade plunging into his spine.

"Dean has told you all?" he asked, sitting in an armchair, legs spread in front of him, wondering how long the pains in his knees were going to persist.

"Yes. They have a rifle and two handblasters now. We have more weapons."

Dean was at the table, his upper lip bearing a pale cream mustache from the gulped glass of buttermilk. "They'll chill them both, then come for us."

"Probably," Krysty agreed. She ran her strong fingers through the curling mane of fiery hair, feeling its sentient length respond to her touch, like a thousand incandescent feathers.

"Should we turn off all of the oil lamps?" Doc suggested. "We don't know how long it might be before they decide to pay us a visit."

"Right." Krysty waved to Dean to turn the wicks down, plunging the house into darkness. "Now, we have to do some serious planning."

KRYSTY REALIZED in the next half hour just how much she had always relied on Ryan when it came to the dealing of death. She was aware that the Slaves of Sin might take it into their crazed skulls to come after them before dawn, so the three of them sat out on the porch, with their blasters drawn, talking through a variety of schemes to rescue Mildred and Jak.

But none of their ideas seemed to hold together.

"They might have chilled them by now," Dean protested. "And us just talking."

"You have to talk before you act," Krysty said. "You've heard your father quote Trader often enough." She hoped the eleven-year-old wouldn't spot that she'd only just made it up.

Doc rubbed at the silvery stubble on his chin. "My belief is that they won't have harmed them. Not yet."

"How do you figure that?" Dean stood and walked along the weathered planks of the veranda. "You saw what that triple sicko did to one of his own people!"

"Right. That is precisely the point that I'm laboring to make, young man. Having had their fill of religious torture and murder for the night, I would believe that they won't want to waste two fresh victims too quickly."

"Could be right." Krysty sighed. "Ryan always said that it was better to be active rather than passive. Go at your enemy before he goes at you."

"Attempt to get your retaliation in first," Doc said. "Admirable in many ways. I'm sure that Marshal Ney would have approved. As would Nathan Bedford Forrest. The firstest with the mostest."

"But they outnumber us four to one. The one strength we have is this building."

"Can only watch three sides from four," Dean argued. "Still sneak up on us."

"I know, I know. Gaia! If we go out against them, we can lose. If we stay here we can lose."

"Let me go scout." Dean stood close to them, his outline just visible in the moonlight that was filtered through a bank of low clouds. "I could be there and back in no time and report what's happening."

Krysty didn't answer, rocking gently back and forth. Finally she said, "No, Dean. That man Simon might be as crazy as a roasted scorpion, but he's not totally stupid. He'll look at it like this. They have two out of the five of us safe in the bag. We know about it pretty quickly, when Mildred and Jak don't return. What do we do? Either we go in like the cavalry and try and stage a rescue, or we hole up here."

Doc coughed. "I fear that our companions will most certainly be put to the torture and then slain within the next twenty-four hours. Do we agree?" Neither of them said anything. "Ah, well, we don't disagree."

"So?" Dean punched his right fist into his left palm. "So what, Doc?"

"I surmise that Simon will want to know what we are doing. He has the numbers, so he could spare three or four to creepy-crawl in the darkness."

Krysty stood. "I think that makes sense, Doc. Yeah. So, let's get ready for them."

DEAN WAS TO REMAIN in the house, moving silently around, catfooted, never staying in one room for more than thirty seconds, checking out the windows on every side, as well as climbing up to the attic and watching from there. He was armed with his own blaster as well as one of the ranch's hunting rifles.

Krysty took the outside perimeter, working on the assumption that she was actually fittest and fastest. She also probably had the best night vision of any of them. She was content to just carry her own Smith & Wesson double-action 640.

"And I shall busy myself by circling the house and also keep a weather eye open for trouble in the barns and outbuildings." Doc rapped the floor with the ferrule of his sword stick. "With this and my Le Mat, I feel total confidence in my ability to rout any number of the ungodly."

"At any sign of trouble, Dean, you open fire. Doc and I head straight back here. You unlock the back door, into the kitchen, so's we can get in."

"Sure."

AS THE NIGHT MOVED ON, Dean was aware of how much the old house settled and shifted, sun-warmed timbers still shrinking, doors and window frames contracting and creaking. Every sound brought the boy spinning around, fingers tight on the butt of his 9 mm Browning, waiting, trembling.

Krysty stood in the cover of the orchard, her nostrils catching the freshness of the apples and the plums, waiting to get her sight adjusted to the darkness. The moon had vanished behind the gathering clouds, and it had become much colder in the past hour. She could see the glow of the camp fires of the religious crazies, taste wood smoke.

Doc stepped as quietly as he could into the largest barn, through the big front doors that were the only entry into the wood-framed building. There was the smell of horses, and he could hear the animals moving a little uneasily, hooves shifting in their stalls, as they caught the scent of a human.

He walked to the far end, where he knew that the bloody-minded mule, Judas, was penned, two clear, empty stalls away from any of the other animals.

"Greetings, you old bastard," Doc said, dodging back as the mule made a lightning-fast attempt to take the ear off his head, the huge curved teeth clicking together, missing by inches. Doc swung his sword stick, rattling the silver lion's-head hilt between Judas's eyes.

The traditional pleasantries exchanged, Doc rubbed his hand down the animal's neck, leaning against the side of the stall. "Maybe we should turn you out, you devil's walking parody. Send the ungodly and unwashed scattering like chaff before the cleansing wind, then return here with Mildred and Jak on your back. Be good to... What?"

The mule had looked suddenly away from him. For a moment Doc thought Judas was going to snap at him again, and he stepped quickly to one side, lifting his cane in readiness. But the long, demonic head was turned toward the doors, the spiteful eyes glinting in the gloom of the barn.

Doc found that someone seemed to have sucked all of the oxygen from the dusty building, and he tried to draw a reassuring breath. "What?" he whispered.

The filtered moonlight that came through the myriad cracks in the walls of the ancient barn gave a strange, undersea quality to the atmosphere, like being inside a wrecked galley, settled on a fathoms-deep reef.

Doc backed away into one of the empty stalls, the butt of the ponderous, gold-engraved Le Mat feeling cold and slick against his hand. He still held the hilt of the sheathed sword stick in his left hand. Realizing this, the old man holstered the revolver and drew the blade of Toledo steel, laying the ebony shell in the straw at his feet.

For a moment he drew the slender sword to his eyes, making out the ornate lettering—*No me saques sin razon; no me envaines sin honor.* His dry lips moved and his shallow breath whispered into the stillness. "Draw me not without reason and sheath me not without honor."

The Le Mat was back in his right hand, the hammer cocked over the buckshot round.

Judas was still restless, his head turning between the back entrance to the building and the stall where Doc was hiding.

KRYSTY KNELT by a trim apple tree, laying her right hand on the rough bark. Her fiery sentient hair was bunched at her nape, packed as tightly against her skull as possible, a sure sign that something was seriously wrong.

She closed her green eyes for a few seconds, trying to concentrate on the "feeling" power of Gaia, the Earth Mother. The air around her seemed to throb with a terrible tension. There was a movement somewhere around her. But it could easily have been the camp of the fladgies, their fires flickering, ruby-bright, out across the desert.

"Careful, Doc," she said quietly.

A FIGURE GHOSTED OUT of the darkness, deep black against the blackness, right in front of Doc's crouching figure. It was so sudden and so silent that it took him by surprise, and he nearly squeezed the trigger on the Le Mat. But his better judgment asserted itself, just in the nick of time, preventing him from firing the gun.

Instead he stood and thrust with the rapier, wrist and arm straight as a die, aiming slightly upward, feeling the needle tip slide between the protecting ribs on the left side of the intruder's body.

It was a perfect, clean kill.

The man dropped to the floor like a sack of meat, shrouded in cotton rags, the only sound in the barn a faint sigh, almost of disappointment.

Doc withdrew the blade, stepping confidently out into the open space between the stalls, aware only of the sudden restlessness of the animals, disturbed by the hot reek of freshly spilled blood—to find himself confronting a second assailant who stood ten feet away, holding a long-hafted hatchet.

At that frozen moment, Doc remembered one of the Trader's sayings that Ryan had often repeated to him. "Pull the trigger too soon and you'll probably be fine. Pull it too late and you'll probably be dead."

But the three and a half pounds of steel, lead and gold remained unfired. "Move and I'll fill you full of holes," Doc said, his voice dry and croaking.

"No, unbeliever," said the cold voice from behind him, along Judas's stall. "*You* move and I'll fill *you* full of fucking holes."

Chapter Thirty-Two

"But they haven't harmed anyone?"

"Not yet."

The speaker was an old woman, bent double, hands knotted with arthritis. "Don't mean they won't."

Ryan nodded. "True enough. But you reckon there's less than a dozen stickies out in the woods?"

"We never counted more than eight," the leader of the small community replied.

J.B. shook his head. Melting snow dappled the shoulders of his worn leather jacket, misting the lenses of his glasses, darkening the fedora. "Only eight. All of them grown men, or some women and children?"

There was a silence.

Ryan's guess had put the population of the small ville at around sixty souls. It was set just north of the old line between Oregon and Washington states, to the east of the Columbia River. The highway was in reasonably good condition, seeming little traveled. According to J.B.'s map, the blacktop should bring them to the crossing of the Snake in a few miles.

The last part of the journey had been relatively uneventful, despite diminishing weather. Twice their progress northwest had been checked by vicious flurries of snow and temperatures that had dropped savagely to twenty below, making the eight-wheeler occasionally difficult to handle on ice-sheathed tracks. Once it was only the remnants of an iron fence that kept them from sliding over a two-hundred-foot drop.

There had been the usual detours to avoid quake-riven trails and a couple of hostile villes that had shown willingness to resist all outlanders. But even the occasional high-powered hunting round did no damage to the armasteel of the wag. Ryan and J.B. ignored these sporadic attacks, not even bothering to return the desultory firing.

Time was still on their side. Since leaving New Mexico, the friends had been nearly a month on the road, leaving them a good two weeks to reach Seattle and track down Abe and the Trader. Easy traveling.

Apart from one minor problem.

They'd almost run out of gas.

The main tanks had been run dry since the previous morning, and now the reserve gauge was trembling into the red. The Armorer's guess had been about another fifty to eighty miles before the laboring engine finally coughed its way into stillness.

And that would leave them stranded in the wilderness, at least one hundred and fifty miles short of their destination.

Which didn't make their planned rendezvous completely out of the question. Just difficult.

Now they'd found themselves in the little settlement of Mitchell Springs, which boasted that it had supplies of gas available for anyone who could raise the necessary amount of jack. Ryan and J.B. couldn't. But the inhabitants of Mitchell Springs were also prepared to involve themselves in some serious trading with the two stone-eyed outlanders.

"Gas for chilled stickies," the leader of the ville repeated. "Chilled stickies. Stickies." He was in his early fifties, with a face covered in scabs that his fingers picked at constantly. He also had an occasional lapse into echolalia, repeating his own words again and again.

His name was Andrew Sheppard.

"How much?"

"Oh, boy, oh boy! How much? Eight stickies." He looked up at the slate sky outside the general store. "I reckon twenty gallons for eight stickies."

Ryan laughed. "Do it yourself. Save twenty gallons of gas. If it's that easy."

"Fifty gallons, gallons."

Ryan was genuinely puzzled. Stickies were accepted to be one of the greatest and most dangerous scourges of all Deathlands. Over the years he had lost a number of good companions to their rending suckered hands.

They moved in loosely knit tribes, often coming out of nowhere to raid isolated villes or lonely homes. Their chief pleasure was to inflict pain on norms, particularly if it could be linked to bright fires or shattering explosions.

Fear of stickies was understandable.

But Mitchell Springs seemed well run, and most of the adult males carried blasters. So, why were they frightened of a handful of the muties?

Ryan sniffed. "Before we get down to the nuts and bolts of this deal," he said, "how about you telling us why you don't go and wipe out these stickies yourselves? Has to be something you aren't telling us."

"No, not really. Oh, boy. Not really."

The crippled woman hawked up phlegm and spit out of the open door onto the frost-dusted earth beyond. "You ain't dealing with triple stupes, Andy Sheppard, by God, you ain't. If you don't tell 'em, then I sure as shit-in-a-hole will."

"Tell them, then, Maggie. Tell them, tell them. See what happens."

"Tell us, Maggie," J.B. urged. "Tell us why you're all so scared of less than two hands of stickies."

THE DEAL WAS STRUCK—twenty gallons of gas for each stickie dead, paid in advance, pumped into the echoing tanks, and a room and food for two nights in Mitchell Springs.

It was dusk, and Ryan and J.B. had just finished a dish of home-fried potatoes and thick slices of wild pig, with a sauce of cinnamon and apples.

"Good," Ryan said. "Bellyful of decent chow and I'm ready to go and carry out some cleansing."

J.B. was staring out of the ill-fitting window at the light flakes of snow that were blowing by, carried on the back of a rising norther.

"Yeah, but..."

Ryan looked at his old friend. "You want out of this?" he asked.

"No. We got paid so..."

"The shitting sickness."

J.B. nodded. "Yeah. Cholera's bad, any day of the rad-blasted week. But when you got the special pick-'em-up-and-knock-'em-down stickie version..."

Ryan stood, the legs of the chair scraping on the rough wooden floor of their cabin. "Better than ninety-nine percent terminal."

"So they say."

"But we can find a good place tomorrow morning. Scout their camp. Four miles to the west, out back of an old hospital. And use the Steyr. And the Uzi if they come at us. No way any of the poor bastards can come close enough to infect us. Don't have to go in among them."

"Guess not."

"What?"

J.B. turned from the window. "They could do this. How come they're so frightened? I reckon they've had a run-in with the stickies and mebbe lost folks to the shitting sickness. Make sense to you?"

"Could be. No point in wondering. We know what we have to do and where we have to go to do it."

MORNING BROUGHT platters of fish chowder and thick slices of fresh-baked bread, a crock of salted butter and a glass jar of strawberry preserve.

"Could drag this out for another three days and still have time to tie up with Trader," J.B. said, easing his leather belt open a notch.

There was a faint scratching sound at the outside of the door of their hut. Ryan glanced across at J.B., who moved silently to pick up the Uzi. He drew his own SIG-Sauer, then stepped over to the door, flattening himself against the white-painted log wall. "Who is it?"

"Me. Maggie. Open up quick before anyone sees me comin' to call."

The old woman limped in, her hair covered in a dark blue shawl, a layer of snow dusting it. She gestured for Ryan to push the door shut.

"What is it?" he asked.

"I'm a Christian woman, outlander. And I can feel the Good Lord a-tappin' on my shoulder, whisperin' in my ear at night, tellin' me that it's close to my time. Race is near run, and I ain't goin' to stand before His gold throne unless I'm full justified. Won't have deaths on my conscience."

"The muties?" J.B. asked, puzzled at her meaning.

"Stupe! You and one-eye here. Not that losin' an eye makes you less fancy, mister. If I was a year or two younger I'd gladly have let you park your boots under my bed."

"You trying to tell us that the good folk plan to chill us?" Ryan said. "After we do the job for them?"

"Course. Get your pretty blasters and their gas returned and that hunk of armasteel parked out back. Now I told you and I'm goin' out again."

"How? When?" The Armorer glanced out of the window into the blurred mix of sleet and snow that was falling steadily over the ville.

"For me to know and you to guess. For a shrimp you ain't so bad lookin', neither." As she pushed past J.B., she made a grab at his crotch, cackling at the rosy blush that flooded his cheeks. Before either of them could say any more, Maggie was gone.

"What now, bro?" the Armorer asked, taking off his glasses and furiously wiping at them.

"Well, we could be well warmed with her if we wanted it." Ryan grinned. "One of those old ladies that I somehow believed right out. How about you?"

"Yeah. So?"

"We go and chill the stickies. Come back and watch our backs. Don't stay a second night. Head out in the wag. That sound like a good plan?"

J.B. replaced his glasses. "Yeah."

"TOO EASY," J.B. whispered, putting his hand over his mouth to check the plumes of breath streaming out into the bitterly cold morning.

The stickies' camp was a collection of ragged tents and brushwood huts, built in the lee of what had probably been the main south wall of the old veterans' hospital. It was the only section of the scattered complex of buildings still standing, the rest of them having been destroyed either by nuking or by earth movements in the following years.

Ryan and J.B. had worked their way within fifty yards, close enough to smell the fires that smoldered in several places around the squalid site. They'd been waiting, hidden in some snow-covered ferns, watching and counting.

"Eight," Ryan said finally.

"Yeah. Six men, one woman and one toddler. We taking the woman and child out?"

"Why not? That's what we're paid for. You know what Trader used to say about stickies."

"Course. The boar and the sow and the cubs. Today's cubs are tomorrow's boars."

Ryan blew on his fingers to keep them warm. "Way they look down there, I reckon another three days or so'll see all of them dead from cholera."

The sickness was glaringly obvious. Even in the short time they'd been watching, two of the male stickies had crawled from their shelters, dragging themselves through the snow, helplessly throwing up. The woman had walked unsteadily toward the hidden norms, squatting less than ten yards away from them, voiding a stinking mess of foul liquid.

After she'd returned to rejoin the other stickies, Ryan rubbed his finger along the stock of the hunting rifle. "Could tell them we'd done it."

"They might come take a look."

"We'll be gone."

"True."

Neither of them liked chilling for the sake of it. Stickies were the most vicious and murderous breed of muties in the land, and it would normally be a positive relief to see a tribe of them, however small, down and dead in the dirt. But these poor, staggering creatures were so wretched, tainted by the killer disease, that it seemed pointless to butcher them. Admittedly they'd taken the load of gas as a part of the deal. But if the victims were dying anyway, Ryan felt no compunction in screwing the cowardly folk of Mitchell Springs.

"Put them out of their misery," J.B. suggested.

"Yeah. Yeah, I guess so. We might as well do it."

He eased the rifle's walnut stock to his shoulder, squinting through the Starlite night scope with the laser image enhancer, waiting for the moment when most of the eight would be out in the open. At such short range he figured that it was highly unlikely that he'd need to use all of the SSG-70's ten rounds of 7.62 rounds.

"Want me to fire a burst and bring them out from cover?" J.B. asked.

"Could do."

There was a gust of wind blowing from the surrounding mountains, whisking up a flurry of the frozen, lying snow. Ryan waited until it had settled before getting ready to give the signal to the Armorer.

"No." The single quiet word came from J.B.

"What?" Ryan kept the rifle to his shoulder, the sight centered on the chest of the little toddler.

"Half left."

Ryan lowered the blaster and moved his head slowly to look in the direction that the Armorer had pointed, seeing that they were no longer the only players in the game of living and dying.

Chapter Thirty-Three

The first light of the false dawn jerked Abe awake. He moaned at the sudden sharp pain that racked his shoulders, elbows, wrists and thighs. The tying had been done well enough to cramp every muscle and tendon in his body. It was like liquid fire coursing through every vein, scorching his heart and lungs when he tried to find a less agonizing position.

One of the gang had come out some time in the previous hour and spit on him, gloating over the helpless prisoner, warning him of the pleasures to come once they got him back to their home ville in the hills.

"Luke got kin that sent us after you and the old bastard. We'll get him an' all. Blood for blood's what we swear by."

If Abe could've gone back a ways and altered time, he might have decided not to bother setting out after Trader at all. It seemed there'd been not much more than hardship, chilling, blood and running.

Now it was going to be an endless time of pain where the final curtain would be dropped on him by the old guy in the hood with the long scythe.

Despite the biting cold and the swirling pain, Abe slithered back into a kind of sleep.

"COME ON, Ryan."

The voice in his ear, breath hot, tickled him, making Abe wince away from the speaker. "Fuck off."

"Quiet, or we both buy the farm. They beat you bad, Ryan, have they?"

Now he was back again in the land of the living. "Trader. That you?"

"Yeah."

"I'm not Ryan."

"What?"

"Not Ryan."

"Who is?"

"Me." Abe was becoming more and more confused, not knowing what was happening.

"Who *are* you?" Trader shifted, the butt of his beloved Armalite scraping on the rocks that Abe had been leaning against. "Fuck that!"

Abe was sliding inexorably toward the ragged edge of panic. Since meeting up again with Trader, he'd noticed several times that the old man was not quite so sharp as he'd once been, subject to the occasional lapse of concentration or memory. Normally it didn't matter that much.

Right now it could easily get both of them butchered by the sleeping gang, only a few paces away near the glowing ashes of their small fire.

"Listen to me, Trader, and keep your fucking voice down, will you?"

"How's that? You don't talk to me like that, Abe."

At least he had the name right this time. "There's the posse chased us, over yonder, Trader. Dawn's close and they'll soon be waking."

"Right."

"So, cut me loose."

Abe had been concentrating on his whispered conversation and hadn't heard the sound of movement behind him. The first warning was the gruff voice.

"You talkin' in your sleep, asshole?"

"Guess I was." He turned his head to where Trader had been crouched, seeing only gray boulders, slick with frost. "Yeah, guess I was."

"I got somethin' to shove in your mouth, you shit-for-brains little bastard. Somethin' good and big and hot and sweet. Mebbe should knock out all your teeth first, so's you don't get it into your head to... Hey, that's good, that. Get it in your *head*. Give some head. Have to—"

"Shut the fuck up, Zach, so's we can all get some sleep. Time for funnin' when we get us all home. Let it lie till then."

"Oh, all right." Zach leaned close to Abe so he could smell the bitter home brew, sour on his breath. "Be back for you tomorrow, sweet thing. Now don't you go 'way, will you?"

ABE DREAMED, a classic dream of anxiety, walking along endless corridors, dripping with rank moisture. The only light came from a pallid green fungus that coated the arched ceiling, reflected in the shallow stream that soaked his bare feet.

He was pursuing a minotaur.

Even in his dream, Abe was puzzled by that. He didn't know what such a mutie creature was, yet in his nightmare there was a clear image of it—tall, with the legs and trunk and arms of a powerful man, but with the head and horns of a great shaggy bull buffalo, bloodred eyes glinting in the gloom.

He could hear it snuffling and grunting, somewhere in the vast maze ahead of him, could almost taste its rank, feral scent. The trail led forever downward, with crossings and turnings every fifty paces or so.

Abe was armed with a long knife, though the point and the edge were hopelessly blunt.

The heavy breathing of the minotaur had faded away into stillness, and Abe was able to relax for a few moments. There was some pressing reason for his pursuit of the mutie beast, but he couldn't quite turn his brain around what that reason was.

Now the noise had started again.

Behind him and not before.

HIS EYES REFUSED to function properly. One of the kicks from the mens' work boots had opened a shallow gash across his forehead. While he'd wriggled and shaken in his dream, Abe had managed to open the cut again, and blood had trickled down and flooded both eye sockets.

But he could hear.

Hear but not understand.

Abe was sure that he was awake, but the functioning part of his brain was feeding him information that made no possible sense at all to him.

A bellowing, tuneless voice sang loudly, somewhere in the blackness behind the helpless man.

"Oh, goodbye to you moaning gaudy sluts,
For we're bound off for high Mexico,
To hunt the fair tuna and the wild buckaroo,
The snow-white cunny and the raw abalone."

Abe tried to speak, but his tongue seemed paralyzed and his lips were clammed together.

Now the singer stopped his chantey and broke into an equally tuneless whistle.

"Trader?" The little ex-gunnner's voice was a tiny, feeble whisper, like the birth mew of a blind kitten.

Abe wondered for a moment whether he might, perhaps, have died during the night. If that was what had happened, then it was undeniably a relief as there'd be no more pain and suffering. But it didn't seem altogether likely to him that the celestial clouds of divine paradise would be sullied by Trader with his whistling and singing. Not unless the old man had also inherited his six feet of cold clay.

"Harps of gold," Abe said, still struggling to open his eyes. "Oh, Jesus, help me."

"What's wrong, Brother Abe? Why're you taking the name of the Lord in vain?"

If it wasn't the mercy of eternal death, then it could only be madness. The posse had been less than a dozen yards away. Why was Trader behaving with such crass insanity?

And why hadn't they...

"Why haven't they chilled you, Trader?" he managed.

"Chilled me, Abe?"

"Yeah." One eye was finally working its way clear, and he blinked, making out Trader's figure, squatting at his right side, silhouetted against the opalescent light of the rising sun.

"Who's going to chill me?" Trader asked, laughing heartily. Pink reflected off the blade of a knife that was beginning to slice through the ropes around Abe's ankles. "Soon have you up and about again. Keep still, or you might get cut."

"The posse is..." Abe's voice rose to a saw-blade scream. "The fucking posse, you triple-stupe old bastard."

Trader patted him on the shoulder. "There, there, Abe. Don't lose that cool of yours. Man who loses a little cool can finish up with the big heat."

Now the first flickerings of hope and realization dawned. "Trader...you haven't?"

"Yeah, I have."

"All of them?"

The last ropes fell away and Abe tried to move, biting his lips so he wouldn't squeal out at the molten agony of blood beginning to circulate again.

"Sure. All of the sons of bitches."

"Didn't hear a thing."

"Razor comes in like a panther in the night."

"You mean you—"

"See for yourself, Abe."

THE SUN WAS RISING clear of the Washington mountains to the east. Abe tottered upright like a weak-kneed old drunk, moaning at the pain, with Trader at his shoulder to steady him over the rough ground. The fire was now completely out, just a pile of soft white ash remaining, with the few unburned stubs of twigs scattered around it.

And the bodies lay in a rough circle around the center of the camp.

Abe already felt sick from the beating and the privation and the lack of anything to drink. But even at his best the sight of the corpses would have brought him to the brink of dropping to his knees to throw up. He had never in all his brutal life seen so much blood in one place.

It was nothing short of a miracle that an old man like the Trader had been able to come creeping in out of the twilight and slit the throat of every member of the posse, without a single one waking to face his death.

He fought for control over his heaving guts, counting the scattered dead. "Eight," he said.

"Never got around to counting them," Trader replied. "Too busy chilling them."

Every single one had a small, deep cut on the right side of his throat, below the ear, opening up the major artery, loosing a torrent of crimson. Death would have come quickly, within a matter of seconds.

"How did you keep them quiet and still while you was slicing them, Trader?"

The older man shrugged his shoulders as though it were such an obvious question it didn't really need an answer. "Just held them down."

"Yeah," Abe said, moving back a few paces as he realized that his feet were dabbling in the edge of the dull lake of blood. There were gallons and gallons, already congealing around the edges, a sticky skin forming on the top. The first blowflies of the morning were beginning to gather for the unbelievable feast.

"No more trouble, Abe."

"Guess not."

"You feeling fit enough to start moving again? There's some bits of rabbit, deer and stuff that they were eating. But I guess it all got kind of covered..."

"I'll wait awhile." He paused. "Thanks, Trader."

"Never should need to thank anyone, you know. Sign of weakness, Abe."

"Sorry." He laughed. "I know. Never apologize, either. Can we get away from here? Smell of death's getting to me."

"Sure thing. Head up for Seattle and wait for Ryan to come and meet us."

"Sounds good."

Chapter Thirty-Four

"Fur hunters," J.B. announced.

There were three men in the group, creeping along the dead ground of a ridge opposite Ryan and the Armorer, invisible to the small diseased band of stickies, but in the full sight of the two friends.

They wore an indistinct mix of rags and tattered animal skins, and all of them were heavily armed. Each man had a single-shot hunting musket in his hands, as well as a brace of pistols stuck in his belt.

"Looks like we might get the job done for us." Ryan shaded his eyes against the freezing wind. "Think they know the muties got the shitting sickness?"

J.B. half turned toward him, lips peeling back over his teeth in a cold, wolfish grin. "Soon find out," he said. "If they stay outside, then they know. If they go into the camp, then they don't know."

It took less than five minutes to reveal that the trio of hunters wasn't aware of the lethally infectious sickness that was ravaging the stickies' settlement.

Two out of the first three shots were clean kills, knocking a pair of males off their feet, to roll and kick in the frosted mud. The third shot clipped another of the muties through the shoulder, kicking him off balance. He struggled, yelping, onto his hands and knees, one arm dangling uselessly, blood pouring into the dirt.

There was screaming and chaos, the hunters breaking from cover, running clumsily toward the ragtag camp. One of them paused by the wounded stickie and smashed the butt of his empty musket into the side of the angular skull. Even at a distance of fifty yards, Ryan and J.B. both heard the clear sound of crushed bone. The mutie slipped onto its face and lay still.

"Three done," Ryan said quietly, keeping the Steyr ready at his shoulder.

The noise brought the other muties out of their shelters, the oldest of them holding a crude spear. He thrust it toward one of their attackers, but the hunter fired his pistol into his chest at point-blank range. There was the dulled explosion of the flintlock and a cloud of black powder smoke. The spear flew into the air, spinning with an infinite slowness before landing point-first in the mud.

"Four," J.B. said.

The fifth and sixth stickie males were bludgeoned to death, sprawling lifeless in the shadow of the wall.

"Kid and the woman left." It crossed Ryan's mind to take out all three of the hunters, but he decided that he might just as well save his ammunition. Simply by breathing in the air of the cholera-infested camp the killers were fifty-fifty to take the last train west. If they got any closer to the muties, the odds would shorten to at least ninety-ten.

One of the norms grabbed the screaming child and cut its throat as easily and effortlessly as if he were gutting a rabbit, tossing the body away.

The woman had a knife and for a few seconds she held the trio of laughing hunters away from her. They circled around as she yelled and cursed, laughing at her, feinting to grab her arm, then pulled back out of range of the blade.

"One of them still got a charge in his blaster," J.B. said. "Looks like they aim to have themselves some fun before they chill her."

"Might as well jump in their graves and shovel the cold dirt in on top of themselves." Ryan laid the Steyr SSG-70 down, easing the action.

The woman was dragged into the largest tent by all three men.

As soon as they were out of sight, Ryan crawled back into deeper cover and stood. "Might as well get going," he said. "They won't let her live. And they'll have a fine, close-combat dose of dying."

Snow was beginning to fall as they set off on the four-mile hike to the ville. The screams had stopped before they'd even traveled a quarter of a mile.

ANDY SHEPPARD and a dozen or so of other citizens waited for Ryan and J.B. as they walked along the main street of Mitchell Springs.

"Boy, oh, boy! What happened? You didn't get to the camp? That it? That it?" A look of shock crossed his face. "You didn't get anyplace inside the camp? In the camp?"

Ryan told the careful truth. "Found the stickies, like you said, by the ruins of the hospital. Eight of them. All looking real sick."

"Yeah?"

"Yeah. There was eight. Now there aren't any."

"You chilled them all?" the old woman asked.

"I told you. When we left the camp they were all dead. Or down and dying. I promise you that your ville won't have any trouble with that group of stickies ever again."

Sheppard grinned, rubbing his hands together. "Oh, boy, that's good news."

"Now we're going," Ryan said, suddenly drawing the SIG-Sauer and leveling it at the man's belt buckle. J.B. had the Uzi cocked and ready.

"Hey, what is this? This?"

"This is the way we leave a ville where we've done a job and got paid in gasoline. And nobody wants any accidents happening to spoil things. Do they?"

Andy Sheppard turned around, his eyes settling on Maggie. "You told them. Oh, boy, oh, boy, you better watch your ass from now on in."

"We hear of any trouble for Maggie when we come back this way in a few weeks, then it'll mean some chilling," J.B. warned. "Starting with you, Sheppard."

"Hey! No hard feelings, feelings, feelings, now."

"Good." Ryan turned to his companion. "Go get the armawag started up, J.B., and bring her along here. I'll stay and keep an eye on our hosts for a while."

"Sure."

Maggie was smiling fit to bust, pulling a shawl up over her sparse silver hair to protect it from the steadily falling snow. "You did good," she said. "Saved 'em makin' decisions. Dirt farmers!" She spit in the street. "They don't need trouble. Too much sun and the crops fail. Too much rain and the crops fail. That's what they understand."

Ryan smiled. "I know it."

Behind him, he heard the clang of the main hatch being thrown back on the LAV-25, followed a few moments later by the throaty roar of the powerful engine.

"Mind if we go inside?" Andy Sheppard asked, shuffling his feet, rubbing his hands together. "It's oh boy cold out here, out here."

"I bet they took our gas and never done what they did the deal on," said a thin-faced man in a heavy trench coat. "How do we know the stickies are dead?"

Ryan turned the blaster toward the speaker, his voice calm and gentle. "Stupe. We have the firepower to just take the gas and chill anyone who tried to stop us. We aren't in the business of playing games." He looked at Sheppard. "No, you can't go in. Just stand there and wait. We'll be gone soon enough."

The hills around were vanishing as the snow fell more heavily, with every sign of turning to a full-blooded blizzard. The temperature was falling fast, and Ryan couldn't wait to get himself snug into the shelter of the wag. And safe out of the little Washington ville where treachery waited behind every watery, insincere smile.

The LAV was rumbling up the grade behind him, but Ryan didn't turn to watch it. He kept his eyes ranging over the group of people, also checking out the windows and doors of the nearby houses for any attempt to coldcock them.

"We didn't mean... Oh, boy, not a thing, not a thing," Andy Sheppard stammered. "Don't need to chill me, mister."

"Not about to do that," Ryan replied. "Water's flowed under the bridge."

"All right, partner," J.B. called. "I got them covered now. Climb aboard."

Ryan backed away, giving a casual wave to the old woman, who dropped him an unsteady curtsy. The metal of the wag was icy to the touch, covered in a thickening layer of fresh snow. He swung himself up and into the main hatch on the turret, the automatic still firmly gripped in his right hand.

"Ready?" the Armorer asked.

"Yeah. Let's go."

He eased himself quickly down the short metal ladder and into the main compartment, dropping the hatch and locking it securely in place.

"Let's go," he repeated.

They'd only driven a mile when the weather closed right in around them, dropping visibility to zero. J.B. had eased down through the gears, but he finally brought the armawag to a halt, calling back to Ryan, just behind him.

"No point going on. Might easily drive straight off the side of the world."

The interior had only just had time to warm up, but the Armorer switched off the engine to conserve their precious fuel and closed the ob slits to keep out the penetrating wind and the driving snow.

They waited in near darkness, as the wag became colder.

"EASING," J.B. said, breaking a long silence between the two old friends.

"Good." Ryan stretched to get some of the stiffness out of his muscles.

"Fancy going up top to keep an eye out for any road problems, Ryan?"

"No."

J.B. laughed. "But you will?"

"Yeah."

RYAN WRAPPED his long white silk scarf around his throat, tucking the weighted ends inside his collar. He hunched his shoulders and blinked into the freezing wind. The snow had almost stopped, but the temperature was still way below freezing and the highway was icy and treacherous.

He glanced down at his chron, seeing that it was already more than three and a half hours since they'd left the ville of Mitchell Springs.

The turbocharged six cylinders roared into life again, and they were once more moving northwest.

They'd only gone a mile or so along the snaking blacktop when Ryan spotted movement ahead of them, three figures, slipping through the rutted snow, about a hundred yards in front.

"I see them." J.B.'s voice crackled in the earphones that were helping to keep Ryan's ears warm.

"Slow right down. I got a feeling that I can guess who they are and ... Yeah."

It was the trio of hunters that they'd seen carrying out the massacre at the stickie's camp. One of them stepped out into the middle of the road, waving his arms over his head. J.B. slowed and stopped fifty paces away from the man.

Ryan called out to him, making sure that the Steyr was very visible. "What do you want?"

The man was flushed, and one hand kept touching himself across the stomach, as if he were in some kind of discomfort. "Supposed to be a ville close by, friend."

"You mean Mitchell Springs?" Ryan kept a careful eye on the other two men.

"Yep, that's it. Far?"

"Take you a good hour in this weather."

"Got caught in the snow. Seems warmer now." He wiped sweat from his pale forehead.

Ryan thought it had actually grown much colder, but he kept quiet.

"Think we can get beds and food there?" one of the other men asked.

"Reckon so."

"They got a medic there?" the third man, who seemed to be breathing unusually hard and fast, queried.

"Don't know." Ryan stared at him. "You sick?"

"We all feel crooked, friend. Some sort of fever. Headaches like the worst of a jolt downer. And we all got us churned up bellies."

"Shitting sickness?" J.B. called from behind the driver's ob slit.

None of the three hunters answered him, looking at one another in silence.

Ryan lowered himself farther into the hatch. "Could be you good old boys been rooting where you shouldn't."

"What the fuck's that mean, mister?"

"Have a real good time in Mitchell Springs. Your sort of folks." Ryan lowered the hatch again, giving J.B. the signal to move on.

The wag started up, past the three dying men, leaving them behind. Ryan watched them out of the rear ob slit, until a bend in the road concealed them from him.

Chapter Thirty-Five

The dead member of the Slaves of Sin that lay at Doc's feet in the rustling stillness of the barn had fouled himself, the stench flooding the darkness.

Doc stood quite still, holding the Le Mat on a second man. But the third member of the flagellants was poised behind him, by Judas's stall, a gun drilling a hole in the old man's back.

"Put it down, unbeliever, now! Now, I said."

Despite the tension of the moment, Doc felt amazingly calm. At last he was going to die. After all the adventures of the time-trawlings and the eternity of loneliness and separation, it was going to end.

Oddly he found that he didn't really mind all that much. He would miss Ryan and Krysty and the others, even miss the stubborn Mildred Wyeth. But he would finally be rejoining his lost wife and children and that didn't seem too bad a trade.

The man facing him was grinning, stumps of broken teeth gleaming in the dusty gloom. "Do like Brother Isaac says, old man."

Whatever happened, Doc was definitely a dead man, drawing on borrowed time with every stolen breath. If he dropped his beloved blaster, then he might live a few minutes longer. More than that if they took him prisoner along with Jak and Mildred, ready to be tortured and butchered. It would then be so much easier for them to fill the inside straight by picking up Krysty and Dean, unaware of the threat.

If he fired, he would certainly kill the fladgie in front of him, to die a heartbeat later, gunned down from behind with no chance to use his rapier. But the explosion would at least give a warning to the others.

"The best surprise is no surprise," he said.

His finger was tightening on the trigger of the Le Mat, when they all had a surprise.

Judas never liked human beings, seeing them only as potential targets for his spleen. The long-haired, sweat-stinking man with the lump of metal in his fist was less than a yard away from the big mule.

It was too great a temptation.

The piercing scream of shock and agony from behind Doc had the simple effect of making him jump, tightening his finger the necessary fraction of an inch and firing the Le Mat.

The single round of 18-gauge grapeshot had little distance to star out and struck the fladgie in the center of the body, knocking him backward as though he'd been struck by a runaway war wag, ripping apart his chest, shattering ribs, shredding his lungs and tearing his heart into rags of bloody muscle.

"By the Three Kennedys!" Doc exclaimed, having the presence of mind to drop the blaster to the straw, neatly switching the sword stick to his right hand, and spinning around ready to confront the third of the attackers.

He peered into the darkness to see a strange sight, a miraculous sight. The fladgie behind him had been hefted off the floor by some unearthly power. His head and shoulders were half inside the nearest stall, bare legs kicking and flailing, his arms waving, his own gun vanished into the straw.

It took Doc several seconds to come to terms with this bizarre apparition, to understand what had happened.

"Judas," he whispered.

The mule had opened its cavernous jaws and clamped them across the side of the wretched fladgie's skull, the teeth sinking in on either side of the man's nose, pulping the left eye and partly severing the left ear. Then it had simply backed away, using its powerful neck muscles to heave its victim off his feet and half into its stall.

Doc stepped carefully past the corpse of the first man he'd chilled, edging around the front of Judas's stall, thrusting his blade into the struggling figure, the classic blow of the assassin, up between the ribs on the left side, under the shoulder blade. He twisted his wrist as he withdrew the blood-slick rapier, maximizing the damage.

"Touché," he whispered, finding that being alive wasn't such a bad thing after all.

The helpless flagellant died far more quickly than he deserved, his bare feet beating a violent tattoo on the scarred boards of the stall. Then his body became limp, hanging in the grip of the mule's jaws.

Judas was angered when he realized that his sport was over, and he tossed his head from side to side, trying to revive his victim.

"Drop him, Judas." Doc leaned over and ruffled the mule's ears, trying to ignore the sound of crunching bone from the skull of the corpse, as the animal ground its jaws together. "You did marvelously and I shall see you well rewarded with an amplitude of fresh provender, picked dew-fresh by mine own self, once this skirmish is satisfactorily completed."

He pulled back just in time as the wily mule cunningly cropped its malfunctioned toy into the trampled straw and snapped at the old man's hand.

Doc sheathed his sword stick in its polished ebony casing and picked up his Le Mat, fumbling in the darkness to adjust the hammer over the cylinder of nine .44s, finding that his fingers were trembling rather more than he'd expected.

KRYSTY HEARD the muffled boom of a blaster and immediately recognized Doc's Le Mat.

"Gaia!"

She had learned enough from Ryan to know that you didn't go rushing heedless toward the scene of danger. Her mind raced over the combat possibilities.

It had to be the Slaves of Sin attacking. She'd felt that sense of overwhelming danger, but hadn't been able to focus sharply enough on it to know for certain where it might be coming from. Now she knew that. From the rear, through the outbuildings.

But there was no way of telling what sort of drama had been played out in the barn where most of the animals were kept. No way of knowing if it had been the first shot heard around the farm, with the whole band of murderous fladgies making an all-out assault, or just a single killer creeping in to try his luck.

There was only one way to find out.

She started to move out of the orchard, circling around to her left, aiming to come in behind the house.

DEAN HAD BEEN in the attic when he heard the soft crump of Doc's Le Mat, sounding like it came from out back, near the largest of the barns.

He ran down the stairs, pausing for a moment just inside the door that opened from the kitchen into the yard. He inched it open and peered into the darkness. For a moment Dean had a glimpse of someone moving quickly around to his left, looking as though they were aiming to circle around toward the orchard.

Dean stepped silently out into the soft dust and started to move toward the barn.

DOC FELT an unaccustomed swell of pride at his achievement. "Well, Apostle Simon, you may well have counted three of your miserable mongrels out, but you won't be counting any of them back in."

With only the most minimal interference of the mule he'd been able to take on and kill three armed men.

Single-handed. His mind filled with what a tale he'd tell Ryan when the one-eyed man returned from his quest for the grail—a certain fetching modesty, a shrug of the shoulders, underplay the achievement.

Doc opened the creaking door of the barn, quite locked away in his victory.

"At least three rogues in green buckram came at me. No, I think that there were six. Three I slew and wounded five others so that they ran scampering for..."

"What's up, Doc?"

The appearance of Dean, combined with the clinical shock that was starting to set its teeth into his mind, brought a fit of giggles from the old man.

"What's up, Doc? That what you said?" He slipped into a strange Bronx-Brooklyn accent. "I knewed I should have made that left turn at Albuquerque!"

"What happened? You hurt in the head, Doc?"

The old man leaned an arm across the skinny shoulders of the boy, feeling a certain comfort in the support. "Not a scratch on me, dear child. But three of the ungodly are currently negotiating their price for a ticket over the Styx with the dark ferryman."

"What?"

Doc fought successfully for a measure of self-control. "Three of the fladgies came in the barn. Helped by Judas, I managed to chill them all."

"Three?" The note of surprise and admiration in the boy's voice made Doc grin with pride.

"All three."

"Reckon I saw a fourth man, heading around toward that shallow draw that runs close by the orchard."

"Where is Krysty?"

"Somewhere out there." He pointed vaguely with the barrel of his 9 mm Browning.

KRYSTY HEARD the panicked breathing of the last of the fladgie intruders as he blundered through the sagebrush toward her, stumbling along the bottom of the narrow twisting arroyo.

The noise of Doc's blaster, muffled by the barn, had probably not reached out across the desert to the camp of the Slaves of Sin. It sounded like there was just the single survivor of the attack, so she figured it would be good tactics to try to take him out silently.

Though Krysty carried a knife, blade-fighting had never been her strong point.

She holstered her own blaster and waited, crouched in the shadow of the steep-sided draw, gathering her breath, clearing her mind of everything except what she was about to do.

The scrambling noise was closer and she straightened, clenching her fists, bracing herself.

The last of the fladgies, called Brother James, was already up against the fear and pain barrier. Three of them, led by Isaac, had gone into the barn. There'd only been the sound of one blaster being fired, and James had waited confidently for them all to reappear so they could get into the house.

He'd waited.

But nobody reappeared and he'd lost his nerve and run, filled with terror. Several of the fladgies had been scared of the black woman and the teenager with the stark white hair and ruby eyes, whispering out of the hearing of the Apostle Simon that they were emissaries of the devil's goat. Though they'd captured them safely and were going to take the next day over their slow deaths, the residual fear remained.

Something had obviously swallowed the others in the darkness, and James wasn't about to get himself sucked into the same slime pit of horror.

He nearly fell on a sidewinder twist in the arroyo, barely keeping his balance.

Recovering just as the moon lanced through from behind the ridge of low cloud, James looked into the glittering green eyes of the fire-headed goddess of death.

Krysty punched at the slightly built man with her right fist, putting all of her body weight and power behind the blow. She aimed at the fladgie's throat, feeling the thyroid cartilage crushed against her knuckles. Even if her victim had been aware enough to try to call for help, it would have been a futile gesture, his vocal cords smashed by the ferocity of the attack.

Krysty followed up with an equally devastating punch from her left fist, aimed a little higher, beneath the point of the chin, fracturing the hyoid bone and causing irreparable damage to the epiglottis.

The religious crazie fell back as though he'd been poleaxed, dropping a large automatic in the dirt. He kicked up the dirt, his mouth open as he fought for breath, making only a faint croaking sound. His hands clutched at his throat.

Krysty took two deep breaths as she looked down at the helpless fladgie. The chiseled sliver points on the toes of her dark blue Western boots had become scratched over the long months, but they were still sharp enough for the purpose.

She judged the distance in the moonlight, seeing a trickle of blood oozing from the choking man's open mouth, ignoring it. She took a quick step in, swinging her right foot like the old vids she'd seen of football kickers. The metal tip of her boot hit precisely where she'd aimed it, beneath the fladgie's left ear.

Krysty turned away immediately, stooping to pick up what she recognized as Mildred's rare Czech revolver. She tucked it in her belt and strode toward the house, leaving the dying man to his solitary passing.

IN THE MOONLIGHT, Dean spotted the glint of cold flame from Krysty's hair, cautiously calling out to her as he and Doc emerged from the shadows of the orchard.

"You okay?"

"Yeah. You two?"

"Doc killed *three* of the crazies," the boy said, his voice breaking into a high, embarrassing squeak with his excitement. "Three aces on the line."

"I got one. Reckon there were any more?"

Doc shook his head. "There were thirteen of them in total, at my latest counting. Surely four of his small band would be all that the lunatic bedlamite would have hazarded.''

''I saw someone by the dry gulch,'' Dean said.

''That'd be the one I got.'' Krysty held out the blaster she'd recovered.

''Mildred's,'' Doc observed. ''It would seem that we would be well-advised to make a prompt move against the remainder of the ungodly.''

''Agreed,'' Krysty said briskly. ''Their chief'll realize, when his men don't come back, that something's gone triple wrong. And he might decide to chill Jak and Mildred and make a run for it.''

''So, we go now?'' Dean grinned.

Krysty looked at him, and the solemn face of Doc Tanner. ''Only three against one, now. Sure. Why not?''

Chapter Thirty-Six

"Blade held low, point up," J.B. said.

Ryan nodded his agreement. "Course. Though you might do better against someone real good with a knife if you break the rules. Go in high with the point down."

The Armorer pondered on that for a while, picking up a dry branch of piñon pine, snapping it across his knee and tossing it into the heart of their fire. "Could be, I suppose. Often works to try the unexpected."

"Not in a Mex standoff." Both of them had encountered that particularly brutal form of frontier dueling, where each man holds one end of a bandanna, or a short length of cord, between his teeth and fights with a knife at close quarters. The rules say that if either of them should break away, then the onlookers will chill them instantly.

"Different rules for that game, all right," J.B. said. "Remember what the Trader used to say about close-combat blade skills?"

Ryan nodded, waving his hand to drive a persistent moth away from his bowl of stew. "Sure. You have to be ready to give your left hand. Your left arm. Mebbe even risk a superficial cut at your face. Let him see your blood and he thinks he's won.''

''And he gets careless.''

''Right. Give up that and you can take his kidney or throat or genitals or eyes. Trade-off's likely the only thing to save your life.''

J.B. leaned back against the padded chair, feet stretched out in front of him, head on one side as he listened to the ferocious wind howling outside the cabin. ''Hard night,'' he said. ''Talking of Trader, it'll be damned strange to meet him again.'' He paused. ''If we ever do.''

''Quiet, he's coming back. Doesn't seem the sort of man to like to talk about knife fights.''

''Nor about Trader.''

The shuffling of feet along the passage grew louder. ''My sight might have taken wing from my eyes, outlanders, but my ears have become rather better than normal. If you want to talk about violence, then feel free. Whatever turns you on, as they used to say before the long winters. You're my guests. And about this Trader person you keep mentioning.''

THE LAV-25 WAS sixteen miles back along the side-trail off Highway 410, with its engine burned out through a cracked piston that had sheared and blown the whole casing apart. It wasn't the kind of damage you thought about repairing.

The snows had been bad, and there were only five days to go before their deadline in Seattle, somewhere around a hundred miles distant.

Ryan had spotted the narrow road off to the right, among tall, white-topped pines, and they'd followed it upward until they reached the isolated cabin, the home of Al Burgoise. In his seventies, close to blind, Al called himself a meditating hermit. "At my age meditation is about all I'm good for."

He'd been living in the lee of Mount Rainier's 14,500-foot shadow for most of his life. He got by with the help of a pack of hunting dogs that were all asleep out back, and by the kindliness of the folks who lived in the nearby small ville of Godfrey Falls.

He was one of the kindest and gentlest men that either Ryan or J.B. had ever met.

They'd asked him whether he felt frightened about being attacked by some of the wolf's-head outlaws who roamed Deathlands. Al had smiled and tugged at his long white beard, shaking his head at the question. His milky eyes turned from man to man.

"To be robbed means you have something worth stealing, friends. Is that not true?"

"Some kill because they have a taste for it," Ryan replied. "Is that not true?"

"I suppose so. Then you will leave here after the blizzard ends thinking that the foolish old man had been unbearably lucky." He smiled broadly. "Is that not true?"

During the evening the two friends found themselves opening up to the old man, talking about the rest of their group back in New Mexico, about their early lives and riding in the big war wags for so many years, and, finally, about the sudden news that Trader lived.

Al had nodded, nursing a large balloon glass of some home-brewed brandy that he'd been happy to share with them, occasionally asking a question or making a quiet, wise comment.

Both J.B. and Ryan were drawn into their hopes and plans for the indeterminate future.

"Settle down with Mildred, and lay the blasters aside," the Armorer said.

"Yeah, all that. And mebbe raise a family while there's time," Ryan added.

"TIME FOR BED." Ryan stood and stretched, feeling a wonderfully warm indolence sliding through his body. "You've been real kind, Al."

"Sure have," J.B. said. "We were lucky to find you up here. Need more of that luck to find Trader."

"If he's alive." Ryan yawned. "Been months since Abe sent us the message."

Al reached out cautiously for his glass, draining the last drops of the golden liquid. "Abe is a small man with a mustache and Trader carries an Armalite. An older man?"

"We didn't tell you that!" Ryan exclaimed, suddenly suspicious, his hand reaching for the SIG-Sauer.

"Please, please. The gun is the last resort of the emotionally immature. You mentioned Trader was an older man. The rest is what I've heard from the local people. Strangers are rare up here, and not always

welcome." He sighed. "Particularly when they go
around with blazing weapons."

J.B. glanced across at Ryan, both of them totally
taken aback by the old hermit's revelations. "You're
saying that you've heard about Trader?"

"I'm sorry to say that I have."

"Been some deaths?" Ryan said, letting his hand
fall away from the butt of the blaster.

Burgoise nodded. "You've traveled Deathlands for
many years. You know how the bush telegraph oper-
ates. Packmen and travelers carry stories and news.
Births and deaths and marriages. My father used to
call it 'hatched, dispatched and matched.' Bad news
and good. Sad and happy. Strangers and dangers. It
often takes less than a day for word to race a hundred
miles and no man can quite explain how that happens."

Ryan nodded. "Yeah. Know what you mean. So
you've heard a lot about Abe and Trader?"

"I didn't know the one name. Not for sure and certain. But the rumor was constant that the older man
was indeed the legendary Trader."

"And?"

There was a pause. The wood in the hearth crackled and spit, sending sparks out onto the stone flags.
"It was not properly seasoned," Al said, his blind eyes
closed, as though he were quite alone.

"Deaths," J.B. prompted.

Burgoise ticked them off on his fingers. "There was
a man slain in a store in a dirt-poor ville in the back-
country. It may be that the blame lay not entirely with

your companions. A posse was raised. They are all family in those places where father lies with daughter and brother with sister. Then a woman was killed and some men by a bridge across a river."

"This was during the chase, was it?" Ryan asked, knowing that at such times Trader became totally ruthless, single-minded to the point of casual brutality, sometimes past that point, taking personal survival above all.

"It was. But I doubt you can wipe the slate clean on those grounds."

"Posse still after them?" J.B. asked, staring into the flames of the fire, as though a part of his mind was out among the snowy hills with his old leader.

"No."

"Gave up?" Ryan queried.

"Dead."

"All of them?"

Al nodded. "Every last man and boy. My informant spoke of somewhere between eight and ten of them."

"He ambush them with his Armalite? And Abe's got that cannon of a Colt Python. I reckon they'd outgun any backwoods posse most days of the week."

"No, Cawdor. When they found what the scavengers had left of the corpses, it was still clear how they'd met their ending. Each one had his throat cut open."

Ryan bit his lip, trying to imagine a scenario that would have led to Trader choosing to take out so many pursuers in that particular way.

J.B. was a little ahead of him. "At night, while they were sleeping. Backtracked and crept up on them in the early hours when they were out it."

"I never figured for Abe being any use at that kind of attack. Tracking and silence weren't that high on his list of things he did well." Ryan's finger reached to touch the deep scar that ran from the corner of his good right eye down to his mouth, thinking deeply, rejecting various ideas, finally deciding. "They caught Abe. Held him. Thought they were safe with just one old man out there, all on his own in the cold and the wet."

"Right." The Armorer nodded his agreement. "That makes good sense. And in he came."

Al sighed. "Like a lean wolf, whose enemies thought him toothless. This Trader is a remarkable man."

"No argument there. So, when was all this chilling? Any news of him since? Know where he might be now, Al?"

The old man smiled at J.B.'s eagerness. "So many questions. Let me see. To take them in order. Some weeks ago. Not really, just the occasional sighting of a pair of ridge runners, seen at twilight against the skyline. And I have no idea where they might be now. The latest word I had was that they had gone away northwest, up toward the dreadful ruins of old Seattle."

"I'm sorry to hear that death still sits at Trader's shoulder, Al." Ryan stood. "But I'd be surprised if most of the corpses didn't deserve their ending."

"I would not argue with that. But the key word is 'most,' is it not? The woman had two little children. Lackbrains, I believe. She fell over a cliff, they say. But your Trader or your Abe shot her first."

"Could've been a reason," J.B. said, his voice betraying his doubt.

"Perhaps." Burgoise's voice betrayed his doubt, as well.

"Chilling sometimes comes around a blind corner and there's no time to think about a reason." J.B. also stood. "We thank you for your hospitality, but we must get to our beds. If the weather eases at all we need to be on the road."

"I understand, Mr. Dix. You have promises that you must try to keep, and you have many miles to go."

"Right."

"Then sleep well, outlanders. I will tidy up here and retire myself. Until the morning..."

THE NEWS OF THE TRADER and his trail of butchery had laid a steel blade between the hermit and his guests. The ease had gone from the previous evening, and their breakfast was hurried and uncomfortable. Conversation was spasmodic, with long silences between the careful words.

The wind had dropped, and there were only a few flakes of snow whispering down from the overcast sky. Al set them right for their destination, standing in the doorway of his cabin as they started off, muffled against the cold. His blind eyes followed the sound of their boots crunching through the white carpet.

"I hope you find what you seek," he shouted.

They didn't reply, eager to get on their way, eager to journey the last miles.

Chapter Thirty-Seven

Trader rubbed at his stomach. "Still feel that pain in my guts," he said. "Not so bad as it was once, but still like swallowing a king crab."

"Could be hunger pains," Abe replied miserably. "My belly keeps rubbing on my backbone. If this snow doesn't ease off, we'll starve."

"No. I saw a rabbit from the mouth of this cave only an hour ago. Hadn't got my Armalite or I'd have taken it."

"So, why don't we get out hunting?"

Trader grinned at the smaller, younger man. "Cold gets in my joints. No hurry, Abe."

"All right, then I'll go and get us something for the pot. And I'll get some more wood for the fire as well."

"Good, good. Have I asked you how long it is to go before our planned rendezvous with Ryan?"

"Only about fifty times a day, Trader." Gradually, over the last months, Abe had lost some of his fear for his old leader, though he still respected him, maybe even more than when he'd ridden the war wags with him. And he could never, ever forget the debt he owed Trader for saving his life from the posse.

"And the answer?"

"We're just five days away from the original deadline. And counting. We need to be a whole lot nearer to the edge of the old ville, Trader."

"We'll move this afternoon and hunt at the same time. Satisfied?"

"Sure."

The weather had been patchy, with some cold clear days followed by several periods of wet snow from a leaden sky. Trails were still difficult, but not impassable. On a bright morning, two days earlier, Abe had climbed to the top of a nearby hill, staring toward the tumbled ruins of Seattle, wondering whether the message had even reached Ryan, J.B. and the others in the far-off baked deserts of the Southwest, and whether he would ever live to see his friends again.

After his escape from the posse, he and Trader had been constantly on the move, only stopping in the many abandoned cabins that were scattered around the Cascades when the weather closed in on them.

It had been a hard time for both of them.

Though they were free of the pursuit, the land was inherently hostile, the cold and snow a constant danger. Abe had sprained an ankle falling badly over the wrecked and rusting remains of an ancient semi, hidden beneath the blizzard. And Trader's variety of old wounds, injuries and illnesses kept him quieter and much less active than usual.

"Should I go and hunt now?"

Trader shook his head. It had been several days since either of them had shaved, and his cheeks and chin were covered with a silvery stubble.

"Leave it awhile. Warmer days coming, Hun. I mean Abe. Let's stay where we are in this good old cave."

What worried Abe was that the "good old cave" had contained a substantial heap of gnawed bones and rotting flesh. As well, there were piles of fairly fresh bear droppings in the woods only a few yards away.

"I'll go later."

"Sure, Abe, sure. You noticed how this place makes your voice sort of echo and sound odd?"

"Yeah. Hollow kind of sound."

"I tell you about the time me and Marsh Folsom came across that cache of—"

"The war wags up in the Apps? Sure you have. But that was thirty years gone."

"I know that," Trader said angrily. "You best stop treating me like your fucking triple-stupe grandpa, Abe, or you'll have my blaster where the sun don't shine."

"Sorry, but you—"

Trader rode over him, ignoring the fact that he'd been in the middle of a sentence. "When Marsh and me found..." Abe stayed silent. Trader looked at him. "Come on, for fuck's sake. Help me out a little."

"When you found that huge store of gas hundred and fifty miles north of the old ville of Boston."

"No." Trader's face brightened. "Though all of that's true. I ever tell you what happened to Marsh Folsom? The way it all ran out for him? I tell you?"

"Plenty of times. But you were going to tell me something different, Trader."

"I was?"

"You was."

"What?"

Abe laughed, the movement shaking a dew-drop of moisture from the end of his beaky, broken nose, into the dangling fronds of his mustache. "You started saying how our voices sounded in this cave and that it reminded you of something."

Trader clapped his hands together. "Sure thing. I got the ace on the line now. Me and Marsh was north of the big lakes. Them days we spent a lot of our hunting time in the north and the east. Good for pre-dark stuff. We found this old . . . kind of a redoubt, I guess it was."

"Using those gateways and mat-trans units. Ryan and the others been into dozens of redoubts all over."

"You told me that scads of times, Abe. I'll believe them when I see them. These jump gates."

Abe didn't bother to correct him, looking out beyond the sinking fire into the dull morning, where snow was already starting to turn to rain.

"This redoubt we found was small. Sort of hidden warehouse for military hardware. Ryan and me . . ." His brow furrowed. "No. This has to be before Ryan and the Armorer came and joined us. Before the war wags, I think. What do you think?"

"Before my time, Trader."

"This place was two floors high and contained forty or fifty rooms. Each of them had once held a different kind of weapon or explosive. Plas-ex, nitro, Semtex, good old black powder even. And any number of grens."

"Frags?"

"Sure. Blue and red implodes. Remotes and nervies. Burners and stuns. Delays and plain hi-ex. Shraps and smokies. Lights and even some hi-alts."

"What kind of firing mechanisms?"

"Both, Abe. Flip-tops and two-step buttons. Seemed to be thousands of them."

"Just you and Marsh Folsom?"

Trader sighed. "Points like this is where my memory gets sort of foggy, Abe. Those days I think I traveled with a handful of good men and women. Five or six of us. Taylor and Rathman. Man who did it was called Wyoming Johnny. Tall with hair that was split half black and half white. Got himself caught in a nasty acid spill, somewhere up near old Cheyenne. Face looked like it was made from minced tomatoes."

"What did he do?"

"What I told him not to. We could see straight off that some of those grens were double edgy. Greasy and sweating. Cases split and rusting here and there. Me and Marsh agreed we'd take a look around, stepping like we was on eggshells. Not risk touching anything. Only take anything that we both thought was safe."

"Wyoming Johnny?"

"I used to think the acid hit his head and made him sort of simple."

"And?"

Trader winced and gave a small gasp of pain as he shifted position. "Sickness hasn't gone away. Just sleeping and waiting its moment. Where was I?"

"In the redoubt with Marsh, Wyoming Johnny and a few others."

"We was in a passage that opened up out back into some old trenches and stuff. Decided that this was too dangerous. Only risk worth taking is the one you have to take. We'd agreed to leave it and move on. We realized that Johnny wasn't with us no more and heard this scream."

"Knew a man once got his jaw torn off by a pre-dark can of tuna and beans," Abe said. "He shook it, and it was just ready and waiting to blow. Kind of hundred-year-old time bomb."

"This was thousands of seventy-year-old grens," Trader said, virtually ignoring the interruption.

"You heard a scream."

"Cry from the soul. 'Fuse came off in my hand. Started ticking.' That was all Wyoming Johnny shouted."

"Well, I'll be hung, quartered and dried for the crows!" Abe said, unconsciously using one of the Trader's own favorite sayings.

"This is the point of the story, don't you see? Where things got seriously weird."

"Go on."

Thoughts of going hunting for rabbits had disappeared for Abe, along with the pangs of hunger.

"What was odd was that time slowed. Oh, I know that everyone always says in time of stress and bloody danger that often seems to happen. But I swear to you that it really did come to pass. We all started running, and I could hear a clock ticking away the time in my brain. Most of those grens would have run off a ten-second timer. Agreed?''

''Sure. Some of those old predark grens can go off anything between zero seconds and never.''

Trader smiled and nodded. ''I was running out of the room where we stood, toward the passage that led to the open and the maze of trenches I mentioned to you. I *did* mention them, didn't I? Yes, I did.''

''You did.''

''But—'' he leaned forward to add emphasis to his words ''—I swear it was in slow motion. The clock was ticking at quarter speed. A single second lasted for four seconds. It was the same with everyone. I heard Wyoming Johnny again. 'Run for your lives,' he said.''

''What happened?''

''I will swear to my dying day that the timing fuse ran for some forty seconds. By that time the rest of us were diving into these deep trenches, all trying not to panic and to avoid the gigantic shock wave we knew would follow.''

''Eyes shut, mouth open, hands over ears.''

''Good, Abe, good.'' He coughed, hawking as though he were about to spit. But didn't. ''I actually glimpsed Wyoming Johnny, framed in the doorway, like a statue, just for that single forever moment. His arms were frozen in the action of pumping him on to-ward safety, his legs sprinting. Head thrown back, hair

streaming behind him, eyes wide, mouth wide as a
bear trap. I will never forget that picture of time
stopped.''

''And?''

Trader sighed. ''The place just blew up. We were all
safe enough. Shocked and deaf, bleeding from every
orifice in the body. But safe.''

''Wyoming Johnny?''

''We found a combat boot we thought might have
been his. The foot inside looked like his, with a toe
missing. But that was all. Nothing else remained.''

''Jesus.'' Abe shook his head. ''Never known that
time slowing myself.''

''Happens.'' Trader stood and moved to the mouth
of the cave, walking with a slight limp. ''Snow's
stopped. I can taste some sun on the way, Abe.''

''Light us the way to a meeting with Ryan.'' Hunger reasserted itself. ''Or a rabbit or some venison.''

''Pass me the blaster. Thanks. Yeah, let's go out
into the world and find us some food, what's your...
I remember. Sure I do. Abe. It's Abe.''

The two men left the empty cave, the fire smoldering to extinction. They picked their way through the
wet slush, over the crest of the hill, finally vanishing
toward Seattle and their meeting.

Chapter Thirty-Eight

Mildred lay on her side, wrists bound behind her, a bruise swelling beneath her right eye, where the Apostle Simon had savagely punched her to demonstrate to his doubting followers that he wasn't scared of her.

Jak, bound hand and foot next to Mildred, had also been beaten to the dirt by the skinny leader of the Slaves of Sin, using his staff with the tortured Christ at its head.

She knew that the albino teenager was awake and fully conscious, because he and Mildred had taken the chance for several snatches of whispered conversation, stolen moments of talk that gave neither of them very much cheer.

"Seen they sent four out toward spread," Jak said. "One got your blaster."

"Yeah. Saw them go. I make it nine left here with us. Haven't heard any shooting from the house."

"Sound might not carry. Been gone good time. Wonder when fladgies start getting worried."

"How long before Krysty, Doc and the boy come out after us, Jak?"

The young man hadn't answered her, his silence telling her everything she needed to know.

A little later, while the Slaves of Sin sat around their largest fire, chanting an interminable dirge about salvation through suffering, Jak had whispered to Mildred again.

"Face facts," he said. "Could be Krysty, Doc and kid chilled. We get chance—*any* chance—must take it. Or torture and chill us. No other hope."

NEARLY AN HOUR had passed, and the flagellants were becoming increasingly restive.

"Apostle Simon, shouldn't we send out searchers to find what's happened?"

But their leader was steadfast. "The Lord will show us the way when He is ready, brothers. He would not allow any of his chosen lambs to stray from the fold and fall among wolves. All we need is patience."

"Why not make Him a sacrifice of these two demon spawn?"

"Or let us scourge ourselves, mightily, that our delicious blood shall freshen the desert as token of our grace and our humble love for Him?"

The Apostle Simon rapped the butt of his staff on the earth. "The moon that was hidden will soon come from behind the clouds. Its light will show us the way."

It had been pitchy dark for three parts of the hour, but everyone could see the bright circle of the moon, about to be revealed from behind the shifting rack of cloud.

"Got one hand nearly free," Jak breathed. "Bit more time is all need."

"Might not get that if they go ahead and murder us because . . . Jesus Christ!"

It seemed that everyone saw the apparition at the same moment, as the moon broke through, flooding the wilderness with its bright silver sheen. It was a young child, a boy, naked except for a white breech-cloth around his loins. His hands were spread, showing the blackness of blood in the center of his palms, a similar mark on both his bare feet. There was a crown of leaves around his forehead, and his face was smeared with ashes. He had appeared from the arroyo that ran toward the distant house, walking slowly toward the paralyzed fladgies, less than sixty yards away from them.

"The Lord Himself," someone gasped.

"Truly the Son of God," a second man whispered in a voice filled with awe.

"It might be a . . . a trick," their leader stammered, his face in the moonlight as pale as whey.

"No trick, Slaves of Sin," said a booming voice from the blackness, somewhere behind the advancing child. "I have sent my dearly beloved among you as a token of how worthy you are of my approval."

Mildred glanced at Jak disbelievingly, her eyes wide. "It's . . ." she began, hushing herself as the albino shook his head at her.

The boy was now a scant twenty yards from the nearest of the religious crazies, his piercing blue eyes gleaming from the shadows of his face.

"We worship You," one of the fladgies shrieked, his nerve breaking, dropping to his knees, hands out in supplication. "Oh, scourge us with your fiery whip, Lord!"

"All of you abase yourselves and make ready to receive my divine punishment," the voice thundered. "For verily I shall seek out the worthy from the impure. By the Three Ken— By the three spears of the divinity, I shall."

Mildred had wriggled around, lifting herself painfully up onto one elbow, staring at the truly bizarre spectacle. Her eyes were caught by a slight movement in the darkness of the sagebrush behind the staring flagellants, the daggers of the moon touching on what looked like living flame.

"Krysty," she breathed.

Now eight of the nine men were on their knees, three of them lying sprawled facedown in the dirt, the light of their fires throwing shadows across them. Only the Apostle Simon was still standing, but he was leaning on his staff as though it were a lifeline between himself and eternity.

"Take me, Blessed One," one of the transfixed men screamed, lifting his scarred, bearded face, a thread of white saliva bubbling from his cracked lips.

The child stopped and lowered his hands, reaching inside the band of white cloth wrapped around his middle. The ringing voice from the blackness behind had risen an octave, showing the sudden edge of tension. "Now we shall reveal the nature of our gifts to reward you all."

"Here comes," Jak said, starting to struggle more openly with the rawhide around his wrists.

"Show us, Messiah!" The eldritch screech came from the Apostle Simon himself.

Dean pulled the massive Browning Hi-Power from its hiding place, already cocked, and opened fire on the helpless fladgies.

Doc ran from the dry gulch, slightly to the right of the boy, his Le Mat spitting out its .36-caliber rounds.

And from behind the paralyzed acolytes of the Apostle Simon, Krysty rose from the ground like a flame-haired avenging angel, firing her Smith & Wesson 640, aiming and firing carefully, picking her targets for the big .38s.

There wasn't a single shot fired in retaliation from the murderous crazies.

Three of them died instantly at Dean's hands, creating mayhem with his powerful blaster, even though he had to shoot it two-handed to achieve any real accuracy.

Two more died on their knees, hands raised, their horrified faces rictuses of terror.

Four managed to get to their feet, including their demented leader.

Mildred watched as one went down, rocked by two bullets from Doc's Civil War pistol. A second dropped dead, half of his face blown away by Krysty.

"Shoot no more! We surrender to your mercy!" the Apostle Simon cried, holding both arms spread wide, like a man awaiting crucifixion.

His last companion finally lost his nerve and turned to flee into the moonlit wilderness, tumbling over and over like a shot rabbit, legs kicking in the dirt, hit between the shoulders by the last of Dean's thirteen rounds.

The desert was still, the only sound the death rattle of one of the fladgies, overlaid by the relentless sighing of the ceaseless wind.

"I will leave this place of blood and never return to it," the leader of the Slaves of Sin stated.

"For fuck's sake cut us free," Jak called, finally breaking one hand loose. Dean holstered his blaster and hurried to kneel by Jak, slicing the ropes off his other wrist and off his ankles. He turned immediately to liberate Mildred.

Krysty stood watching Simon, Doc covering him from the other side of the campsite. Already the stench of death hung heavy in the firelight.

Jak stood, reaching a slender hand to assist Mildred to her feet. She rubbed her wrists, chafing life back into them, looking around her at the litter of corpses.

"Thanks for turning up, friends," she said. "Beginning to think that the sand was running out of the glass for us. Nice trick, Dean. Nice voice, Doc."

The old man dropped a low bow to her. "Praise from you, ma'am, is praise redoubled. But the bulk of your thanks should lie with Mistress Wroth, who was the dramaturge and inspiration for our little playlet."

"What happened to four men sent in?" Jak asked, looking around and retrieving his Colt Python from the dead fingers of one of the flagellants.

"Krysty chilled one and Doc wasted the other three," Dean told them.

Mildred's mouth dropped. "Doc chilled... You mean... Three of them? What'd he do, breathe on them after a meal of garlic and wild onions?"

"Delighted to see that you are returned to your former misanthropic and waspish self, Dr. Wyeth." Doc favored her with another bow.

"I should've known," the Apostle Simon said. "When my men didn't return, I should've known."

"You didn't," Doc stated, "because you got shit for brains."

"The day will come, child of Shaitan, when you will writhe on the white-hot grill and your skin will blister and sear and your eyes boil and your hair smoke from your skull. Then you will feel sorry for what you have done here this night."

"Fuck you, stupe!" The boy drew his blaster and squeezed the trigger. The only result being the dry click of the hammer on an empty chamber.

The Apostle Simon threw back his long, narrow head and laughed out loud, waving his staff in triumph. "There! See how my Lord of pain defeats your feeble demon's power. Nothing can harm me, nothing."

"Wrong," Jak said very quietly, shooting the leader of the flagellants through the lower stomach with the Python. The .357 full-metal-jacket round left a small, black entrance hole, less than an inch from Simon's navel, hitting the spine and angling off sideways, tearing into the liver and exiting through the small of the back, taking out a chunk of flesh the size of a dinner plate.

The staff flew into the air, clattering down toward the heart of the fire with a great starburst of crimson and orange sparks that rose high into the still air.

Simon staggered but didn't fall immediately, his head turning to see the blazing destruction of his symbol of power.

"Missed me," he said.

"You wish." Jak holstered his blaster and turned away, starting to walk back toward his home, knowing with total certainty that the man was doomed.

Simon sank to his knees, his system still holding off the rending agony that his wound deserved. "I will sit down," he announced with a peculiar dignity.

Dean had reloaded his Browning with bullets that he'd hidden in his breechclout, and he leveled the gun at the kneeling figure. Jak was twenty yards away and he didn't even look back, calling to the boy over his shoulder.

"No. Done."

Dean hesitated a moment, glancing at the other three. Doc shook his head, as did Mildred. Krysty smiled at him. "Jak's right," she said. "Let's go and have some food and catch up on our sleep. You never know. Ryan and the others might come back tomorrow."

THE APOSTLE SIMON lay down and watched the five figures walk away from him, throwing long stark shadows in the bright moonlight.

He felt the first spasm of pain and he moaned, sniffed and wiped his nose on the back of his hand. "Like my Dad used to say... Be back here some lucky day."

Then the blood stopped flowing and he died.

Chapter Thirty-Nine

The day was bitterly cold, with a dazzling sun hanging at the center of an untouched blue sky. From east to west and north to south, there wasn't even the hint of a cloud. All around it seemed that you could reach out and touch the perfection of the snow-covered mountains.

The cold air had the unmistakable scent of salt, from the Cific Ocean only a few miles away, beyond the ruins of old Seattle. Here and there it was possible to make out the thin tendrils of cooking fires, among the stumps of the nuked city buildings. But whatever ate there, ate alone.

The oppressive wet weather of the past three days had vanished, and it had snowed during the previous night as the temperature dropped well below freezing.

Now, an hour after dawn, it was a heaven of morning.

Ryan and J.B. had found no cover, waking up to find their sleeping bags were crusted with frozen snow, which crackled when they moved.

"Last day of the last week," Ryan said as he stooped, trying to get a fire going to warm them up and dry their clothes and heat some oatmeal.

"Now we'll see." J.B. checked that the cold hadn't affected any of his blasters.

"Yeah, we'll see."

THEY HAD DECIDED that the best place to begin the final stage of their search would be to pick a high spot with a view over Seattle from the east. There was a particular hill that suited their purpose and they had been working their way toward it, occasionally slipping on the icy trail.

Apart from the scattered fires among the ruins, there didn't seem to be a living soul within fifty miles of them.

There had been a pair of white-pelted hares gamboling in a clearing among the pines, as they climbed higher, who'd totally ignored them.

In a valley to their right they spotted a small herd of deer, picking its way delicately through the frosted grass. J.B. had nudged Ryan and pointed to the Steyr on his shoulder, but he'd shaken his head.

"Bullet on a still, cold morning like this might be heard twenty miles off. Could attract Abe and Trader. If they're anywhere near. Could attract anyone else."

It was hard work, and both men were panting as they neared the crest of the small mountain.

"You can make out the sea from here," Ryan said, pausing for breath.

"Yeah. Look at the Cascades back yonder."

A few more paces brought them to the top, giving them the ultimate view, all the way around.

Now they could see the far side of the slope, bisected by a narrow hunting path. Two figures were about a hundred yards below them, struggling upward through the deeper snow. The smaller man was sliding and falling, a little way to the rear.

The leader, using the butt of what looked like an old Armalite rifle to help himself, was gray-haired, tall and erect. He spotted the pair on the ridge above him immediately and stopped for a single heartbeat. Then he lifted his blaster above his head in an unmistakable gesture.

"There they are," Ryan breathed.

Asian warmongers draw the U.S. into a Pacific showdown

STONY MAN™ 13
WARHEAD

Tactical nuclear weapons have been hijacked in Russia, and the clues point to their being in the possession of a group of North Koreans, Cambodians and Vietnamese, all allied with Chinese hard-liners to solidify Communist rule in Southeast Asia. The warheads are powerful enough to decimate the population of a large city, or destroy an entire port or airport facility, and are dangerous tools of extortion.

When the warheads are traced to one of the largest military installations in Southeast Asia, Stony Man Farm puts together a recovery mission.

Back to the beginning . . .

DEATH LANDS ®

PILGRIMAGE TO HELL $4.99

Out of the ruins of worldwide nuclear devastation emerged Deathlands, a world that conspired against survival. Ryan Cawdor and his roving band of post-holocaust survivors begin their quest for survival in a world gone mad.

RED HOLOCAUST $4.99

Ryan and his warriors must battle against roaming bands of survivors from Russia who are using Alaska as a staging ground for an impending invasion of America.

NEUTRON SOLSTICE $4.99

Deep in the heart of Dixie, Ryan and his companions come upon a small group of survivors who are striving to recreate life as it was once known.

CRATER LAKE $4.99

Near what was once the Pacific Northwest, Ryan's band discovers a beautiful valley untouched by the nuclear blast that changed the world forever.

HOMEWARD BOUND $4.99

Emerging from a gateway in the ruins of New York City, Ryan decides it is time to face his power-mad brother—and avenge the deaths of his father and older brother.

Here's your chance to find out how it all began!